The Break-up Before Christmas

ALSO BY CHARLOTTE BARNES

A Walk in the Park
The Break-up Before Christmas

THE
Breakup
BEFORE
CHRISTMAS

CHARLOTTE BARNES

Choc Lit
A JOFFE BOOKS COMPANY

Choc Lit, London
A Joffe Books company
www.choc-lit.com

First published in Great Britain in 2025

© Charlotte Barnes 2025

Cover art by Jarmila Takač

ISBN: 978-1781899090

For my own remarkable mum,

You are still, and will always be,
the best Mum in every story that I write.
Thank you for telling me to sit down
and write the bloody book.

PART ONE

CHAPTER ONE

It was easy to be Dear Dotty in London. Easier still in the middle of the seasonal shift; that move from summer to autumn, when everything became particularly photogenic. Dear Dotty was a big fan of sitting outside boutique coffee shops with her friends and drinking flat whites. Dear Dotty worked on her column in trendy outdoor locations while taking pictures of her laptop in perfectly shadowed window seats and on park benches. She read a lot of translated literature, always bought the latest copy of *Vogue*, and regularly went running in Gymshark gear every other morning.

In no uncertain terms, Dear Dotty was the perfectly stylised 'It-girl' with a romanticised existence and ample platforms through which to share that with her loyal readers.

Dotty was different.

Dotty hated flat whites. She could never write on a park bench owing to her squirrel-like attention span. *Vogue* always made her feel entirely inept when it came to piecing together an outfit, so she avoided it much like any other woman might avoid a smear test. Sweating in public was one of Dotty's biggest fears, no matter how much confidence her Gymshark attire instilled in her.

Instead, Dotty enjoyed takeaways, romance novels, and pink wine — and she was only too happy to partake in all these things, preferably all at once and from the comfort of her own home.

Such were the two distinct sides of my personality. I was especially grateful to Instagram for allowing them to coexist.

It's not that I didn't like life in London. On the contrary, I *loved* life in London. I loved that I could get a pizza delivered at the most hideous hour of the morning. I loved that I could see tourists by the hundreds and experience the joy of the city all over again through their startled, wide-eyed expressions. I loved that I could discover my favourite new musician just by walking down a street and spotting a busker I hadn't heard before. I loved that I could see both green spaces and offensive traffic within a five-minute walk of each other — it's strange, but it's true. I loved that I could see a play whenever I felt like it, safe in the knowledge that a theatre was never more than a few stops on the Tube from home. And safe in the knowledge, too, that the Underground was right there waiting whenever I needed to hop, skip, or jump to the other side of this great city. Which, admittedly, didn't happen often these days. But it was nice to have the option. However, much like the woman I am named after, the older I got the more I firmly believed in the adage that there really is no place like home.

By the grace of some higher being, my girlfriend Caitlin and I managed to secure a *relatively* affordable two-bedroom flat in Islington, London, some four years ago. Since then, we haven't stopped tweaking and styling the space. Caitlin was kind enough to let me take over the spare bedroom as a home office. The space was brilliantly bare, featuring a clear glass desk, a comfortable bucket-seat office chair, and a pile of magazines — mostly *Vogue* — that I'd been collecting for photo ops over the last six months. Every few months I had a clear-out and started all over again with the latest issues of things. There was a single wall lined with books, organised by colour, and I never knew where anything was. But it photographed well.

With such a beautiful and curated space at my disposal, it was a shame that I instead opted to do most of my work smack bang in the middle of our living room floor. It was another beautifully designed space with bookshelves galore, exposed brick walls, and plush matching sofas in a dark teal colour that really made the room pop against all the copper pipework lamps that Caitlin and I had treated ourselves to last Christmas. Because yes, I admit it, since collapsing headfirst into our thirties, new lamps for the living room were our idea of a treat.

The living room was open plan, leading to the kitchen-diner where Caitlin was making tea for us both — and tutting.

'Are you going to make me ask?' I was sitting cross-legged with my laptop balanced awkwardly in my lap. I couldn't even see her. I could only hear the intermittent tut-tut over the sound of traffic drifting in from the open window.

'Why do you even have that spare room? Why aren't we using it for something more . . . exciting?'

'What's more exciting than colour-coded bookshelves?'

Caitlin wandered over and set my steaming cup down on the coffee table next to me. 'It worries me that you would even ask that.' She was wearing high-top socks that looked like they belonged to a professional athlete and a charcoal T-shirt with a Medusa head on the front. When she turned to walk away, I caught a hint of boxer shorts. Her wild curls bounced about behind her as she tutted her way back to the kitchen.

She was still the most beautiful woman I'd seen in my life. *But for the love of everything, please stop tutting.*

'Thanks for the tea.'

'What are we doing today?' She acted as though I hadn't spoken at all.

'What do you mean?' My attention was back on the screen. I had a deadline to beat, and some solid life advice to come up with for 'Forty and Feeling It': a woman who had spent so much time focused on her children's lives, she wasn't sure what to do with her own. 'Were we meant to

4

be doing something today?' I asked when she didn't reply. Though I have to confess, most of my attention was fixed on the Amazon page full of self-help books I'd just clicked into. I was good at giving advice. Most days I felt sure of that. There was just something about Forty and Feeling It's dilemma that had me stuck in a rut. Ironically.

'I just thought . . .'

When she didn't finish whatever the just-a-thought was, I closed my laptop. I grabbed my tea and my phone to try my best at taking an aerial shot of myself holding said tea perfectly central to the space between my still folded legs.

'Is that for Dear Dotty?' Caitlin's tone was *almost* spiteful. It was a total mismatch against the question, which seemed fair and innocent enough.

'I've posted a lot of "out and about" stuff recently and Elza has asked me to try to make the page more economical.'

Elza was my editor. More like a handler, really. It had been her idea to start the Dear Dotty Instagram account in the first place. I'd spent a hard eight months telling her it wouldn't take off. Now, she rolled out an I-told-you-so with every performance review. But given that I'd somehow become one of the magazine's defining features, she didn't give me too much of a hard time for it.

When she didn't respond, I spoke again. 'So, are we meant to be doing something today?'

'I just thought we might.' Caitlin's mouth bunched up to the side. I'd seen pictures of her when she was a kid — she wore exactly the same expression, then and now, whenever she was even slightly annoyed. Six months into our relationship, her mum tipped me off and told me that's what that face meant. Since then, I've always tried to tread carefully around the narrowed eyes, the gathered lips, the half-sentences.

'Why don't we go out for lunch?' I suggested.

She thought about her answer for much longer than I expected. I was *sure* the suggestion had been a sound one, and yet—

'What about a picnic somewhere?' she countered. 'The weather is so pretty, and we could make up a little basket of . . . I don't know, bits.' She shrugged. 'What do you think?'

'I think it sounds like a lot more effort than getting an outdoor table somewhere.'

Caitlin shook her head and sipped her tea. I wondered whether she was buying herself a second to cool down before she answered. The counteroffer obviously hadn't been what she was expecting; her lips were still bunched for one thing. But really, in a world of deadlines, who even has time for a picnic? I gave up on taking the picture I was after, put my tea back on the table, and took a low-angle photograph of the mug with the exposed brick behind it instead.

'Let me help you,' Caitlin said.

I felt like I'd been hit over the head with an olive branch. 'You don't have to, really.'

Though she'd never outright said it, Caitlin hated the social media side of my work. @DearDotty wasn't authentic, she'd said. But then @noplacelikehome, my personal account, was hardly brimming with excitement: mine and Caitlin's slipper-socked feet in front of a large television screen. Our jumbo drinks at a cinema screening of the latest Marvel release. The newest Beth O'Leary novel lying on our coffee table with head exploding emojis as the caption.

@DearDotty looked a lot better on paper than I did. And that's how you could tell she wasn't real.

'Honestly, it's fine.' She reached down to take my phone from me. 'But I want a really good outdoor table at a really good restaurant, and I want a long walk through Hyde Park after we've eaten.'

I thought carefully about her demands. 'I want lots of casual photographs that take at least thirty attempts to get.'

Caitlin rolled her eyes. 'Deal.'

But once Caitlin stood on the sofa I was leaning against and hovered over me from behind, it only took twelve attempts to get the tea shot.

I thought that might be a good omen for the day ahead.

CHAPTER TWO

Nothing says 'Happy Monday' like being pressed up against a crowd of complete strangers on the Tube. Though they weren't all *total* strangers, of course, given that I pressed up against a lot of them on most of my Monday morning jaunts.

There was Man Laughing At Instagram Reels, Woman Trying To Read Her Book, and perhaps the most admirable character of them all, Woman Trying To Do Her Make-Up. There had been more than one occasion when I considered offering to help her — hold her mirror, maybe — but she didn't have the kind of face that welcomed such an interaction. And frankly, who could blame her on a Monday morning?

By the time we pulled into Piccadilly Circus she had everything done but her lips. Someone jostled into her on our way out of the carriage — while someone else made mooing noises in the background as we herded — and she seemed to think better of trying to apply her bright red lipstick with so much disruption around her, which I thought was wise. If she'd got any closer to her face with that lipstick, I think I would have knocked it out of her hand before someone else had the chance to knock her elbow or bump into her side on.

Shortly after that, the Underground spat me back out into the open air, and I lost sight of my Monday morning comrades. They were replaced by other stock characters who were hurriedly knocking into and dodging each other on the pavement, making their way to their respective offices. There were fewer suits in Soho than in other parts of London, so at least while people moved around me in a blur, they did so with the odd splash of colour.

I stopped en route to grab a fruit tea from my favourite coffee shop that was close to the office. There were already customers spilling out the door, but there's something to be said for knowing the managers well enough that they'll bump you to the front of the line.

'Dotty! Tea?'

'Fruit, please, Alex,' I shouted back to the absolute dismay of the thirteen people in front of me. I flashed a self-conscious smile at the man directly ahead, who actually turned and stared. 'Morning,' I managed, and he grunted in reply. I felt a genuine flood of relief when Alex passed the tea over the counter to me and told me he'd add it to my tab. All the better for a hasty escape. 'You're a babe. Have a fab day.'

I stood on the pavement opposite the shop front, held my to-go cup at arm's length, and snapped a picture with the shop name conveniently positioned over the top of my drink. Then I added it to the Dear Dotty Instagram account's story. I'd pop it on the grid later, along with a Monday wrap-up to get the week rolling.

It took three minutes and two sips of piping hot tea to get the rest of the way to work. There were four delays from the main entrance to my office, which was tucked away at the back of the building, as people exchanged good mornings and asked how the weekend had been. As nice as the interactions were, there was something to be said for working from the quiet of my living room when it came to getting into the headspace of a reader, which also made hitting deadlines that bit easier.

All About Us was a weekly print publication, but since the 'Dear Dotty' column had really taken off, it had become a *daily* feature on the website, where updates were much faster and readership was into the bonkers numbers (technical term). So yes, while socialising was good for the soul and all, it was hard to work consistently in the office without a number of—

'Did you dial this one in, Dotty, or what?'

—distractions.

'Morning, Elza.'

'Don't you "morning, Elza" me.' She snatched my cup from the corner of my desk, took a sip, and winced. 'There's literally no caffeine in this.'

'No, but now there is your saliva, which I think borders on sexual harassment in the workplace.' I propped my elbows on the desk and balanced my head in my palms. 'You may as well have just leaned over here and kissed me.'

'Cute.' Elza slapped a loose sheet of paper on my desk. 'Forty and Feeling It tells you that she's feeling lost with her life and you recommend three self-help books? She's a woman who's devoted her life to making sure *other* people's lives are running okay and now she's bloody lost because her children are growing up. Come on, Dotty!'

I sighed. 'You're right. I should have recommended more books.'

'No, Dotts, you should have given her advice!' I opened my mouth to reply but Elza held up her hand to stop me. 'Better advice than to try reading a book.'

'I find it usually helps me.'

'Well, wait until you're forty and then it won't.'

I pulled my tea back towards me, then second-guessed taking a sip. But for fear of causing offence, I fidgeted with the cup between my hands instead, twirling it in one direction and then the other. 'I was under a bit of pressure to get it done. I . . . Ugh.' I dropped my head back and stared at the ceiling. 'You're right, it was terrible advice. I'll redo it.'

'Choose another letter.'

'But—'

'No. No "but", no anything. Pick another letter — something easy. Get your laptop out; we'll choose something together.' Elza pulled a free chair from a desk behind me and yanked it around to my side. There was no getting out of this. 'While you're waiting for your laptop to boot up, you can tell me all about your problems at home.'

I guffawed, and that is not a word I use lightly, but there's no other way to describe the sound that erupted out of me. 'I don't have problems at home.'

'Then what was distracting you from this column?'

'I . . .' It was a false start. I'd pre-empted that an answer would come once I'd opened my mouth, and yet . . . 'Caitlin and I had a lunch reservation and I was in a rush.'

'Mhmm.' Elza leaned over me to click into my inbox. 'There, first one up. *Help: I'm in love with my best friend.* Bang out four hundred words on what a terrible idea it is to pursue this. I want a finished copy in my inbox by the time *I* take you out for a lunch reservation.'

I thinned my lips and squinted at the email subject.

'What?'

'I don't know, it . . . it's just old, isn't it? Hasn't *everyone* been in love with their best friend at one time or another?' I looked up just in time to catch Elza's frown. 'Okay, those of us who are capable of human emotion have been in love with our best friend at one time or another.'

Elza slapped my upper arm, albeit playfully. 'I'm capable of human emotion.' She pushed away from my desk and ushered the chair back. 'But not when it comes to deadlines, so copy by lunchtime, please and thank you.' I made another disapproving noise as I clicked into the email. 'Dotty, do you enjoy being an advice columnist?'

'This is a trick question,' I said, without looking up from my screen. 'And yes.'

'Well then, enjoy.'

Elza whirled back into her office with a soft click of the door closing behind her.

I hadn't planned to be an advice columnist. Like every other Creative Writing student in the country, I, was going to be a novelist. And once upon a time, I truly did believe that in

10

an elitist industry that's haemorrhaging money, I was going to be the exception to the rule. Unfortunately, while I was working out how to be that exception, I'd been haemorrhaging a fair bit of money myself — and being in the throes of a new relationship at the time hadn't helped matters either. Caitlin and I were in the first months of working hard to impress each other, not officially a couple yet but certainly working towards it, and that took funding. So, I wound up taking an agency gig for holiday cover at an undisclosed magazine that turned out to be *All About Us*. The holiday cover was for 'Ask Eleanor', an older woman who, depending on the day you asked, would often openly admit she was lucky her husband even let her have a job. Where's the head exploding emoji when you need it?

But by the time my temporary contract was coming to an end, they were asking Eleanor to clear out her advice columnist's desk and consider copyediting for them instead. Meanwhile, the PR team was busy planning a swift introduction to 'Dear Dotty'.

Nearly ten years later, I was still writing letters to strangers for a living.

Oh, and I still hadn't written a novel.

Dear Dotty,

It's a tale as old as time. I'm in love with my best friend. I don't think he sees me in the same way. I really don't. But I can't unsee him that way since we went for a weekend away with his parents recently. Everything about it just made me feel like we were basically already a couple, and now I can't shake the feeling. Could we be? Is it such a terrible idea? I keep wanting to tell him how I'm feeling about it all but I'm terrified of losing him!! It genuinely would break my heart to lose the friendship. But I'm worried about what happens if these feelings persist.

Help!! With hugs and thanks—
I'm in love with my best friend xx

CHAPTER THREE

I loved Caitlin like a toddler loves their blankie. It was disgusting, and maybe even slightly cliché, but nevertheless true. What I didn't love, was Caitlin's family.

So, no one could possibly imagine the unbridled *lack* of joy I felt at having to spend my Saturday — at the end of a long week — hauling myself across London to the iconic Notting Hill, to knock on the door of Caitlin's parents' home and then stand outside shuffling awkwardly from one foot to the other while Caitlin and I waited for 'the help' to answer. All the while, I was still wondering whether I was even properly dressed for this. I was wearing a thin, loose-fit white jumper complete with skintight jeans and a pair of heels I found while raiding Caitlin's shoe trunk that morning. I didn't believe in footwear that made me feel uncomfortable, but Caitlin's mother believed discomfort equalled fashionable.

Henry — the so-called help, who had been working with (for?) Caitlin's parents for so long that they tried to pass him off as family — seemed to be taking his time. So I filled the quiet by scanning the houses around us and playing a game of *Where would I live if I had money to burn?* We were surrounded by homes that had a starting price of I-don't-belong-here pounds, complete with six zeros trailing behind those price tags. Nothing made me feel more separate from Caitlin than being here. She was a Londoner to her core, and her family had worked their way up through the ranks to this fine establishment. It was now occupied by just her parents, even though the house had so many bedrooms that I hadn't been able to find them all yet.

It was a world away from Alfriston, where I'd grown up and where Mum still lived in a cottage that her own grandmother had left to her some twenty-odd years ago. Otherwise, we never would have been able to afford to touch the property ladder there, never mind set a foot on it — and money was an even harder thing to come by after Dad left. That was another point of contrast between Caitlin's family and mine: hers was still fully formed. Mine was just me and Mum, and it had been for as long as I could remember. Dad and I weren't in touch and hadn't been since I'd found out about his affair. Of course, I was a loyalist to being on Team Mum, then and always. Plus, not only were Mum and I fiercely loyal, but we actually liked each other.

'You didn't have to come, you know?' Caitlin's tone pulled my attention away from the rich greenery and back to her. 'I told you, I could have come on my own.'

I'd been an advice columnist for nearly a decade. I knew a relationship trap when I saw one. So I smiled, reached across for her hand, and squeezed. 'Of course I had to come. It's your sister's baby . . . party. I wouldn't have missed it.'

Caitlin knew me well enough to know that this was a lie. I didn't understand what the event was, which made it harder still to muster any enthusiasm for being here. It wasn't a gender reveal party — because Caitlin's sister, Ellen, and her husband, Donnie, wanted to be surprised this time — but it wasn't a baby shower either. Ellen and Donnie had such a brood of children at home that they already had everything they could possibly need to raise another child. So I'd been calling it a baby party to anyone who happened to ask what my weekend plans were, and I'd rolled my eyes every time I said it. But now I only widened my smile.

And Caitlin saw right through it. 'You're a terrible liar.'

'I think you'll find I'm actually a very good liar. You just know me too well.'

Caitlin laughed, and the sound broke the tension we'd carried with us all morning.

'I'm glad you're here.' She leaned in to kiss my cheek. 'Especially because you don't want to be.'

'I didn't say that I didn't want—'

Henry snatched the door open in the middle of my protest, and I made a mental note to buy him something extra nice for Christmas this year. 'Ladies, my apologies. The children, they're . . . I mean, I . . .'

Caitlin reached forward to squeeze his shoulder. 'It's okay, Henry. We know.'

Henry laughed, but it sounded tired and defeated. Then he stepped aside to welcome us into the house. 'The adults are in the kitchen. The children have been relegated to your father's old study. There's a lot of mayhem in there.'

'In the kitchen?' I joked.

'No, in the . . . *Oh.*' Henry broke into a smile when he caught on. 'Very good, Dorothy.'

That was another joy of visiting Caitlin's family: they didn't believe in nicknames. Even though I'd been Dotty to everyone since I was knee-high to a grasshopper, here I was Dorothy. It inevitably meant that I was also quite rude when I visited Caitlin's folks — mostly because I never registered that someone was actually talking to me when they said that name. That was my excuse, anyway. I also took great issue with the fact that everyone managed to call Donnie, Donnie. All because his parents happened to put that on his bloody birth certificate, rather than Donald, which they obviously should have done.

We followed Henry into the kitchen, where Olivia and Peter, Caitlin's mum and dad, were propped with their arms around each other as though they were about to be photo-graphed for an interior spread. Ellen was awkwardly resting on a barstool across the island from them, and Donnie was stood with his arm around her. It crossed my mind that he might be holding her up. Most of the socialising happened in the kitchen, owing to the sofa in the living room being far too expensive to actually sit on. I thought Olivia and Peter might have made allowances for their heavily pregnant daughter, though.

On the far end of the island, between these two couples, stood Edward, Caitlin's brother, and the nondescript woman he'd brought along for the occasion. She was definitely differ-ent from the last woman I'd seen him with, but not so much so that I could actually put my finger on it. Edward was a mas-ter of the uncanny when it came to choosing his girlfriends.

'Ah, girls!' Olivia crooned when she saw us. Her heels click-clacked across the floor as she made her way over, arms already open. Peter soon followed. It wasn't until Olivia released us from her deadly squeeze that I noticed Caitlin's dad was making a show of looking around behind us. He winked when he caught me looking.

'No brood following you two around yet, then?'

Oh, good, the baby jokes have started.

'Hi, sweets,' Ellen said to Caitlin. She would never call me that. She struggled to get up from her seat.

'Don't! I'll come to you.' Caitlin passed me the small gift bag she'd been holding — because it wasn't right to turn up empty-handed, even for the baby who had everything — and then rushed over to her sister.

'You know I'm only joking with you, Dorothy,' Peter said. He gave my shoulder a squeeze, and I laughed along like I believed him even though we both probably knew that I didn't. 'Can I get you a drink?'

'Oh, I'll just have what you're having, don't go to any trouble,' I drifted back across the room with him and handed the bag to Donnie. 'It's just a little something—' I bit back on an urge to apologise '—to welcome Junior into the family.'

'Ah, thanks, Dorothy. You shouldn't have.' He took the bag and pulled me into a one-armed hug. 'Nice to see you and Caitlin. Well' — he glanced behind him and laughed — 'it'll be nice to see her when they've finished clucking.'

Caitlin was now sitting on the stool next to Ellen, and the pair were so wrapped up in their chatter that neither of them answered when Peter offered them a drink. He laughed, shrugged, and went back to whatever he was mixing.

'Dorothy, sweetheart, make yourself at home,' Olivia said, in a tone that made it sound like an instruction. She pointed to the one empty chair around the island, and I made a point of pressing my thigh against Caitlin's as I took the seat next to her — if only to remind her I was there.

She glanced around. 'You okay, babe?'

'Your dad asked whether you wanted a drink.'

'Oh' — she turned — 'sorry, Daddy, I'll have whatever Dorothy is having.'

'You're both having Long Island iced teas then.' Peter pushed two glasses across the counter to us. 'No reason for either of you not to be drinking, I suppose?' He chuckled loudly at his joke, and Caitlin laughed along.

I was too busy taking thirsty mouthfuls of my cocktail through a bright pink straw to laugh with them.

CHAPTER FOUR

It wasn't that the baby party was a complete disaster. In fact, it wasn't a disaster at all. Ellen was delighted with all the presents she and Donnie received, even though they hadn't asked for anything — and she seemed especially pleased with the wine-tasting voucher that Olivia had bought for her.

'For when this is all over with,' the grandmother-to-be had said, as though speaking of a traumatic experience.

But even though everything had *seemingly* gone smoothly, something also very clearly hadn't. When Caitlin and I were travelling home from the family gathering, she'd turned to me and said, 'Did you mean what you said when you were talking to my dad earlier?'

It had been a long afternoon. Peter and I had spoken *a lot*. So my natural response — as anyone's natural response in that situation would have been, I think — was to answer, 'Can you be more specific, babe?'

Caitlin had turned to look out of the taxi's window and sighed. 'Never mind.'

Two days later, and she had said fifty-two words to me in that time. I know that because, while staring at the ceiling on the first night and wondering what I'd done wrong, I tallied up everything she'd said. And the tired, illogical part of my brain decided to carry on tallying things up the next day. Most of her words were made up of 'no, thank you' or 'yes, please' when I asked her things. I found myself asking whether she wanted tea, what she wanted for dinner, whether the light-coloured washing had been done yet, specifically so I could get a response out of her.

On the evening of the third day, I wandered over to the sofa where Caitlin was curled up with a book, and I placed a large glass of chilled white wine on the coffee table in front of her. This in itself was an olive branch, given that I was a steadfast drinker of pink wine. But I placed my own glass of white alongside hers, and then curled up in the empty spot beside her.

'Everything okay?' I asked.

'Mhmm.'

I leaned forward to grab my laptop from the table. If we weren't going to talk, then I was at least going to get some work done. It was two hours and three glasses of wine later when we gave up on our frosty, but somehow companionable, quiet.

'I won't have another,' Caitlin said. She started to struggle up from the sofa. 'I've got an early work thing *and* a late work thing tomorrow.' She sounded exhausted by the sheer thought of both.

'Is it anything I can help with?' I stood up and wandered to the kitchen to drop our empties off in the sink.

Caitlin made a noise that was half laugh, half sigh. 'You can try washing those glasses up before you come to bed.' She pulled me to her and kissed me on the corner of my mouth. It was a slow, lingering kind of kiss, and I wondered whether this meant we'd cracked through the ice of the last couple of days. 'But short of having a meal ready for when I'm home, there's not really anything. Do you mind?'

I frowned. 'Do I mind cooking?'

'Well, yeah.'

'Why would I . . . Never mind, no, of course I don't mind cooking.'

'Okay, then.' She kissed me again, firmer this time. There was no lingering. 'I'll see you in a sec.'

Caitlin trod away in the direction of the bedroom and left me standing clueless in the kitchen. *Why would I* mind *cooking her dinner?*

I began to overthink as I stood swilling our glasses, and the three cups I'd left abandoned around the kitchen over the day, too. I washed, swilled, and set things to drain, still wondering about Caitlin's comment. But on my journey to turn off the lamps around the flat, it occurred to me that this might just be me finding *another* thing to overthink. With the flat in darkness, I followed Caitlin into our room, where she was miraculously already tucked up in bed with the lights out. So I changed from comfies to comfier — writing clothes to sleeping ones — and climbed in next to her.

It took me all of five minutes to realise that I wasn't going to sleep anytime soon, though. So I ferreted my phone out from my bedside table, turned the brightness down, and Googled: 'easy romantic recipes'. I filtered the website to only show things with two chef's hats — not *quite* a beginner's rating, but certainly an easy one — and browsed through their ideas. After thirty minutes and twelve recipes, I'd decided on baked sea bass with lemon caper dressing. I was only mildly deterred by the fact that the sea bass itself required two ingredients — sea bass and olive oil — while the accompanying dressing required approximately one million things to make. But I remained determined. I copied everything into a note on my phone, quickly Googled whether Tesco Extra was likely to stock lemon caper dressing — turns out that was a hard no — and then I factored food shopping into my plan for the following day.

***

People think there aren't any drawbacks to working from home. Believe me, there are. The main being that, for much of your working life when you're working from home, it's entirely possible to forget that there's somewhere you actually need to be.

That's how I wound up half-dressed with my head in a cupboard, holding a shoe in one hand and my mobile in the other. I'd also be lying if I said that five minutes ago those two items hadn't got a little muddled. But after a minute of talking into my shoe and getting no response, I made a hasty swap and asked my mum how much of what I'd been saying she'd heard.

'You got your shoe confused with your phone, didn't you?' she said it as though I did this sort of thing regularly. 'Sweetheart, why didn't you set an alarm?'

'Because before I went to sleep, our psychic linking told me that you'd call and wake me.' I felt a pang of elation when I finally found the other shoe wedged at the back of my cupboard. I yanked it free, threw both in the general direction of the doorway, then ferreted through my clothes to find a top that would go with stylishly ripped jeans. Or rather, the first clean pair of jeans I happened to find when I fell out of bed ten minutes ago. 'I looked at recipes, fell asleep and forgot to set an alarm. But you called, so all is well.'

'I mean, all isn't well, that's *why* I called. I was telling you about Nancy two doors down—'

'Is all well with *you*, Mum?'

There was a decently sized pause. 'Well, yes, but—'

'Then could I possibly call you back when I get on my train?'

'You mean that Underground contraption.'

'Yes, that Underground contraption.' I tried to keep the contempt out of my voice. There were times when I didn't feel London enough for London. Anyone from outside the city limits will know precisely what I mean. But whenever I spoke to my mum, who could only ever call me from one or two rooms in her house because her signal was so shocking, I realised that I'd acclimatised to the city better than I'd realised. 'I love you, deeply, but I am running so late, Mum.'

'You don't get signal on the Underground.'

I froze. It was my turn for a lengthy pause. I actually did get signal there these days, because London had moved up in the world of 4G. But it didn't seem like a life lesson worth introducing to Mum *right* at this moment. 'No, you're right, you don't.'

'You're a rude, rude young woman and I love you.'

'Thanks so much for understanding, Mum. Love you.'

It took another ten minutes for me to get out of the flat. Then the best part of forty-five minutes on top of that to get to Soho, where I ran straight into Elza standing outside our office building. She had a stern expression, a cigarette, and a foot that I thought had likely been hard-tapping the pavement not thirty seconds ago.

'So, Dotty, when I say I've got the media team to arrange fresh Dear Dotty headshots, and when I email to say, "Dotty, make sure you're not late for the photoshoot on Wednesday", you take that to mean what, exactly?'

'Elza, I'm sorry. There was this whole thing with a raccoon. It swept right into my apartment, wrecked the place and—'

'You can't talk your way out of this with a *Friends* reference.'

I tried to keep the surprise from my face. I hadn't had Elza pegged for the *Friends* generation. 'I really am sorry. I completely overslept and got waylaid by Mum, but I am here.'

'You look gorgeous, by the way.' She said it with such bite that it somehow sounded like an insult. 'Woe is me, for having outgrown the days of being able to rush across London in casual clothing and still look like a bloody model at the other end. Get in,' she pointed to the door. 'Carlos is waiting for you in the downstairs studio.'

* * *

Needless to say, what should have been a quick photoshoot turned into nearly a full day of it. There was the photoshoot itself, then the feedback from the shoot, where Elza made me look at unedited pictures of myself and choose my favourites

22

to be edited. Then there was lunch with Carlos, because after all, 'He's travelled all this way.' Elza laid on the guilt thick, apparently forgetting that I knew full well Carlos lived in a loft conversion *in Soho*. Next, there was an impromptu meeting with Elza to discuss the Dear Dotty column for that week, and to blitz through submissions to the Dotty inbox, before talking through the possibility of my getting an assistant to help filter those submissions, which seemed to be growing in number by the week. I nearly asked whether having an assistant would mean I could send them to these unscheduled office days instead, so I could stay at home writing, but even I was aware of the potential to read that as ungrateful. Even though it wasn't intended to be (lazy, yes, but certainly not ungrateful).

By the time I tumbled through the door to the flat later that afternoon, the last thing on my mind was lemon caper dressing.

'I could go for some fish though,' I said to no one. I freed my phone from the back pocket of my jeans and texted Caitlin to ask when she'd be back. She replied immediately to say I had another three hours. Then she texted again to ask what was for dinner.

I didn't reply, because when you've been in a relationship with someone for nearly ten years there's sometimes a need for an air of mystery. That, and I wasn't altogether convinced that the whole sea bass thing would work out. I trod from the living room to the kitchen to set the kettle boiling and fetched my laptop from my bag by the front door. The afternoon setup looked like sunshine through an open window with a steaming cup in front of it, and my laptop just in the corner of the photo square. I posted it to the Dear Dotty Instagram account — 'Who doesn't love London in this light?' — and then went over the letters that Elza and I had chosen that afternoon.

There was a young woman asking for advice on how to sensitively break up with her partner, an older man asking for

23

advice on how to respectfully approach women these days, and what sounded like a teenager querying their sexuality. We'd picked them for variety, but they were all stark reminders of how bloody lucky I was that people trusted me with their problems and wanted my advice at all.

I hadn't planned to start writing my answers. But I wagered they would need to be *so* carefully worded that starting sooner rather than later mightn't be a bad idea. What *was* a bad idea was starting them when I was meant to be in charge of making dinner. Because it was a full two-and-a-bit hours later when I came up for air, and even then, it was only because my phone had pinged with a message: Caitlin, saying she was on her way home. I saved the document, slammed the laptop closed, and went into overdrive. I hurriedly placed candles on the dining table, positioned wine glasses, and checked the fridge for chilled white, before turning the oven to a low heat and typing out a few rushed taps on my phone. Then I waited. The hum of the oven was an unwelcome percussion to my nervousness. It was a toss-up whether Caitlin would arrive home before everything was ready, and I didn't like the odds of her being okay with having to wait for dinner after such a long day and—

The buzzer to the apartment sounded.

Arses. I slapped my forehead. *No, wait, Caitlin wouldn't—*

I hopped and skipped down the stairs to the main door of the building and heaved a deep sigh of relief when I saw Pedro standing there with a large white carrier bag in hand, no doubt steaming with fresh fish and thrice-cooked chips. I ferreted a tip out of my back pocket and thanked him at least four times before closing the door and rushing back upstairs.

I slid the cardboard boxes into the oven to keep warm, lit the candles, and poured myself a splash of pink wine to enjoy while I waited for my love to come home.

CHAPTER FIVE

Elouise, Tots, and Marissa were already sitting at a table for four in a glorious patch of sunshine. Brunch outside with friends was undoubtedly one of the perks of London life. As I battled the madding crowds on the pavements to get closer to them — which, incidentally, is *not* one of the perks of life here — I could see that they had already ordered our drinks.

I waved to catch Tots's attention, and when she waved back, the other girls turned and gestured their greetings too. We were an unlikely friendship group: the model, the accountant, the journalist, and the advice columnist. Under different circumstances, we might have made the perfect sit-com cast. In real life, though, we were the archetypal friends who, by luck and chance, had been thrown together in first-year university accommodation, and we'd managed to stick out our friendships in the years since. These girls were, in no uncertain terms, a lifeline — not least because they put up with my ridiculous stunts for the sake of a good picture.

'You are absolute angels.' I dropped my bag alongside the empty seat that was waiting for me and sized up the spread on the table: three flat whites and a tall green mulch that looked like Elouise's answer to a cleanse. I kissed them one after the other on the cheek while we gushed our hellos. 'Mind if I get this over with?'

'We'd rather you did,' Marissa answered with a wink.

I held onto her shoulder to steady myself as I climbed up onto my seat, and opened my camera app. Marissa kept a firm hand around my calf while I shifted this way then the other to get everything inside the gridded version of my camera screen. I snapped one, two, three images, then changed the settings to take another four with a different filter. The girls had become accustomed to this Instagram routine. The stylised flat whites, the trendy table layout, versus the drinks we would *actually* order, and the pastries we would inhale.

'I'm sorry—'

I turned and nearly knocked over the waiter with the movement.

'—but is everything okay, miss?'

'Oh, fantastic,' Elouise answered dryly.

I saw Tots's shoulders shrug with a laugh.

I clambered down from my lofty perch, holding onto Marissa's shoulder again until I was steady on the ground. 'Everything is so great, thank you. But, could you actually swap this order around a bit for us, please?'

The young man looked at the table, then at my friends — who had clearly been no fuss at all in the thirty minutes they'd been here without me — and yet here I was, asking, 'Could you take the three flat whites back? And El, are you keeping that thing?'

'It's a kale smoothie, and yes.'

'Okay, can we sub out the three flat whites for three breakfast teas, please? And — actually, sorry, girls, is breakfast tea okay for you both?' I waited for Tots's and Marissa's murmurings of approval before turning to the waiter again. 'Three breakfast teas, and three croissants, butter and jam if you have it.'

'Ah, hello?' Elouise piped up. '*Three*?'

'I thought you were on a cleanse,' Marissa answered, her voice breaking with a laugh.

26

'Could you make that four, please? Thank you so much.'
I flashed the waiter my sweetest smile and ferreted a ten-pound
note from the back pocket of my jeans. 'I'm really sorry for
the inconvenience.'

I never really knew what passed for a good tip in London.
But given that this poor sod had double the work, just so I
could have a cluster of good shots for Dear Dotty, I thought
a tenner was the least he deserved. He assured me it was no
trouble at all — as he took the money — and then he started
to gather up the things on the table. Elouise set a protective
hand around the bottom of her glass as though she were afraid
the waiter might snatch it.

'Don't worry, babe, literally no one wants that,' Tots said.
'Jesus, it's just a juice drink.'

'And you're giving up caffeine altogether?'

'I'm sorry, what?' I snapped in answer to Marissa's question. My head shot around to Elouise then. 'Altogether?'

'It's just for a few weeks while I do this bloody cleanse.'

'Is it your agent making you do this?' Tots asked, her
head buried in her handbag as she tried to search out her
trusted vape. 'Aha! Or are you actually doing this of your own
volition? I'm not sure which one of the two I find least offensive, if I'm honest, but I think it would help to know.' She
took a thirsty inhale and exhaled a plume of fruit salad — or
something that claimed to be it, at least. 'You're a mile tall,
isn't that enough in your industry?'

Elouise sipped her drink and grimaced. 'Please. Nothing
is enough in my industry.'

'Then, why do it?' Marissa leaned back in her chair to
make way for the waiter, who was leaning over her with a
one-person pot of tea. I noticed it was a different waiter this
time, and a shudder of near-embarrassment moved through
me. 'If nothing is enough, then—'

'Ladies,' I interrupted, 'given that Marissa, you work
anything up to eighteen hours a day crunching numbers, and

27

Tots? You were literally shaken off your last freelance job due to a *bomb scare*, I'm not sure our hands are clean.'

'And what about Dear Dotty?' Tots asked with a raised eyebrow.

'What about her?'

Marissa giggled. 'Breaking waiters' hearts all over London, making their jobs even—'

'I tipped him!'

'You're right, she *is* a Londoner now,' Elouise butted in, and I felt a whiplash sting at the subject change.

'Since when have I been a Londoner?'

'Since your idea of a romantic meal for two is something you paid someone else to cook and deliver to your door in time for your girlfriend to get home,' Tots answered as a smirk spread over her face.

'Now that we're on the subject, I don't understand what's even so bad about that,' Marissa chimed in. The majority of her concentration was still focused on pouring *just* the right amount of milk into her tea to keep it a good colour. 'Dotty is busy, Caitlin is busy; you don't always have time to throw a meal together, and sometimes you eat for convenience.'

'That's true,' Elouise agreed. 'Hey Marissa, how *is* your love life these days?'

Tots made an 'Ooh' noise from across the table, meanwhile Marissa's face looked thoroughly unimpressed next to me. 'I'm really glad I booked time out of my eighteen-hour workday to come and have brunch with you bitches.'

'Speaking of which,' I craned around in my seat to look for the waiter, *any* waiter, 'do you think he forgot our pastries?'

'Aren't we eating, like, proper food anyway?' Tots said. 'I could murder fish and thrice-cooked chips.'

There was a chorus of laughter in answer to her comment. Meanwhile, I huffed and started to pour my own tea. Despite her falling in line with the funniness of it, I wholeheartedly agreed with Marissa, *obviously. What's the issue with ordering in at the end of two long workdays?* The fact that it had been my turn to cook had nothing to do with it.

'I wouldn't have minded if Caitlin surprised me with fish and chips at the end of a long day.' When I saw the expressions on my friends' faces I began to wonder whether they'd changed the topic already.

'Honey,' Elouise leaned across the table and held out her hand, 'we're just teasing.'

I reached across and she squeezed my hand. 'No, I know, it's just . . . Caitlin seems really put out by it, and I . . . Oh, I don't know. It doesn't matter.'

'Hey!' Marissa cupped my shoulder with her palm. 'Of course it matters.'

'Do you think Caitlin's issue is that a lot of love actually goes into homemade cooking over convenience cooking, and you might have picked the wrong thing out of the two when she'd specifically told you which one she wanted?'

It felt a little like Tots had slapped me with her menu. And from a sideways look at Elouise and Marissa, I could tell they both felt the same.

Tots's mouth bobbed open, closed, open again. A puff of air escaped her, shortly followed by a nervous high-pitched sound. 'I mean, what the hell do I know? I haven't had sex in nearly a year, you really shouldn't be listening to me.'

'Ah, um.' The waiter — waiter number one — lingered by the table. Tots's face reddened as she looked up at him, and I heard a snort escape Marissa. 'I brought the croissants that you . . . I'll just, if I can . . .' He took great care to avoid leaning over Tots to set the plate down on the table, then muttered something about a colleague coming to take our food order shortly.

By the time he was a safe distance from Tots the Siren, we'd all erupted into wild laughter befitting of Banshees. It didn't matter that people stared. And for a few minutes, it didn't matter that Caitlin hadn't appreciated my thrice-cooked chips.

Elouise tucked a small measure of croissant into her mouth while the rest of us tore into ours.

'Anyway,' I spoke around perfect flakes, 'that's my news. What have I missed in everyone else's world while I've been letting down my girlfriend?'

29

'You didn't let her down!' Marissa erupted. Tots made a show of flicking pastry crumbs off her face. I couldn't help but laugh, even though I was sure Marissa's outburst couldn't have reached *that* far. 'It was one meal, one time. Besides, you show up for people in the ways that count, Dotts. Don't sell yourself short on that.'

I made a noise like I didn't quite agree — mostly because I didn't.

'Don't give me that,' Tots chimed in then, 'it was literally two months ago, if that, you cancelled with Caitlin at the last minute because Marissa got roped into that networking thing with her sleazy client.'

'And you were a *fantastic* girlfriend to me all night,' Marissa added.

I smiled. 'But I stood Caitlin up for that.'

'To help a friend,' Elouise answered flatly. 'It hardly counts as bad behaviour.'

'Besides, what about the time you dressed up like a cock-tail waitress and absolutely saved Caitlin's backside at the PR event she put on?' Tots said, tearing free a fresh mouthful of dough. 'Or literally last month, when *she* cancelled last minute on you for that' — she clicked her fingers, trying to remember the finer details — 'whatever it was.'

'Didn't she lose track of time having drinks with friends?' Elouise asked. She took a sip of her drink and winced. 'God, I hate this.'

'Right, that's it.' I turned and looked for a waiter. 'I'm ordering you a tea.'

'I can't have tea!'

'You can have decaf. Excuse me? Miss?' It was a waitress who came to our table this time, and she took my order as though she had no idea what our previous indiscretions had been that morning. 'Can we get a decaf tea with skimmed milk, please? Thank you so much.'

When I turned back around Elouise gave me a soft smile, and Tots, who was licking her fingers clean of jam, said, 'See, no one in the world could accuse you of being uncaring, Dotty. You're just caring in non-home-cooked meal ways.' She winked. 'Now, can we *please* look at the menu?'

'You literally *just* finished your croissant,' Elouise protested.

'Hey,' I leapt in, 'she's gotta keep that big, beautiful brain of hers well fed if she's going to take down the politicians and sleazebuckets of the world with her scathing, well-written journalism.'

'See,' Tots added, 'caring in a non-home-cooked meal way. Just like I said.'

Dear Dotty,

I am the single friend. It feels like I should be writing that with capital letters. I'm sure it bothers my friends much more than it actually bothers me. I'm thirty-six now and for the last six years, if not longer, they've tried setting me up with their other single friends and nothing has stuck. At this point I think I'm going along with it all out of politeness rather than want. Because honestly, I'm not sure I want a relationship. I love all my couple friends so much and there are times when I do utterly envy them. But there are also times when one hasn't done the washing or the other hasn't bought the right food shopping or the other has arranged for a visit to the in-laws without checking first, and the arguments galore that break out over the silliest of things just makes me wonder. Am I meant to be alone? Do you think some of us are? And, should we all be a bit more open to that possibility?

Please, give me your best honesty,
Alone But Not Lonely xxx

CHAPTER SIX

One week and five home-cooked meals later, I sought sanctuary outside of my home and office. It wasn't my day to go into work, and I couldn't stand the questions that would come with my unexpected arrival. But I also couldn't tolerate being at home anymore, either. Now, I didn't know whether it was the fish and chips incident — as it had come to be known — or the proverbial corks wedged up either nostril, but Caitlin was actually becoming close to impossible to be around. So that morning, I packed up my laptop and notebook, put on one of my nicest summer dresses — black, covered in white flowers, with a wide base that kicked out a satisfying swoosh when I twirled around (and absolutely not warm enough for the weather that day) — and did the only thing that any sane, self-preserving person would have done.

I lied to my girlfriend.

'You didn't mention having to go in for a meeting,' she said. Her nose was so clogged with mucus that it was hard to know whether she sounded suspicious or not.

'It's just this thing that Elza wants me to pop along to, so we can throw some ideas around for the future of the column. I think she said something about an assistant, too.' I pulled that truth from *deep* within my memory. 'I'm not sure. Anyway, can I get you anything while I'm out?'

I left with a veritable shopping list of cold and flu medications to source from somewhere on my travels. But I also had a sunny spot and a window seat at a coffee shop that was completely new to me.

It felt a little like bliss just to sit and breathe and be. I was ten minutes into my sitting when I remembered why I was actually there: to work. A helpful waitress, leaning over me with a steaming mug of fruit tea, snapped me out of my quiet sighs and admiration of the sunny day, reminding me why I'd set up camp. When she asked if there was anything else she could get for me, I bit back the temptation to bring more pastries into my life. I was sure that if I totted up the amount I'd spent on socialising and feeding myself, I could have bought my mum's house outright by now.

'I'm fine, thank you,' I answered with a smile and then turned back to my view.

'I'm sorry . . .' the waitress continued. 'This is, well, embarrassing. But, you're not . . . I mean, are you . . .' She laughed at herself, sighed, and shook her hands, as though trying to physically shift the nerves she was clearly nursing. 'Are you Dear Dotty?'

It felt as though someone had pinched colour into my cheeks. This didn't happen often, admittedly. But when it did, I always felt a little like I wanted the ground to crack open, swallow me whole, and then seal over again just to be sure that no one chased after me. The Dear Dotty Instagram account was the most front-facing thing I had for the column, but it still didn't have my actual face on it. Whenever I snapped and papped London streets, it was coffee shops and window views and the best parks to visit with your partner. It was never me — never just Dotty. *She must know me from my column headshot*, I realised then, not for the first time.

I flashed her a thin smile and held out my hand. 'That's me.'

She reciprocated with an enthusiastic shake. 'Oh my god. I'm Jenny. I'm *such* a massive fan. I actually dumped my last boyfriend *because* of you.'

'Oh, I . . . Ah, that's—' *Holy heck, what do you say to that?*

'It's not a bad thing,' she rushed to add, obviously spotting the sheer horror that had taken over my face, 'he really wasn't good for me, and I read a story about someone in such a similar situation and you' — she paused to laugh — 'you point blank told this person to dump their partner, and it was genuinely like you were talking to me, like, talking right at me. And now I'm with someone who is actually nice to me and . . . Gosh, I'm just — I feel like I *owe* you.'

'That's so lovely to hear, honestly, but you don't owe me any—'

'What's your favourite pastry? Cake? Anything? I can see if we have it? On the house.'

Ah, well, now that changes things . . .

Five minutes later I'd taken thirteen pictures of the masterpiece that was a generous slice of carrot cake, complete with a pot of ridiculously thick cream to douse it in. It was then I remembered that Caitlin didn't actually know where I was, and the cake tasted of guilt and bad decision-making from the very first mouthful.

While I was chewing through my guilt-cake, I read and reread Alone But Not Lonely's letter. It wasn't a hard letter, not really. And yet, I couldn't quite decide what route I was meant to take with my advice. Should I tell them to shush and let their friends carry on trying to set them up, even though my letter-writer clearly didn't want that? Or should I be honest and say, *You're right, Lonely One, sometimes being on your own is just fine*? Frankly, I worried a little about what it might say about *me* if I were to admit that on a public forum. Would Caitlin find it and read into it? Would it be the catalyst for more awkward evenings and unspoken tensions? Of which there had been more than enough already, over the last couple of weeks especially. I rubbed hard at my forehead and stared out of the window, as though I might find an answer, standing across the street from me, jumping up and down and waving its arms in delight that I'd finally spotted it. I didn't like that I'd managed to tie this back to Caitlin. Caitlin, who most definitely hadn't read my column in at least five years. But when prodded with the question of being alone but not lonely, I couldn't help but wonder whether there was part of me — in my long-term, easy-going, very settled relationship — that, lately, had felt more Lonely But Not Alone.

But then an even more disturbing thought arrived in the wake of that first one: *Is Caitlin lonely sometimes, too?* It was a knee-jerk reaction to grab my phone then and tap out a text to see how she was feeling. I followed it immediately with a second text to ask whether there was anything she needed — apart from the list I already had. It was a balm to my panic that she put three kisses at the end of her message when she replied. It was childish, but kisses were still currency in our relationship — a throwback to some time between 1995 and 2015, when the amount of kisses determined the intensity of someone's feelings for you.

After replying to tell her that I wouldn't be much longer and promising a dinner of mashed potatoes with melted cheese (which I remained convinced was how I'd won her heart in the first place), I settled down to write my letter back.

No, Alone But Not Lonely, relationships aren't for everyone, I would say, *but they are worth having when you find the right person to share one with.* Now all I needed to do was write that in such a way that Elza didn't print the column, chew it up, and vomit it back over my desk like a disgruntled housecat when she saw me next.

* * *

The overwhelming London heat had started to dip into something that warranted a thin cardigan if you were out too late or too early. Caitlin had finally recovered from her annual cold — or 'this plague' as she'd been referring to it before

36

her nose unblocked — and I'd mostly recovered from my Lonely But Not Alone incident. I wasn't lonely, not really. Especially when Caitlin came out of her Lemsip haze of hatred and started speaking to me like I was a normal human being again, rather than a chambermaid, or a plague doctor.

I wrote back to Alone But Not Lonely to tell them, in no uncertain terms, that no, there wasn't anything wrong with not wanting a relationship, right now or ever. They were well within their rights to tell their friends to pipe down and enjoy them for the token happily single friend that they were, with no need for romantic intervention. Elza didn't quite vomit the article back into my inbox, but she did tell me to be less 'soapbox' about it — which, for her, counted as kind editorial input. I tweaked the column, resubmitted the letter, and put all thoughts of loneliness out of my mind . . . until two days after my response letter was uploaded to the magazine's website when I made the *stupid* mistake of reading the comments on the page which I would ordinarily *never* do. But I was far too emotionally attached and as a result, couldn't help but press the tip of my finger to the wound to see whether it was still tender. The first comment read: *Really Dotts!? You don't think sooner or later we all NEED someone!?*

I slammed my laptop closed and took my tea over to the open window in the living room. The street below was busy with bikes ringing bells, drivers tooting horns at the bikes, and people on one side of the street hollering their hellos to people on the other. And like a confused kid playing a competitive sport without knowing the rules, I ran between wondering whether I was content in this moment, or lonely in it. *Content-lonely-content-lonely*. I hurried between the two like a game of touch tag while I finished my tea. When there was nothing but dregs left in the bottom of my mug, I did the only sensible thing I could think of: I drafted four responses to the top comment on my letter, deleted them all, and then made another cup of tea.

* * *

By the time Caitlin came home that night, the flat was an absolute wonderland, if I do say so myself. I had pulled the blinds down to shut out the last of the low-hanging sun outside and closed the windows, too, despite it turning the living room into greenhouse levels of hot. But it was the only way to set the right tone for the movie night I had envisioned — a potential remedy to our various ills. Fairy lights now hung around every mirror and picture frame in our living area. There were tealight candles in various coloured jars dotted around the room, too, complete with all of the soft blankets I could find, every throw cushion Caitlin had ever pointlessly brought home with her, and our pillows from the bed. It was by no means an understatement to consider our sofa a fort of soft things.

The coffee table was covered with mixed nuts, crisps, mini cheese and tomato pizzas and, I'll admit, a lot of other things that had photographed well when I'd snapped some shots for future use. There were also two bottles of white chilling in the fridge and a two-litre bottle of Coke Zero set to chill, too — another of Caitlin's favourite things. I'd also bought hazelnut hot chocolate, mini marshmallows, and whipped cream in case we were actually awake — or not in a food coma — long enough to make it to a second film. It was the ideal home movie night, complete with three of Caitlin's favourite films stacked on the coffee table. We were a streaming household, so the DVD cases were largely there for gesture — I wasn't sure we even had anything to play them on — but I wanted something that would complete the look.

And after all this, I waited for the inevitable click and bustle of Caitlin arriving home . . .

'Dotts, I'm . . . *Oh*.'

Caitlin was dumbstruck as she wandered into the room.

'Welcome to London's most select cinema screening,' I announced. I couldn't be sure whether it was the atmospheric lighting or whether she was actually a little aglow with the surprise of it all. 'Tonight, we're offering *Dirty Dancing, Moulin*

Rouge, and *Notting Hill* for your viewing pleasure, even though that last one feels a bit on the nose.'

Caitlin stood with a hand on each cheek and a wide smile between. 'Dotty, this is . . . Why did you . . .' She threw her hands up. 'Do you know what, it doesn't matter why, this is bloody lovely.' She pulled me in for a slow kiss that made my lips numb and my heart loud. 'Christ, you hate all of those films, too,' she said as she pulled away, still clutching my hand.

'I do not *hate* them, I just think they're too . . .'

'Romantic?'

I frowned. 'Hello' — I gestured to the room — 'do I look like someone who's afraid of a little romance?'

'Oh, babe, you really do have no idea sometimes.' She tapped my cheek tenderly, but the gesture didn't feel right for what she'd just said. *Am I afraid of a little romance?* Before I had the chance to speak the thought aloud, Caitlin wandered to the coffee table to assess our feast. 'You got all of my favourite things, Dotts, I . . .' She petered out and shook her head. 'This is perfect, it really is.' She wandered back to kiss me again, a soft one this time, on the corner of my mouth. 'Thank you for this. It's been a pig of a day and this, well, this just changes everything.'

I beamed. 'Then my work here is done. Wine?'

'White?'

'Of course,' I shouted back, already on my way to the kitchen. 'The DVDs are for effect, by the way, but I have got all of those in our watch list ready if you want to throw the set on.'

'How's *Dirty Dancing* sound?'

Like torture. 'Perfect.' I poured Caitlin a large measure of white and myself a splash of pink, then went back to the living room. Caitlin had already managed to burrow into the soft furnishings. When I went to set her drink on the table she made a grabbing gesture for me to pass it to her. 'It really has been a day, eh?'

She smiled. 'More like, it really has been a couple of weeks.' She paused to sip, and I waited in anticipation of a fuller explanation. 'I just haven't been feeling great about . . . stuff, I suppose.' She took another sip, then handed me her glass to put down.

But that seemed to be the end of the conversation, as Caitlin clicked into the film, pulled back the blankets, and patted the space for me to scooch in alongside her. I wanted to push, to ask whether it was only the cold, or something else, something bigger, that had made the last couple of weeks so hard. But I was genuinely scared of ruining what felt like an evening with a lot of promise, especially when I saw the Cheshire Cat contentment on Caitlin's face. So, I parked myself on the sofa, lifted an arm, and let her curl in against me without any further comment.

We were half an hour into the film when Caitlin spoke again. 'Is this whole night a prelude to a night at Claridge's next week by any chance?'

Claridge's was one of the city's finer dining establishments. Packed rich with Art Deco glam, a waiting list as long as your arm, and a menu made up of truffles and food that all seemed to originate from somewhere: Cornish lamb, Norfolk black chicken, Severn & Wye smoked salmon. Caitlin had been to a snazzy public relations event there for work a year or two back, and we'd browsed the menu well in advance — her with starry eyes, me with absolute terror. Caitlin's family regularly dined out at this sort of restaurant; she was practically raised on these kinds of menus. It was a far cry from the chain pubs Mum and I had treated ourselves to on *very* special occasions when I was a kid.

After Caitlin's visit there, she'd spoken about Carlingford oysters daily for a good month. I had a vague memory of promising to take her one day — despite the terror — but we hadn't quite gotten around to it. It seemed a leap to go from a makeshift home cinema night to a restaurant that would swallow our monthly allowance for rent, bills, and a food shop.

I decided to go along with her joke. 'Yep, mhm, sure thing. I'll be wearing a suit, and I'll pick you out a nice dress. I'll collect you from work, and we'll make a real party of it.'

'Why do you think I'm joking?'

'Why do you think I am?' I kissed the crown of her head. But of course we were both joking. *Claridge's? For an average date night?* I squeezed Caitlin, gave her another kiss, then turned my attention back to the film, where Patrick Swayze was rolling his hips in a way that bordered on the erotic. *Claridge's?* I huffed a quiet laugh, and we spent the rest of the film in comfortable, companionable quiet.

41

CHAPTER SEVEN

Despite the previous break in temperature, the heat in London grew to unbearable levels in the days that followed. Apparently this was the last push of a heatwave, a kickback from summer that wasn't ready to give way fully to autumn just yet. Everyone seemed to be making the most of it: the city was overflowing with full beer gardens, outdoor brunching, and wanders through the parks. My Instagram feed was awash with images of friends enjoying themselves in the sun.

Meanwhile, my @noplacelikehome Instagram account — my *actual* account, that is — boasted nothing more than back-to-back pictures of me eating homemade ice lollies that I stripped from the freezer one after the other, as though my very life depended on the sugar intake. There had been many a time when I'd thought of suggesting to Caitlin that we invest in an air conditioning unit for the flat for weeks such as these. Or at the very least an industrial fan. That week, though, while the heat tore through London, the inside of the flat became veritably frosty — ice lollies aside. It was more to do with Caitlin than anything else, who was becoming increasingly distant as the week wore on. I didn't know what had happened this time — and it was starting to feel like a trend, that I would upset her without meaning to, without even knowing how I'd done so. And even though I *should* have asked what I'd done, I also knew that I had a mountain of Dear Dotty letters to wade through, while being painfully aware that Elza had put a mystery meeting in my diary for the end of the week, too. I had my own stresses: Elza never planned meetings without context. She was honourable like that — she liked people to know in advance when she was coming for them. Because of this, and because of Elza having entirely ignored my email asking what the meeting was for, it felt as though I was already juggling enough fires. So, I let Caitlin be quiet and have her space. I reasoned that once the Friday meeting was out of the way, I could tackle Caitlin.

And then I went and got myself another ice lolly.

* * *

On the day of the dreaded meeting, I waltzed through London in a bright white dress that was polka-dot patterned with tiny sunflowers. It wasn't the most professional attire, but it was also the only clothing I could stand to wear with the temperature pushing thirty. I darted and dodged my way to the office in a mad hurry and then desperately tried to find reasons *not* to go inside when I arrived. *Maybe I should go and get pastries*, I wondered. *But what if it's not just us? What if I need more than just pastries for two people?* Then I spiralled into thinking of all the situations that might involve *more* than two people. By the time I was climbing the stairs to Elza's floor, I'd actually managed to convince myself there would be a panel of HR personnel waiting for me on the other side of the frosted glass window that barred my view.

So imagine my shock — and utter bloody relief — when I walked through the door.

'Surprise!'

The entire team was waiting for me, in a room adorned with banners, bottles of wine, and cakes galore.

Thank God I didn't stop for cakes.

'Darling Dotty.' Elza approached with an arm out-stretched for a hug, which would have perhaps been the most surprising thing of all, had she seen it through. Instead, she snatched a small glass of pink wine from a nearby tray — I was touched that they'd even bought my favourite booze — and she went in to rub softly at the top of my arm instead. 'Your face is a picture. What were you expecting?'

'I . . .' I accepted the glass and immediately took a sip before laughing. 'Not this!'

'It's ten years of Dear Dotty! We couldn't let that go uncelebrated. Look' — she led me towards a string of bunting hanging over a nearby window — 'we printed your most pop-ular columns and had these made. Aren't they fantastic?'

They really were. So fantastic that I felt tears pricking at the corners of my eyes. I reached up to pinch one of the col-umns between my finger and thumb, and squinted as though trying to make out the writing from this distance. It bought me the time I needed to blink back the feeling.

'Don't worry about snapping pictures either, unless you want them for feeling's sake. We had the team come in and do a proper sweep of the room before you got here. I'll make sure they're emailed over.'

I rolled my eyes. 'Thanks, Elza.'

'Come on, you're a commodity.'

'Thank you, I think?'

'You're welcome. Now work the room.' She tapped me lightly on the backside. 'There are a lot of people here who want to tell you how brilliant you are.'

I swallowed my small measure of wine in two thirsty mouthfuls and grabbed another glass on my way to say hello to Richard — the poor man who had no doubt been tasked with taking the aforementioned photographs.

After Richard I said hello to Claire, and Marie, and Abigail, Ian, and David, and Lance, and then somehow I was four glasses of wine in and heady as a kitten on catnip for its first time. I had been too nervous to eat anything that morning, but between the empty stomach and the heat, the wine now seemed to be sloshing about my tummy, arms, and legs alike, creating that joyous tingly feeling that comes with the early stretch of intoxication. So, when Elza clambered up onto a vacant desk, tapping at her wine glass with a pen, I took the opportunity to stuff no fewer than *two* strawberry iced cupcakes in my mouth at once. I chewed behind my hand and swallowed in such a rush that I needed another swig of wine to wash the food down. Then pretended to laugh along with my colleagues at whatever Elza had just said.

'Dotty, come up here a second, would you?'

My eyes widened as the room turned to me. 'On the desk?'

Elza huffed a laugh as though this was the most ridiculous question I'd ever asked her — which it definitely wasn't. 'Yes, Dotts, on the desk.'

Ever the gent, Richard held my hand to steady me while I stepped on the chair and then onto the desk alongside Elza. Thank goodness the desk had been empty to begin with; otherwise I hated to think what pens, mugs, and miscellaneous personal items I might have sent flying as Elza and I fidgeted next to each other.

She wrapped an arm around me then and I felt myself go frigid. 'This woman has worked *tirelessly* since she started here with us. And I know some of you have known her for a long old time now' — she paused to laugh — 'ten years in fact.' Everyone seemed to find that hilarious, including Abigail, who definitely overdid it with her belch of a laugh from the back of the room. 'And some of you have only known her a short time. But either way, I have known Dotty and her work ethic since she started here. I have known her to sacrifice personal plans. I have known her to work through weekends, and I have seen her make it her personal mission to reply to every single entry in her inbox, *not* just the letters we're publishing.' I wondered whether she was going somewhere with

45

this, or whether it had become *Elza's* mission to parade me in front of my colleagues as a workplace model. My cheeks were burning the same shade of pink as the wine now. 'I have seen her shape Dear Dotty into something beautiful, and Dotts' — she turned to me — 'it's been an honour to work with you.'

Unprompted, the entire room erupted into semi-drunken applause, and I'm woman enough to admit that I cried then. Not a whopping great blubber of feeling, but a small well of it gathered in each eye and unsteadily perched there. A tear tumbled down each cheek when Richard helped me down from the desk and said, 'She's right you know, Dotts. You're something else to work with.' He winked, too. Not the sleazy London lad-about-town wink. But the supportive, proud wink that my dad might have given me, if he had existed.

It was well outside of work hours by the time the cakes and bottles had run dry. There were some people who'd escaped early, citing childcare arrangements and evening plans as their excuses. Then there were those of us upending our glasses one last time to make absolutely sure they were empty. Elza had just finished the last vanilla cupcake of the bunch when I drew up next to her, wearing the loose and happy smile of a drunk woman who'd spent the afternoon celebrating her achievements.

Elza licked icing from her finger. 'You look very pleased with yourself. I take it we did well with our little surprise?'

I clutched my chest. 'Oh, Elza, you did so much more than well. I didn't expect anything at all for the ten years, never mind something—'

'I meant every word, Dotts,' she interrupted me. 'You give your all to this place and it doesn't go unnoticed. Now, home or away?'

I looked around the room one last time. 'Home.'

Elza pulled her phone from her trouser pocket. 'I'll order you an Uber.'

'Oh, I can take the—'

'You're drunk and it's too bloody warm. Take an Uber.'

I laughed. 'Thank you, Elza.' I turned and gestured to the bunting. 'Would it be okay if I kept some of that? Is that silly?'

'Absolutely ludicrous.' She winked at me. 'I'll make sure it's wound up and left on your desk.'

'Thank you, Elza, for all of this.' I gestured to the room. 'And for taking a chance on me.'

She shrugged off the comment. 'Best chance I've ever taken. So you're welcome.'

In the back of the taxi, I texted Caitlin to let her know I'd been blindsided by the afternoon's celebrations. I followed it up with a flurry of pictures showing the room in various states of party antics, including an image of Elza standing on the desk, which I sent without context. It occurred to me that it might lend itself well to a caption contest over breakfast the next day. She didn't reply, even though the messages immediately appeared as read. So I texted again to say I was nearly home. But she didn't reply to that either.

CHAPTER EIGHT

I didn't notice the card until the morning after.

After the card, I noticed the flowers. Then the missing overnight bag.

I made a strong tea, tucked myself onto the windowsill to let in the early morning breeze, and called the only person I knew would be awake at that time. The phone rang out three times before—

'Is everything okay?'

'I messed up, Marissa.'

I heard the shuffling of papers in the background. 'Give me a second.' Marissa moved around on the other end of the line and I imagined her excusing herself from a room of people who were also already crunching numbers, despite it being the weekend. 'What's happened?'

'Caitlin and I have been together for ten years.'

There was a long pause. 'I wouldn't say that's you messing up.'

'Is my *forgetting* that we've been together for ten years me messing up?'

'Ah.' Then there came an even longer pause. 'Well, yes, that's you—'

'Bugger, bugger, bugger,' I chanted. 'What the hell is the matter with me?'

'That's a very separate line of questioning. First, what's happened with Caitlin?'

I sighed and regaled her with the story. The joke about the expensive dinner — which I now realised hadn't been a joke at all — and the frostiness that came after. The tension when she was clearly upset with me about something I'd said, which I still didn't even remember saying. 'Something I'd said to her dad, I think? But I don't know, I . . .' I reached for an ending to that sentence but couldn't find one. Instead, I finished with the missing overnight bag, the open *Happy Anniversary* card propped on the kitchen table, and the flowers deliberately draped over the top of my closed laptop, where Caitlin knew I would find them.

'Have you called her?'

'No, I . . .' I faltered in the face of the question. 'I called you.'

'Do you know where she'll have gone?'

'Her parents,' I answered without hesitation that time. Years ago, Caitlin and I had made a quiet agreement that if either of us were ever to make a mistake — though that felt like somewhat of an understatement here — we wouldn't immediately run to our friends. Instead, like adults, we'd run home. We both believed that friends were notorious for being less forgiving, though I thought this situation might stretch the limits of Caitlin's parents' own abilities to forgive. But still, we'd promised each other that we wouldn't ever air our dirty laundry with people that the misbehaving party would later have to face on a regular basis, once the storm had subsided. It had felt like a very grown-up agreement at the time. And Caitlin was a sucker for keeping promises.

'Will you go over?'

'And do what?'

'Apologise, Dotty,' she snapped. 'You mess up, you say sorry.'

I ran a hand through my hair and rested my head against the edge of the window frame. I was grateful for the cool breeze that swept in at that moment and eased the creeping hangover heat stretching across my forehead.

'What's the matter with me, Marissa? How could I— Why would I do this?'

'Babe.' She softened then. 'It's not like you've done this on purpose.' When I didn't answer she added, 'I assume?'

I huffed a laugh. 'No, I definitely didn't.'

'Then tell her you're sorry. Order flowers, buy something expensive, book a table at the restaurant she mentioned. Make it right.'

'Thank you.'

'For what, giving advice to the advice columnist?' There was a laugh breaking through as she spoke. 'Seriously, Dotts, it's bad, but it isn't game-over, relationship-ending bad. Unless that's what you think you want?'

'What? Of course it isn't, no, Marissa, I— No, just—'

'I'm just making sure,' she interrupted me with her soothing voice. I wondered whether it was the same tone she used at work when she had to call people to let them know their investments were tanking. 'There's a way back from it, Dotty, I promise.'

Somehow, even though I am a grown woman — independent and not ignorant of life's changeability — that promise made all the difference.

I turned my head to look at London as it unfolded into a fresh day. Someone on the street below was juggling too many to-go coffee cups at once, and the few shopfronts within view were opening their mouths to welcome in customers.

I thanked Marissa somewhere between three and five times before eventually letting her go. She told me to call her later and I promised I would.

But first, I needed to know how quickly I could get flowers delivered to Caitlin's parents' house. For good measure, I also ordered a twelve-inch cookie with *I'm sorry* inscribed in icing, because extra gestures couldn't possibly hurt right now. And I knew Caitlin's appetite hit its peak whenever she was upset about something. I paid the premium charge for express delivery — they would be there by five that afternoon — and then jumped through hoops to get a reservation at Claridge's. It ended up being a precarious balancing act between accepting their heinous waiting times for a weekend table, while also trying to work out when Caitlin might have forgiven me (enough) to stand sitting across from me at dinner. I didn't like my odds for the following weekend, but blind optimism told me to book the table anyway.

I had just settled back on the window ledge with my second cup of tea when Tots called me.

'I hear you dropped the ball.' It was a subtle hint that Marissa had asked her to check on me throughout the day. She kept me company until my mug was empty. 'Do you want me to come over?'

I sighed. 'Honestly, Tots, that's a lovely offer but I've got a hangover threatening to kick in. I think I just really need a bath hot enough to boil a lobster alive, and then maybe a lie down in a darkened room.'

'Sounds like a fantastic plan.' I heard the crackle of her vape. 'Call me if you need me? I'm free all day. Elouise and I were going to go shopping later, for nothing in particular, if you fancy wallowing with us.'

'I love you. Tell Elouise I love her, too.'

Even after the call had ended, I didn't make any move towards the bathroom. Instead, I sat and stared at the clock and checked WhatsApp for a reply. I saw Caitlin go online three times, and every time she did, I started to type a message — only to hastily delete it when I saw her go offline again.

I was one buttered crumpet and half a litre of water into my hangover when I feebly tapped out, *I'm sorry. I know I messed up. Xxx,* and hit send before I could talk myself out of it. It was a weak follow-up to the four missed calls I'd already left her, but I reasoned the WhatsApp blue ticks would at least let me know whether she'd seen the message — even if she chose not to reply.

In the hours that followed — with no word from Caitlin — I cleaned the kitchen, including the oven, and the bathroom, took a lukewarm bath for fear of dehydrating myself further, and cleared the handful of letters that had arrived for Dear Dotty overnight. Somehow, only half the day had gone by in that time, and I found myself wondering what Caitlin and I would be doing now, if I hadn't completely cocked up our special occasion. *What do we even do on weekends?* I thought as I thumbed my way through Netflix, looking for a true crime documentary that might lift my spirits — a thought that only made me feel like an even worse person than I already did.

I fell asleep sometime during episode three of *How to Become a Cult Leader*. It wasn't something I necessarily aspired to, but it made for good background noise. It was the shrill chirp of my phone announcing a new message that pulled me out of naptime, though. Earlier in the day I'd left it on a startlingly loud volume to make sure I didn't miss a message. This one was a delivery notification: Caitlin had the flowers.

I restarted episode three and constantly checked WhatsApp for signs of life.

Marissa messaged me once — *Any news?* — and Tots twice. The first time she asked whether I'd heard from Caitlin. The second, she asked whether I fancied drinking away my hangover. I was sorely tempted to take her up on the offer, but the thought of venturing outside to a cocktail bar in a heatwave sent a ripple of nausea through my lower abdomen and all the way up to my throat.

It was two episodes later when the message I'd been waiting for finally arrived. Caitlin's name, complete with the small pink love heart that I'd added to her contact listing some seven years ago, appeared on my phone screen. I pulled in a deep breath and opened WhatsApp.

Thanks for the gifts but our anniversary was yesterday.

Then I balled up tightly on the sofa and allowed myself the luxury of a snotty, messy, loud, and ugly cry.

Dear Dotty,

I am lost. Somehow, I've staggered into my mid-thirties without ever stopping to evaluate what I want from my life and now I'm on the high jump of making some hard and horrible decisions. My long-term partner has lost his lustre. He never makes an effort anymore, always opts to stay in instead of going out and never wants to try new things. Recently I heard him tell someone that we're 'fine just as we are' and now I can't stop thinking about it. Are we fine just as we are? And even if that's true, is just fine enough? I might not know what I want from life in the big picture but I'm not convinced that rambling on is enough for me, even though it clearly is for him, but I don't know what that means for me or for us. Is it time to focus on my life, my needs, or is that me being selfish? I have a 'just fine' relationship, and life. Should that be enough?

Tell me, what would Dotty do?
Restless, unappreciated, but fine x

CHAPTER NINE

I took to working everywhere but at the flat. Even though Caitlin would ordinarily have been at work herself, somehow her not being there, even during the day, created a deafening silence. The discomfort of which felt how I imagined tinnitus might.

That afternoon, I took myself to Hyde Park with my laptop, a flask of tea, and a beaker of homemade lemonade that I'd impulse-purchased before looking for a shady patch of grass.

I took pictures galore before eventually settling down to look over the most recent letters in my inbox. Over the afternoon, I managed three responses, another beaker of lemonade, and a blueberry muffin the size of my fist. Three hours passed at a beautiful speed, peppered with people-watching and deep breaths where I could escape the harsh reality that my partner of ten years was no longer speaking to me.

I let out a jagged sigh and checked my watch. Somewhere across the city, Caitlin was packing up work for the day and making her way back to her parents' house, where another *I'm sorry* gift would be waiting. This time it was a plush, knitted green cardigan that I'd spied in her New Look basket last month. I'd scoured the wilds of the New Look website to find said cardigan and once again paid a small fortune for next day delivery.

Penance was getting expensive.

* * *

The heat was dipping out of the day when I pushed back into the flat. I hadn't been able to stand the thought of beans on toast for a third night in a row, so I'd grabbed a misguided McDonald's en route, despite knowing it would need five minutes in the oven when I got there. I was finalising my plan of action — put the oven on to heat, change into cotton slob-about-the-house trousers, find a fresh true crime documentary to watch — when I heard a thud from the bedroom. I froze, McDonald's bag still in hand, and looked around the kitchen for an easy weapon of defence. It was times like these I wished Caitlin and I were adult enough to own a knife block. I turned to yank open the nearest drawer and cringed at the crash of cutlery that knocked together as my hand pulled back with what turned out to be a ladle.

'You're home.'

The voice came from the doorway behind me and I *literally* screamed. A great and embarrassing high-pitched sound, coupled with my weapon of choice thumping to the floor and my hands flying up to cradle my chest where my heart was beating an audible thrum.

Caitlin reached to grab the ladle from where it had landed between us. 'Good job you weren't still holding that drink.' She set it down on the kitchen counter, then moved around me, opened the fridge, and yanked free a bottle of white. 'I won't get in your way, I'm just getting ready.'

I only just noticed that Caitlin was wearing out-out clothes. Her hair was straightened, making it long enough to trail well past her shoulders, and ending in such a severe line that it made me wonder whether she'd had it trimmed. Her eye make-up was smoky and smudged to perfection, and her brilliant red lipstick, neat and shaped to her cupid's bow, popped even more against the black dress she was wearing. It was thin-strapped, with a small panel missing at the front that showed Caitlin's quiet sternum tattoo. It was a symbol she'd got because she thought it meant *recovery*, though I'd always joked that it was more likely just a cute design her tattooist had come up with. In her free hand she was holding a pair of black strappy heels that absolutely weren't designed for comfort or speed.

'You're going out?'

She was leaning over, steadying herself on a dining table chair while she fixed the strap on one shoe. 'It's David and Elaine's engagement party.'

'Oh, bugger!' My hand flew to my head as I remembered. It was on the calendar and everything! *Silly, silly Dotty.* David and Elaine were two of Caitlin's friends that I'd inherited, such is the way when you're in a long-term relationship. They were both accountants and painfully boring, but they were also very good people. Before planning their engagement party, they'd actually emailed out an online poll to make sure they chose a date that was convenient for everyone invited. 'Give me five minutes and—'

Caitlin snorted. 'You're not serious?' she said as she caught a glimpse of my face. She had both shoes on now, making her a good three inches taller than me. Between that and her tone, I felt a little like I'd drunk the wrong potion and shrunk to the size of a dormouse. 'You've got plans' — she nodded to the food on the table — 'and we haven't spoken in nearly a week.'

My mouth was suddenly dry. 'I sent things, I sent apologies,' I eventually managed.

'Thank you for the . . .' Caitlin narrowed her eyes, choosing the next words carefully. 'Thanks for the *things*, but our anniversary was over a week ago.'

'They weren't *for* our anniversary—'

'No, Dotts, because I got *nothing* from you for our anniversary.'

I sighed and ran a hand through my hair. I realised how much I was sweating as I let my palm rest on the back of my neck. 'Caitlin, I've told you how sorry I am, and I genuinely am. I . . . Honestly, it's beyond me how I could have forgotten something so important, because *of course* it's important, and I want to . . . There must be a way to make it up to you, there has to be, and I want to do that, whatever it is, whatever you need.'

Caitlin huffed, dropped her head back, and stared at the ceiling. A short, sharp laugh fell out of her, like a small nugget dropping onto the floor, and she turned back to look at me. 'How is it that you remembered your bloody work anniversary but not ours?'

'That's different,' I protested. It was a knee-jerk reaction, and not at all thought out.

'How?!'

'Well, they threw me a party to start with!'

Silly, silly Dotty. No sooner had the ill-considered answer emerged than she was on her way to the front door. 'Caitlin, wait. That was stupid and ridiculous, but honestly, I *would* have forgotten I'd been at the magazine for ten years unless Elza had prompted me, and . . .'

'And what, Dotty?' she snapped. 'What more do you have to add?'

I hated how Caitlin looked at me, then. Her expression was full of disappointment and defeat, and maybe even irritation at how much of her fun evening this conversation was eating into. She had already grabbed her bag and her neatly wrapped gift and had one hand on the door handle, ready to leave. I knew that to turn her around, to get her to face me fully, I needed something good, something with impact. But everything I thought of died in a small ball on my tongue before the words could even come out. To my shame, it really seemed as though I had nothing better than the implication that if Caitlin had only thrown me a party, I would have remembered our anniversary. *Silly, silly Dotty.*

'Caitlin, I'm just sorry. I miss you. And I want to make things right.'

'Okay.' She shrugged. 'I need to go.'

'That's it?'

She made a sad sounding laugh. It was a defeated noise. 'What more is there right now? Whatever fix there is for this, Dotty, it isn't going to happen in the next ten minutes, and I have somewhere I need to be, so—'

'Will you even be home tonight?'

Caitlin glanced over her shoulder with one hand still on the door handle. 'I don't know.'

Then she left in such a hurry that even if I'd thought of something good to say, I wouldn't have had the chance to say it. She slammed the door with a force that I took to be her way of punctuating the end of the conversation.

I lingered in the hallway for so long that it bordered on the cinematic. Between that and the cold McDonald's I ate alone while perched on the windowsill in the half hour that followed, I wagered I was about ready for a movie montage with a suitably tragic power ballad soundtrack.

* * *

She didn't come home.

I called her, and even resorted to calling David and Elaine the day after the party, but neither of them answered. It made me wonder — *worry* — whether Caitlin had broken our promise never to speak of the other's cock-ups to friends. If she had broken the promise, then what might that mean?

I tried to write through the panic of that thought, two days after the party, three days after, but when I smashed straight into a wall of what can only be described as advice columnists' block, where I simply could not give another word of advice to anyone on any matter, I played the only sensible card I had left. I emailed my council of advisers to ask for a Zoom meeting.

It was difficult to get all the moving parts together in a physical space at such short notice. Mum was available, but also a million miles away (not really, but it sometimes felt that way). Marissa squeezed panic calls into her lunch break (which often lasted for a full twenty minutes before someone needed her). Elouise was on location somewhere and Tots was presumably also on location — though her precise whereabouts remained undisclosed when she emailed to say she could make a Zoom call anyway. True to form, they all found time later that same day.

'Liz! How are you doing?' Elouise beamed, with her full face of professional make-up, when my mum appeared on the screen. 'It's been so long since we saw you.'

'Oh, I know, love, but you know how I feel about London.' Her face said it all.

Marissa laughed. 'I think we all feel like that about London sometimes.'

'I don't know,' Tots answered while she pulled on the window dressing behind her that seemed to be blocking out a stream of sunshine, 'I find that I miss London when I'm actually not there.'

'Right' — Marissa was typing as she spoke — 'and where are you exactly?'

'Ladies,' I interrupted, 'I would love for this to be a social thing, but I'm having a *minor* crisis of . . . everything.'

Mum huffed. 'Dotty, don't oversell things.'

'I can't even write,' I snapped.

Marissa stopped typing.

Elouise put down the hand that was adding more make-up to her face.

'Oh. That's . . . Well, if you can't work, then . . .'

'Then it must be something bloody terrible,' Tots tied up Mum's sentence for her.

And I spent the next ten minutes explaining to them precisely how bloody terrible it all was. It became a highlight reel of horrors as I explained the sheer amount of money I'd spent trying to spoil Caitlin into speaking to me again, and the strained results I'd gotten in return.

'Dotty, love, you know gifts can't fix problems,' Mum commented.

'But they never make anything worse, do they?' Elouise asked.

'No,' Mum answered, 'no, I suppose . . .'

'And she flat out won't speak to you, at all?' Tots steered the conversation back towards a helpful, albeit painful, terrain. 'Have you tried just turning up at her parents' house?'

I squinted at the suggestion. 'No.'

'Because?'

'Because that's a step too far,' Marissa answered, the tap-tap-tap of her keys echoing in the background. 'Caitlin's parents are already involved, because she's suddenly living there. But if you actually go round there and Caitlin decides she doesn't want to talk then you're left on the doorstep talking to one of Caitlin's parents, and frankly, although what you did was pretty bloody terrible, I'm not sure it's terrible enough to deserve that.'

'Marissa's right,' Elouise added, 'confronting the parents is for cheaters, not forgetfulness.'

'I think forgetfulness is something of an understatement, love,' Mum said, though I wished that she hadn't. The comment made me flinch. 'We're talking about something quite big here, aren't we?'

'But we're also talking about a *very* busy person,' Tots chimed in, 'and one who prides work over pretty much everything.'

'I do not—'

'Dotty, don't even deny it.' The force of Marissa's statement was doubled by the fact that she'd stopped typing again. 'Work is everything to you. Otherwise, why didn't the work party make you think, hey, didn't something else important happen about ten years ago? Even having forgotten the anniversary, you still didn't remember when prompted. You'd never be like that over a work matter. And that's okay.' She rushed to add that last part, as though realising she needed a balm to soothe everything she'd said beforehand. 'You're allowed to love what you do.'

'But . . .' I hesitated, avoiding eye contact with the camera as I answered. 'It shouldn't be everything, should it? There's a bit more happening in life, isn't there?'

'*Is* there?' Marissa answered.

'From experience,' Mum spoke gently. It sounded like she was about to break bad news to us all. 'There actually is, my loves, yes. There's a lot more, when it comes down to it. I'm not saying you shouldn't work, darling Dotty, because I know how much you love what you do, but if you're losing your way with other things — Caitlin, for instance — it might be worth thinking of ways to put more energy there. If that sounds like something you want?'

It felt like a question I should have had a more immediate answer to. Even I didn't like how long I hesitated. 'Of course I want to put energy into Caitlin. I'm so . . . comfortable in the life we have together. I don't want to lose that.'

Elouise narrowed her eyes, opened her mouth, and shook her head. Then she sank back into silence while Tots took the lead. 'I say give her time.'

'And space,' Elouise added, thankful for Tots's prompt.

'So you're saying, what? I should just leave her alone?'

'Well, hounding her doesn't seem to have worked.' Marissa was already typing again.

'Love, why don't you use this time to think about what *you* want?'

'I already know what I want, Mum.'

'Okay.' She shrugged in the same she-knows-something-I-don't way that she might have done when I was a child. 'So we're opting for space?'

'Agreed,' the girls all chimed in one after the other.

'Speaking of space . . .'

I laughed. 'Thank you, Marissa, for affording me your twenty-minute lunch hour.'

'Any time, babe. Ladies, always a pleasure,' she said before catapulting her screen to black without a more conventional goodbye.

One by one, after that, they all disconnected from the call, leaving me alone on my sofa with nothing but my laptop screen and time to think . . .

* * *

After spending three hours reading magazine articles allegedly designed to help you work out what you want from life, I decided that taking time to think was both overrated and dangerous.

I had started the morning a little lost, but comfortable with my place in the world. By mid-afternoon, I didn't know whether I wanted the life I had, or whether it was time for me to *Eat, Pray, Love* myself into travelling, a new career or basket weaving. But they weren't things I truly wanted, surely?

In the end, I had to force myself to close my laptop before I wrote a hasty letter of resignation to Elza, which she wouldn't have accepted anyway. It was still a glorious day outside — cardigan weather but very much warm — and I decided to make the most of this 'time to think' by taking myself out for coffee and cake. *Lots* of cake. It mightn't have been the bigger picture thinking that this time was meant to be, but a sugar rush was all I could convince myself of by that point in the day.

There was a sweet café a comfortable distance from the flat, and I wandered there with my laptop in case inspiration should strike. I managed to grab myself an outside table, conveniently positioned in a beam of afternoon sunshine, and I ordered a hot chocolate, even though it didn't match the weather, and I told myself this was me honouring what I wanted. Again, I wasn't sure it was exactly what my mum had in mind, but it helped to start small.

When the waitress brought my order out, I politely declined the offer of anything else and instead wedged myself comfortably in my patch of sun, eyes closed and ears open, listening to the percussion of a semi-busy London street. Before I reached to take my first sip, I pulled out my phone, stood, and put one foot on my chair to hoist myself into a better photo-taking position. I hadn't even managed a single shot when I lost my footing, slipped from the chair, and landed squarely with my face in the small mound of whipped cream on top of my drink.

'Oh my god, are you okay?' came from the table across from me. Meanwhile, I was sure I heard a snicker from the table on the other side.

I tried to laugh it off, even though there was a growing pain in my shin and a peak of whipped cream on my nose intruding on my vision.

'That'll teach me,' I joked with the kinder of the onlookers.

Really, Dotty, this is what you want? I wondered, as I reached for a napkin. *This* is *what you want?* I questioned myself again, as I rubbed my aching leg. I took the first sip of my spoiled drink and felt instantly soothed by its warmth. But still, the same thought chased itself around my head, drowning out the London street. It could only be soothed by a big belly breath that came out shaky, expelling the final shock of the fall.

I took another sip of my drink and decided it actually tasted that bit better for not having had its picture taken.

CHAPTER TEN

Taking time to think didn't last long. I managed to give Caitlin an additional two days of space, until the swell of my own noise-making around the flat was driving me to the brink of what I genuinely believed was something like insanity. Then I texted her, saying that we really needed to talk at some point. I instantly regretted my tone. Caitlin was a highly intelligent individual — emotional and otherwise — and my reopening gambit had been to tell her something she must already know.

I sighed, threw my phone on the kitchen counter, and went back to cleaning the oven. It was my second attempt at this since she'd left. The first had been a trial run, where I was mostly working out exactly which of the many materials under the kitchen sink might be fit for purpose when it came to the job. For this second attempt, I was up to my elbows in Marigolds, scrubbing with a homemade baking soda paste and feeling every bit the Stepford wife for having been domesticated enough to Google the best ways to clean an oven. I'd misguidedly told myself that this would earn me brownie points, as though the oven had been the cause of the collision in our relationship.

When my phone chirped from the countertop, my head shot up at such a speed and with no spatial awareness, that I ended up whacking the back of my loud brain against the edge of the oven. All for a message that read: *You're right. We need to talk. I'll be home later.*

I sank to my knees on the kitchen floor. I felt like replying to say she could save herself the trouble of a break-up monologue — it was clear enough from her tone. But instead of fury-typing something that would only — *could only* — make the situation worse, I stayed fixed to the spot on the floor — a floor that, only an hour ago, had been swept clean of a week's worth of toast crumbs, evidence of what I'd been living on while Caitlin had been away — and stared into the open mouth of the oven.

It would take another thirty minutes for the baking soda to strip the grime.

* * *

'Later' was a relative timeframe. But I went out on a limb and guessed that Caitlin meant she'd be home after work, which gave me the majority of the day to stew.

When I'd run out of letters to answer — who would have ever thought I'd wish *more* problems on my loyal readers? — and the oven was clean enough to eat dinner out of, I wrapped myself in my best black and white polka-dot dress, with a mustard cardigan for comfort, and took myself out into London. Selfridges had never been one of my favourite places, but it was big enough — and loud enough — to get lost in for the afternoon.

My first stop was the cupcake store, where I ate not one but *two* cupcakes, each of which was the size of my fist. And while they knocked a considerable dent in my not so considerable spending limit for the day — which admittedly, in a place like Selfridges, wasn't much of a spending limit at all — the sugar rush did give me a surge of something like confidence.

I read and reread Caitlin's message while I washed my baked goods down with delicious tea, and by the time I dusted myself free from icing sugar stains, I'd managed to convince myself that stuff mightn't be as bad at home as I'd first imagined them to be. What had I expected from a message from Caitlin, exactly? A heart emoji and our standard number of kisses? She was mad at me, madder than she'd ever been. But you don't just walk away from ten years because you're mad. You don't just leave.

'Could I get one of those to go, please?' I pointed to a jam and cream contraption hidden behind the counter and watched as the young waitress boxed everything neatly with a bow, a smile, and overall much more care than I thought anyone else in this whole place might give to their job — even the magicians on the make-up counters. I tried to match her cheery expression. 'Thank you. Have a great day.'

'Aw, thanks. You too.'

It wasn't a great day, and it probably wouldn't turn out otherwise — there was, after all, a Big Talk on the horizon — but I managed to make sure it wasn't a terrible one. I browsed the accessories, the jewellery, the make-up, and made a mental list of things to come back and browse through again for Caitlin at Christmas. Planning ahead made the panic quieter, too, and gave my sugary confidence that little bit more time to bloom. In total, I killed three hours in the shop *and* didn't spend all of my budget, so by the time I was strolling up the road to our flat, I felt every bit like I'd blown away the detritus of the morning and fixed myself up nicely for whatever was waiting on the other side of that front door. Of course, that was because I was overly cocksure and fuelled by cupcakes. It had never occurred to me that what would be waiting for me was—

'Caitlin?' I shouted along the hallway. 'Caitlin, are these bags from your parents'?' Even as I asked the question, I was all too aware of its ridiculousness. Caitlin had taken a string of overnight bags to her mum and dad's. These weren't overnight bags. They were long-haul flight ones — one of which was responsible for the throbbing that bloomed in my little toe after I enthusiastically booted it on entry.

66

I rounded the corner into the kitchen and found Caitlin sitting with her hands clasped together on the table in front of her. There was a slip of paper in the centre of the table, too, but I couldn't catch sight of what was written on it.

'I didn't realise you'd be home by this time, I wouldn't have gone out if I'd—'

'I didn't make it very clear in my message,' she interrupted. I managed to swallow the urge to say that at least that was something we agreed on. 'It gave me time to get some things sorted, anyway. Do you want to sit down?'

Not really, I thought, but I took it to be more of an instruction than a question. I pulled out the chair opposite her and glanced at the sheet of paper again as I sat. Now I could see all too clearly what was written at the top of it: *Dear Dotty* . . .

Caitlin took a deep breath. 'Do you remember a letter from "Restless, unappreciated, but fine"? It came through to your inbox and you—'

'I remember it.'

'Do you remember the advice you gave to the person who sent it?'

I rested my elbows on the table and put my head in my hands as I stared at her. The penny dropped. 'Please tell me you didn't.'

'Do you remember the advice?' she repeated.

I ran a hand through my hair and dropped back with a thump against the wooden chair. Caitlin had wanted kitchen chairs with fabric, I remembered, but I'd told her that we'd never spend enough time actually *in* the kitchen to worry about whether the chairs would be comfortable for hours on end.

Of course, I remembered the advice.

'I told her to leave her partner.'

She huffed a laugh. 'Point-blank, no holding back. "Your partner doesn't sound like they're invested in the relationship anymore, which is horrible, but it does happen. That doesn't mean you need to fix it, though",' she read from the sheet in front of her. I wanted to beg her to stop. "'You're only responsible for yourself in this life, and if your partner seems like they've checked out of the relationship then maybe they have, and maybe you should too. There's no shame in calling time. Leave. Find your lustre.'"

Caitlin pushed the sheet of paper towards me then. 'I always did trust your advice more than anyone else's.'

PART TWO

CHAPTER ELEVEN

Two weeks later...

Caitlin said I could keep the flat. So at least I wasn't homeless *and* single. She said I'd spent so long making it 'Instagram friendly' that it hardly felt like a home to her anyway — which was tosh. The real reason she hated it was because there were so many romanticised images of my laptop balanced on an open window ledge overlooking the city and she was always sure some superfan would be crazy enough to work out where we lived. I told her that was ridiculous, that no Dear Dotty reader could ever be that desperate for an autograph. But telling someone they're being ridiculous in the middle of an argument isn't helpful. Something that an advice columnist should, apparently, know.

In the weeks following the break-up, we swapped the usual awkward messages shared between two people slowly trying to unpick the stitching that holds their lives together. I could keep the flat. Could she come round for the rest of her clothes? She'd found things of mine she'd accidentally packed. Did I want my copy of *Breakfast at Tiffany's* back? I tapped out a message telling her that Truman Capote was the least of my concerns. I hadn't even noticed him missing from the bookshelf in the living room, despite the sparse landscape it now was.

I may have been keeping the flat, but visit by visit, Caitlin had determinedly started to clean out everything she owned from its innards. I was out every time she visited — by my decision, not her request. She never made it sound like it was a problem for me to be there. But who in their right mind would happily linger in a doorway and watch their partner of ten years work out which books to take from the cosy nook of your once shared living room? So instead, she always gave me advance notice, and I made a concerted effort to be quietly walking the streets of London, like a Dickensian orphan, whenever Caitlin needed to come by.

Now, I was officially living alone for the first time in my adult life. The world was still moving though, and there were now mornings when the weather was too chilly for me to sit by the open window with that first cup of tea.

Instead, I worked more and more in my home office. It was one of the few spaces that Caitlin hadn't inhabited while we'd lived together, which meant there was nothing for me to miss while I was in there. The photo frame that had sat in the corner of my desk, boasting a picture of us — me planting a firm kiss on the side of her cheek, her smile wide and beaming — stared at me. So I threw it in the bin, and poof: it was like Caitlin had never happened.

Until I needed more tea, or the loo, or to sleep. Then there she was again.

* * *

I was wrapping up my response to the last email in the Dear Dotty inbox and was already at a loss for what I could or should do next. The girls all knew about the split, as did Mum. Although I hadn't told anyone at work, it was an easy guess that something outside of Dear Dotty's stylised life must be happening, because I hadn't been into the office at all since Caitlin's departure. So I suppose I should have expected—

'Hello?'

I snatched at my phone the instant it started to hum across the desk.

'I'm downstairs.'

'Oh, I . . .' I looked around the room as though Elza might be here for an unplanned flat inspection. 'I . . . Did we—'

'Dotts, don't make a thing of it. Come down, I'm taking you out.'

I glanced down at the sweat socks, the dark red joggers, and the loose-fitting shirt I was wearing. 'Do you mind coming up, Elza? I'm sorry, you've caught me a little off guard.' I let out an awkward laugh. 'I'm not exactly real-world presentable at the minute.'

'Have you left the flat for anything more than teabags and milk since she left you?'

My mouth fell open. I wasn't shocked, as such, but dumbstruck. *How does she—*

'I know a cry for help when I hear one,' she said, as though answering something I hadn't even got round to voicing, which was oh so typical of the great and wise Elza. 'I'm going to pop down the road to that quaint little building that passes for a coffee shop and get myself a drink. By the time I can see the bottom of my glass, I want you there.'

Quaint though the coffee shop was, it wasn't anywhere near trendy enough to serve her a flat white in a glass. I didn't tell her that though. It sounded like the last thing she needed to hear.

* * *

If Elza had told me that she planned to whisk me off to the centre of London, I would have worn something more presentable than ripped jeans and a linen shirt. Thank goodness

72

I'd at least opted for brogues over Converse, or we never would have gotten in anywhere. When we arrived at The Dorchester, I grabbed us a table with a wholesome view and was still busy fussing with my clothes when Elza came back with a tray of drinks: two Pornstar Martinis and their accompanying Prosecco shots.

'Stop fussing with your outfit,' she ordered. 'It's London, you look chic.'

'No, *you* look chic.'

Elza was wearing a slim-fitting black dress that was cut in a V-neck at the front and back, and a burnt orange wrap that matched the seasonal shift taking place around us. She'd paired that with simple but ridiculously strappy heels, and it was a wonder to me how she'd got to and from the bar without developing a limp, or at least letting out a whimper. 'Did you come straight from the office?'

'Mm. When you didn't turn up for our meeting I thought it was time for a little intervention.'

My eyes widened. My mouth would have likely dropped open, too, if my bottom lip hadn't already been firmly pressed to the rim of my glass. I rushed through a swallow before speaking. 'Elza, I'm so sorry, I—'

She held her palm up to stop me. 'I've been dumped before, too. I know the distraction of it.'

It was the second shock blow. 'Who would *dare* dump you?'

Elza smiled and stared out the window as she answered. 'He was called Anthony. I was young and naïve, and I honestly thought love lasted as long as you wanted it to, if you only worked at it.' She paused to sip her drink, and I sipped mine again for something to do. 'But it isn't like that. Things fall apart every day, Dotty; you know that much from your readers. But things also fall together. You'll be fine.'

I huffed a laugh.

'I'm serious,' she said, and it showed in her tone. 'You'll be fine.'

73

I fidgeted with the stem of my glass, turning it in a circle to give myself something to focus on. I couldn't bring myself to look at her when I asked, 'What happened? With Anthony, I mean.'

Elza sighed. I chanced a look up and saw her expression fixed beyond the window again. She smiled. It was a thin-lipped, sad sort of smile. 'I worked too hard. I worked too hard and he hated it. So I worked less, worked hard at our relationship, and he seemed to hate that, too. He said I wasn't being authentic. I was miserable without my work.'

'Bold statement.'

She turned to face me. 'He was right.' She pushed her drink to one side to make more space on the table, and rested her clasped hands between us. 'Dotty, believe me when I tell you that I understand the heartache of losing someone you thought you'd have for a long time. It's ugly and messy and it may get messier still. But you, my girl, will be fine. You might even feel relieved, if you give yourself the chance to.' I opened my mouth to dispute her claims, and she must have sensed what was coming because she held up a hand to pause me again. 'You will be fine.'

I let the statement hang between us for a second. 'Thank you, Elza.'

'You're welcome. Now, let's talk about Dear Dotty.'

I laughed. 'Of course, let's swap from sentimental right around to practical.'

'You can't be sentimental all the time if you want to get anywhere in this world, Dotts. You also can't let your work slip.'

I was outraged by the mere suggestion. 'I'll have you know that inbox is *empty*.'

'But you're not uploading fresh content to your social media platforms.'

'I am!'

'You are not, Dotty. Those leaves are spring green if ever I saw it and the leaves outside are *orange*. You're recycling pictures. You're not out and about.'

'How is anyone to know that?' I snapped.

Elza held her palm outstretched towards me. 'Give me your phone.'

I leaned to one side to free it from my back pocket. 'I don't like where this is going.'

'Now, smile for me.' I didn't see what Elza had clicked into, but when she held the phone up with the camera lens pointed straight at me it became clear. I didn't have make-up on, my hair was on its third day without a wash, and I was pretty sure this shirt was bottom-of-the-wash-pile creased. 'We'll filter it before we post it,' she said as though guessing my concern. 'Hold your drink up as though you're taking a sip.'

I snatched the glass and chugged two mouthfuls as I heard the camera click at least five times.

'Fantastic. Now, do that again but be gazing out of the window . . .'

It took Elza another three Pornstar Martinis to get twenty-one pictures out of me in total.

By that point, I was merry enough to post three of them without so much as a lighting tweak.

CHAPTER TWELVE

While the chat with Elza was nice and all, everyone in the world knows by now that niceness doesn't fix heartache. *Nothing much does*, I thought, as I felt around on the coffee table to grab my phone, which was howling with yet another call from one of the girls. I rejected it, again, groaned the language of my people — the heartbroken and hungover, that is — and rolled over on the sofa for another two hours of sleep. This had been the routine for nearly two weeks straight.

I couldn't stand to see my friends, not because I didn't want to, but simply because I couldn't handle the thought of them trying to cheer me up and failing, then trying again, and so the cycle would continue until they eventually get bored of my anguish and stopped trying altogether. It was, I reasoned, better not to give them the opportunity at all. And that's the thought I held onto while a steel-drum band worked a lap around my cranium and I tried desperately to sleep through another painfully bright morning in London. Because perish the thought that I move to close the living room blinds.

This same laziness carried me through until lunchtime. At which point my mouth was so dry that I wondered whether I'd unknowingly taken a trek around the Sahara, rather than a lengthy nap. I was relieved to find that the headache had at least eased. But I was so thirsty that, after stumbling to the kitchen, I found the only thing that could possibly quench my thirst was to stick my head directly under the cold tap. I lapped at the flow of water like a dog who'd been dragged for a summer walk around Hyde Park and *just* as I started to feel something close to hydrated, my phone howled again. True to form, hangovers have always made me somewhat tetchy — so the curt ring caught me so off guard that I slammed my head upwards from the tap and immediately into an open cupboard door.

'Bugger!'

Of course, it would be the cupboard where the wine glasses were kept.

I rubbed the back of my head as I hurried toward the coffee table, snatched up the handset and said, 'What?'

There was a pause before my mum asked, 'Do you always answer the phone like that?'

'Oh, Mum, I'm sorry, I . . .' I dropped onto the sofa and angled myself into a patch of sunshine reaching from the window. Its warmth was much more palatable, now, after a morning of extra sleep. 'I thought you were going to be one of the girls.'

She laughed. 'I'm not sure that excuses it, Dotty.'

'No, no, I suppose it doesn't.' Guilt jabbed me in the stomach — or maybe it was the slosh of leftover wine knocking against the amount of water I'd just managed to guzzle. Either way, there was something moving in my lower belly, and it didn't feel great. 'How are you?'

'Oh, love, I'm fine. You know me.'

'Everything okay at home?'

'Of course, of course. There are new neighbours moving in across the way so everyone's all aflutter about that.' She giggled, a schoolgirl sound, and I could picture the childish delight that would have been on her face, too. 'It's quite funny, really, seeing everyone quite so up in arms about it. It's two chaps, a very lovely couple. I got talking to them in the shop a couple of days ago actually. I told them about you and—'

'This isn't going to be one of those, they're gay, so I told them about my gay daughter things, is it?' I interrupted her, my voice flat. I was already prepped to be unimpressed by whatever she was about to tell me.

But when her answer came, she sounded like I'd pricked her joyous balloon with a carving knife. 'No, Dotty. Joseph, he was holding a copy of the magazine, so I told him that my daughter is Dear Dotty and, well, they were delighted, you know. *The* Dear Dotty. So, I . . . well, I told them all about you.'

'Christ, Mum, I'm sorry.' I leaned forward, ran a hand through my hair and pulled in a deep breath. 'I'm a cow, I'm sorry.'

'You aren't a cow, Dotty. Don't say that about yourself.'

'Well, I'm not a very nice . . .' I tried to think of a counter animal. 'Person.' I gave up.

'You are. But you're not going through a very nice thing.'

I huffed a laugh. 'I'll say.'

'Actually, love, that's why I'm calling. Tots called me and—'

'Oh, Mum, look, I'm sorry, she shouldn't have—'

'She's worried,' she cut across me. 'Her, Elouise, and Marissa all are. They said you haven't been answering their calls.' She said it with a questioning tone, and when I didn't answer she pushed, 'Is that right?'

'I haven't been, no.'

'Love, you can't isolate yourself like this. It won't help, you know?'

'Dumping my stuff on their doorsteps won't help either, though.'

She huffed. 'Isn't that what friends are for, my lovely Dotty? How many heartbreaks have you helped them through over the years, hm?' I could hear a smile teasing at the outskirts of her voice.

It was a hard question to answer. I wasn't sure any-one would ever dare to break Marissa's heart, lest she run a comprehensive overview of their tax history and report them for minor indiscretions. Tots and Elouise were different kettles of fish, though. Over the years Elouise had had more heartbreaks than I'd had bottles of wine, and given recent drinking habits that really was saying something. Meanwhile, Tots always seemed more heartbroken when she'd broken someone else's heart. She had a tough skin in her work life, but when it came to romance, she was deathly afraid of being the Bad Guy.

'A few.'

'Dozen,' Mum added. I spluttered a laugh. 'Dotty, imagine this is a column.'

I groaned. 'I'm not sure I like where this is going.'

'Hear me out…'

I wondered how long it had taken Mum to come up with this ploy. I could imagine her sitting at the kitchen table, nursing her morning cup of tea and brainstorming ideas before ringing me. Knowing her, she'd probably had a whole sheet full of potential plans to try and soften me with, and I wondered what the others might have been. There was probably a suggestion for a dating app, because Mum tended to believe she was trendy whenever she mentioned one. There was undoubtedly also mention of a new hobby, too, because that had been Mum's answer to most things for the longest time. And then there was this — this golden nugget that most of the world held onto in hard times: *What would you say to someone else in this situation?* Of course, I would have steadfastly advised *against* drinking alone in the flat you shared with your former partner, while working your way through the cheapest wines the corner shop had to offer. As a rule, I tended to swerve away from advice that would cost me my job. But then, I'd always known it's much easier to give advice than it is to take it.

'What do you tell people, when they're going through a break-up?'

'Keep busy.' That had always been my generic starting point.

'And?'

'Have a clear-out.'

'Okay, and?'

'Spend time with people you love,' I answered flatly.

'So?'

I sighed. 'So I'll call the girls.'

'Do you promise?'

'Yes, Mum.'

'With a pinky held out?'

I laughed. This had been our thing — well, one of our things — since I was a teenager. Mum had caught me sneaking out to a party that I hadn't even asked I could go to because I'd been so convinced she'd say no. When she caught me with one leg unceremoniously hanging out of my bedroom window and a rattling backpack that happened to be stocked with two bottles of cheap white that I'd lifted from the kitchen, she hadn't been mad at all. If anything, she'd seemed sad that I hadn't thought of just asking her. 'I'm not a dragon, Dotty,' she'd said, 'I understand young people like their illicit endeavours.' I could remember stifling a laugh at the phrase. From that point on, Mum made me promise that whenever I wanted something, or needed to speak to her about something, I would. She'd sat alongside me on the sofa, tucked an arm around my shoulder, and held out her pinky finger. 'Promise?'

I smiled over the memory and stuck out the little finger of my left hand. 'With a pinky held out.'

'Thank you, love.' I imagined her sitting there with her own pinky held out, too. 'And if you really can't stand to be around your normal life, you could always move home for a while, spend some time with your dear old Mum.'

'You aren't old,' I replied, 'but nice try.'

I wasn't in the least bit surprised that that suggestion had made it onto her shortlist of bright ideas.

'Call them today, would you, love?'

'As soon as we get off the phone.'

'I love you, Dotty. You'll be okay.'

I smiled, even though I could feel sadness pulling at the edges of the expression. 'So people keep telling me.'

'Well,' she lingered, 'sometimes people are right.'

Mum and I said our goodbyes after I'd promised — again, with a pinky and everything — that I'd call the girls that same day. I didn't quite manage it as soon as I got off the phone.

First, there came the litre of water, complete with three slices of cucumber and a candid window snap for the social media. Then there came the bacon sandwich. After that, I finally felt human enough to handle Tots and her—

'Well, it's about goddamn time!'

—tender love and support . . .

CHAPTER THIRTEEN

Marissa picked a lively bistro for a late afternoon meal. Which we all knew translated to her having been at work since the crack of dawn, and she wanted somewhere close to the office so she could stumble out and meet us. And yet, somehow, I was still the last to arrive. I waltzed in feeling every bit the glamour puss in my black linen dress that kicked out in a twirl when I moved, set off with strappy black sandals and a squat, square handbag that was just about big enough for my phone alone. My hair was loose and natural, my make-up minimal. I followed the advice that I'd give to anyone else in my situation: do things that make you feel good. Channelling my inner starlet with simple and stunning fashion choices happened to be one of my feel-good things.

I picked out the girls at a table just inside the open windows of the restaurant. Even though London's summer had died a death to give way to autumn, I was thankful that they'd grabbed a seat with a breeze. I edged my way through the other diners to make my way to them and I was just in the middle of removing my outlandishly expensive sunglasses — another thing that made me feel good: spending money — when Marissa greeted me with a cocked eyebrow and a tone.

'Are you trying to be Audrey Hepburn?'

I silently folded down the arms of my glasses and averted her gaze. 'No, I'm just in mourning.'

'Lord help us all,' Tots said from behind her menu.

Elouise stood and held out an arm to hug me. 'Ignore them, Dotty. I think you look fantastic.' She greeted me with a big squeeze, and as soon as the body contact hit me I appreciated that it had been exactly what I needed. What with being a recluse and all, I realised only then that I couldn't remember the last time I'd felt the touch of another human being, and I felt the sad weight of that when Elouise pulled away. 'Gorgeous, utterly gorgeous.' She dropped back into her seat. 'And not at all like you've been ignoring your friends and quietly drinking away your problems for the best part of three weeks.'

I pulled out the empty seat and sat down. 'Okay, okay. Any other jabs that you want to get out of the way before we order?'

'Oh, they'll be liberally scattered throughout the meal,' Tots said with a wink.

Marissa leaned forward and gave my arm a soft squeeze. 'We've just been worried about you, Dotty, that's all. You know that, right?'

'I do know that and . . .' I pulled in a greedy mouthful of air, 'and I'm sorry that I've been missing in action. I haven't . . . well, I haven't really known what to do with myself, honestly.'

'Apart from topping up London's recycling banks.'

'Yes, Tots, apart from drinking lots of wine. I think we've established that much.' I narrowed my eyes and smirked. 'I've just felt a little . . .'

'Lost?' Elouise suggested.

I nodded. 'Lost.'

'You know what'll help with that?' Tots asked.

'This should be good,' Marissa answered as she reached for her own menu.

Tots slapped her arm. 'I wasn't going to say anything bad! I was going to say' — she leaned forward, lowered her menu, and pointed to the sharers section — 'this mini pizza tasting board that comes complete with *three* types of garlic bread. *Three*, Dotty. Don't even *try* to tell me that that isn't going to help you find yourself.'

I laughed and reached across to squeeze her hand. 'You're right, Tots, you're so, so right. Three different types of garlic bread are exactly where I'll find myself.'

* * *

Tots wasn't altogether wrong; I did find myself in that garlic bread. I found myself stuffed, smelly, and utterly content, surrounded by laughter and women who, especially after three cocktails, I couldn't have loved more if I'd tried.

I was two hours into their company and already questioning why I'd wasted quite so much of the Caitlin break-up *not* being with them. Elouise had entertained us wildly with her latest on-set dramas — 'Honestly, he wanted me to wear the snake *around* my neck, like I'm some sort of Britney Spears throwback' — while Tots told us everything she could about her latest story involving a corrupt politician — 'There are so many of them these days, it's not like you'll guess which one I'm talking about' — and I was just settling in for the latest work grumbles from Marissa when the mood of the table changed entirely.

Elouise's face dropped, as though seeing the ghost of romances past, and I saw her try and fail to subtly nudge Tots beneath the table. Marissa caught their exchange, too, and even though she carried on talking, she was patiently trying to catch a glance behind me at whatever had caught the girls' attention.

I smiled and stirred my cocktail. It was a fruity number with a wedge of pineapple poking out from the top that made me want to run away to the beach.

'Babe,' Elouise started in her tamest voice, 'I don't want this to be awkward—'

'But Caitlin just walked in,' I finished her sentence.

'How the f—'

'Come on, Tots. I've seen enough romantic comedies to know what just happened.'

'Do you want to leave?' Marissa asked quietly.

I shook my head. 'I'm okay, thanks though, sweetheart.' I sucked in a breath and stirred my drink some more. The silence on the table was so severe that even over the background noise of the bistro I could hear my ice clinking against the side of my glass. 'Does she look fantastic?'

'Utterly terrible,' Tots answered too quickly.

I sighed and rested my elbows on the table. 'How the hell is London so small? So help me, you can't swing a stick without knocking into someone you've slept with.'

'Well, Tots definitely can't,' Marissa said. It was obviously a desperate attempt to change the mood. And even though it was a valiant and fair effort, it didn't quite stick.

I laboured long and hard over whether to ask the clear follow-up question. The answer to it shouldn't have mattered; not least because the answer wasn't technically any of my business. But I couldn't help myself.

'Is she with someone?'

The girls didn't need to answer. I caught their hooded looks before they even had time to decide between them whether to lie or not. That's when my cool slipped, and I turned around at such a speed that I took out Marissa's cocktail in the process. Over the cries of 'It doesn't matter, it doesn't matter', while Tots helped her mop up the mess, there was a sudden whooshing sound in my ears, too. It sounded as though a high tide was trying to break a seawall in winter — the slam of water on concrete over and over again, catching the inside of my skull with every swing. *Of course she's with someone.*

Caitlin was wearing a brilliant white shirt dress that was so fantastically bright I thought it must be brand new. She was forever mixing her colours and whites by mistake. It was set off by a brown band of leather tied in the centre that perfectly highlighted her waist. I couldn't see what shoes she'd paired it with because, on my journey down her tall form, I stalled partway when I saw that her hand was clasped with another — someone she was guiding across the restaurant. My eyes moved up to the other woman, starting with her high-waisted Mom jeans and the loose-fit black T-shirt tucked in. Tattoos peeked out from both T-shirt sleeves, and long hair crept low past her shoulders. She was a brunette but a darker shade than I'd expected Caitlin to go for. There was a tangle of low-hanging thin gold chains around her neck and—

'Oh God.'

Elouise set a hand softly on my shoulder. 'Dotty?'

'Oh God. That's . . . I know her. I know the woman that she's—'

'Maybe they're just friends,' Elouise said. The comment was hurried and panicked, and it was met with a derisory snort from Tots. I heard an arm slap, which I was sure would have been Marissa.

Caitlin and 'Lili from The Gym', as I'd always known her, walked across the room together, their hands clasped the entire time. Of course, Caitlin might have just been guiding the perfectly toned woman across a busy space, holding on to her so as not to lose her in the din.

But as they sat down at a table for two, I wasn't sure where Lili slapping Caitlin's backside and kissing her cheek fitted into the narrative of them just being friends. Or the narrative that Caitlin used to tell me, about how Lili was just a good gym buddy, and how there definitely, absolutely wasn't anything to worry about. Because Lili, with the perfect body and the refined life that was so good she didn't even *have* an Instagram account — because she didn't feel the need to share everything with the world — *that* Lili absolutely *wasn't* Caitlin's type, so what could I possibly have to worry about and—

'I think I'd like to leave now.'

The statement emerged from me quietly, mouse-like, but the girls heard it. There were hurried sounds from behind me as they started to collect their things and mine. Marissa said she'd get the bill. Tots said they'd wait for her outside, then corrected herself and said 'No, we'll meet you . . .' I lost the name of where she said, but I guessed it would be another watering hole. Then Elouise was guiding me up and out of my seat.

'Put these on, sugar. They complete your outfit.' She handed me my sunglasses, which I took from her absentmindedly without fully knowing how I was even completing the action. 'Flick your hair back and imagine someone with their fingers tucked just beneath your chin. There's nothing like big shades and a head held high to complete a look.'

I managed a weak smile. 'Thank you, El.'

'No need to thank us.' I was flanked by Tots, then, carrying my bag for me. 'We love you, Dotty, this is exactly what we're here for.'

And I'd never felt more grateful for that reminder.

CHAPTER FOURTEEN

The only reason I knew Elza was drawing the meeting to a close was because she said my name.

'Dotty, can you stay behind for a minute?'

Panic gripped my stomach in a vice. Of course, I hadn't been present for the last hour! Of course, I didn't care what Sophia was doing for the travel section, nor Claire for the fashion section. All I cared about was whether Caitlin and Lili were having brunch in a high rise somewhere that overlooked London, or doing exciting things like going to the theatre, eating in posh restaurants, and attending art exhibitions. Or maybe they were just curled up on the sofa doing nothing at all, like Caitlin and I used to. Somehow, I couldn't decide which version of the story I was telling myself was worse.

'They're doing all of the exciting things that you never wanted to do, that's your worry?' Tots had pointedly asked when I'd voiced similar concerns to her during a late-night phone call. It had killed me that she was right, and it had only made these idle, ugly fantasies that bit more trying. I was starting to hate every square inch of London owing to the sheer possibility that Caitlin might be living her best life out there now — without me. But the hardest thing of all was that I couldn't work out whether it was Fear of Missing Out *with Caitlin*, or just Fear of Missing Out that was driving my female rage. To my shame, I was inclined to suspect the latter.

Elza waited until the final few members of staff had trickled out of the room before shutting the door behind them. She picked up a blueberry muffin and a can of Diet Coke from the centre of the conference table and set both down in front of me.

'How are you doing?' she asked as she sat down opposite me. I was suddenly grateful for the sheer size of the table — it meant there was a good metre and a half between us. 'I mean, how are you *really* doing, Dotty?'

I narrowed my eyes. 'Fine, thank you.'

'Eat your muffin,' she nodded, 'you look like you need the sugar.'

I wasn't altogether sure what the comment meant. But never one to turn down free food, I pulled the muffin closer and started to pick at the blue dots peppered across the top. I couldn't stand the thought of the drink, though. The hiss and fizz and spit bubbling away in my stomach would do nothing for the slosh of nerves already sitting there.

'I want to talk about your last submissions for the column.' She pulled her laptop from the head of the table, opened it, and maintained a stoic silence while she looked for whatever it was she needed.

Meanwhile, I frantically scanned my lazy brain to try to remember who had written in, what they'd said and, perhaps most importantly, what on earth I'd said in return. 'This woman, Lonely and Longing.' *Bugger.* 'She writes in to tell you that she's recovering from a break-up, from a long-term relationship no less, and she doesn't know what to do about suddenly feeling so lonely.' Elza delivered these details in a flat tone. She'd never made a secret of the fact that she didn't exactly have time for other people's problems — which made her vested interest in my well-being that bit more baffling. 'Can you remember what you told her?'

I sighed and lowered my gaze. 'I told her to get a dog.'

'Mm.' She mulled over my comment, even though she must have had my full response right there in front of her. She squinted at the laptop screen as though searching the words for a hidden meaning, perhaps something redemptive that might mean my advice was sounder than she'd originally thought. But alas, when she looked up again, I recognised the expression: her eyes down to slits; her mouth bunched up at the corner. *That's disappointment, right there.*

I picked at the top of the muffin, breaking off a decent enough chunk to wedge into my mouth and keep it full.

'Do you think you should get a dog, Dotty?'

'I'm sorry?' I spoke around the sponge. I couldn't help it. I should have taken a bigger chunk, I realised. No, I should have eaten the whole muffin in a single sweep.

'Do you think you should get a dog?' she repeated.

'I . . .' I exhaled hard, stumped by her question. 'I've never thought about getting a dog.'

'Even though you're lonely?'

'I wouldn't say I'm lonely, Elza.' *Affronted, maybe, but certainly not lonely.*

'You're in a similar situation. Recently bereaved—'

'It wasn't a death!'

'It was a loss.'

I pushed the muffin away pointedly and rested my arms on the table. 'Elza, I honestly think I preferred the version of this conversation where you take me out for cocktails.'

At least that made her laugh. 'I think you need a break,' she announced.

My head jerked back. 'From work?'

'*No!*' The horror in her reaction was strangely comforting. *I'd lost enough already*, I thought, *it would be unfair to snatch work away, too.* Besides which, without work I would be just another bum slouching around their London apartment until the mid-hours of the afternoon. At least *with* work, I could do that under the guise of being productive. 'You can work from anywhere, Dotty. You don't *need* to be in London.'

'But where . . .'

Elza sighed in such a way that I sensed she was losing patience with the situation. 'Don't think I didn't see you searching for flights to LA during the meeting this morning, Dotty. But you aren't Kate Winslet, and this isn't *The* bloody *Holiday*. If there's somewhere else you want to be, then be there.'

'LA?'

'Anywhere.' She stood and started to walk towards the doorway, even though the discussion felt far from over. Scratch that: even though I still wasn't sure what the discussion was about. It felt like it had started in one place — my work — but somehow wound its way into another — my living arrangements. But honestly, who could really afford an apartment in London *and* a trip to LA for no good reason? It had been idle browsing, a fantasy, nothing more, and yet . . .

'I think you need some time away, Dotty, is what I'm trying to say. Your advice, it's . . .' I didn't like where that pause was going. 'It's fine, it's working, just about. But it isn't Dotty, it isn't *you*, and I think some distance from London, from the home you shared with . . .'

'Caitlin.'

'Caitlin, right. I think some distance from there might help you get some perspective. Think about it, okay?' Elza grabbed for the door without even waiting for my nod, which, admittedly, was a hesitant nod at best. 'Oh' — she turned back — 'rewrite the Lonely column, too, would you? Be a bit more . . . inventive.'

'Okay, sure, I can . . . I'll . . .'

Quite frankly I didn't know what I could do, or what I would do. But given that Elza didn't stick around long enough to hear a weak promise from me, it didn't seem to matter all that much.

I was left with my half-eaten muffin, feeling deflated, defeated and—

'Lonely,' I admitted to the empty room.

I collected my things slowly, already knowing that I didn't have the guts to stay in the office for the day and risk seeing Elza again, but knowing, too, that I couldn't much stand the thought of heading home either. Which left me with only one real option . . .

* * *

I ordered Supernova's House Cheeseburger with a portion of hand-cut fries and a Coke. Their menu was simple but inspired. And given that I couldn't even decide whether I felt level-headed enough to go home for the afternoon, heading to a local burger joint with a menu made up of just a handful of items really helped when it came to the element of (in) decision. The queue was offensive, as was so often the case — they were, after all, exceptionally good burgers — but once the gruelling task of flipping a coin between one burger and another was done with, I reasoned this at least meant my hardest decisions were effectively made for the day, and I tipped the server extra because of that.

'Dashing out for lunch?' a voice caught my attention as I lingered at the edge of the counter. I turned and found a tall, conventionally handsome man about my age, who looked every bit the part of a Londoner. He was wearing a crisp shirt with the top two buttons undone, paired with a pinstripe suit — although the jacket was slung over his arm, and in the mixed-message heat of the overcast day, I couldn't blame him.

I smiled. 'Just treating myself.'

'I hear that. I'm straight back to the office after this.'

'Me too,' I lied, with the sinking realisation that I still needed to decide where I would actually eat my burger and fries. 'Sometimes you just want something different from the slush at the canteen, don't you?'

The man laughed and I noticed a dimple pinch at the side of his mouth. 'Slush is the word. Whereabouts do you—' His question cut off when one of the servers from behind the counter shouted a name that the man reacted to. He was Matthew, it turned out, and his burger, fries, and sundae were served up. 'That's me' — he gestured with the boxes — 'enjoy.'

'You too.'

It was nearly another ten minutes before my own name was yelled, and like a full house in a strange game of Bingo I threw my hand up in response to the call-out. In the waiting time, I had been jostled and hustled by the surrounding customers, all of whom were clearly becoming more irate as the lunch hour wore on, so I was glad to make my escape. But at least the waiting time had given me the chance to work out where I was going next. Soho Square Gardens were only a five-minute walk away, at a quick pace, so I wandered over there with my burger, fries and drink in tow, and tried very, *very* hard not to think about what I might do after that. Even though the answer was obvious: I had a column to rewrite.

The weather had turned slightly, but I managed to find a quiet bench shielded from the gentle winds to devour my lunch. The burger turned out to be just the distraction I needed, too. I deconstructed it — which is to say, I freed the pickles from the melted slabs of American cheese and ate those first — and chewed my way through the meal in absolute silence. I shovelled fries into my mouth, guzzled my drink, and chewed through more of my burger which was so tasty it may have actually been illegal. And all I did during that time was watch everyone around me. There weren't any thoughts of Caitlin or Elza or the column, even though I couldn't work out exactly how I'd managed to switch all of that off in the space of a single sitting.

'Unless this really is magic,' I said quietly to no one at all as I licked the last of the house sauce from my fingers.

But then, magic really did happen. As I folded my empty fry wrapper into my burger box and drained the last of my drink, the column sprang back to mind — complete with an answer. The *right* answer. I freed my laptop from my bag at such a speed that anyone would have been forgiven for thinking an actual emergency was taking place, but I was scared of losing the seed of the idea. I crossed my legs, balanced my laptop on one knee, and opened a new Word document:

Dear Lonely and Longing,
I hear you. But hear me: the first thing you need to do is
start taking yourself on dates . . .

CHAPTER FIFTEEN

Tots and Elouise were slumped on opposite ends of my sofa with Marissa on speakerphone between them. Meanwhile, I was perched on my window ledge, paying only the tiniest bit of attention to the conversation that was unfolding. We'd been at it for nearly thirty minutes, and my interest had withered after about three. Elouise was right in the middle of saying something about London being good for the soul when Tots reminded her that she actually spent most of her working life outside of London, on location shoots.

'Whose side are you on?' Elouise snapped back.

'I'm not sure it's about taking sides,' Marissa chimed in from the handset. 'Isn't it more about supporting Dotty's decision-making and helping her to listen to what she actually wants to do in her life right now?'

'Hear, hear,' I added from the window. My comment was met with an eye roll from Elouise, though, who only slumped further into the pillows behind her. 'Els, I really think you're making more out of this than you need to.'

'Babe' — Tots inched forward — 'I think Elouise's worry is that what you're actually doing is running away from a problem rather than taking steps to fix it, and that maybe, right now, being around your friends and around people who love you is more appropriate.'

'So you're on *my* side now?' Elouise added.

'It looks that way, doesn't it, but I can always be on Dotty's side again, if you'd prefer?' Tots matched her, snarky tone for snarky tone.

There was a loud huff from the speaker then. 'Dotty, how long do you think you'll be away for, if you do go?'

'Well, I am going,' I answered Marissa, who seemed to be the only middle ground voice out of the lot of us, 'and honestly, I don't know how long for, I just think that—'

'Christ, what if you don't come back?'

I huffed a laugh. 'Elouise, this is home, of course I'll come back.'

'Will you call?'

'If I do, will you answer?' I cocked an eyebrow at her. Elouise was notorious for not answering phone calls or text messages. Though I'd found that she was mostly always available through her direct messages on Instagram. 'I'll call you as often as you'd like. And we can video call still, all of us. I'm not falling off the edge of the earth!'

There was a look swapped between her and Tots, then a loaded expression that I couldn't quite decipher the meaning of. Until Elouise threw her arms in the air in a defeated gesture, complete with a sulky glance my way.

And that seemed to decide it. Marissa said her goodbyes and, if I wasn't mistaken, I thought there was a crack of emotion in her voice. Meanwhile, Tots offered to help me pack, and Elouise hunted through the cupboards, looking for a bottle of wine to open.

'You won't find any!' I eventually shouted through to her from the bedroom.

'Why not?'

'I'm on a booze cleanse.'

'Good grief,' she answered in a low tone, albeit not quite lowered enough, 'I just can't catch a break.'

By the time the afternoon drew to a close, we'd managed to decide on a farewell takeaway without another argument erupting. Although I did have to acquiesce to Elouise's demand for two bottles of wine between us for the evening ahead. She and Tots went to collect enough Vietnamese food to feed a small army, and they returned with Marissa in tow as well. And, as good fortune — for Elouise — would have it, Marissa had also thought to grab a bottle of something sparkling on her travels. We dotted ourselves around my living room and ate so much food that even Elouise was popping the button of her jeans to make space for an expanding stomach — 'That'll be an extra two pounds of joy I've gained there, I'm not worried' — and one by one my friends fell asleep for our last impromptu slumber party.

And the next morning, just like that, I was leaving London.

* * *

When I was younger, catching the train anywhere had always felt like a luxury. My friends and I would escape the confines of country living thanks to the Great British Railways system, and for a day at a time we got a taste of city life, the likes of which we'd never known before. I think that was probably what seeded my early interest in London: the perceived glamour of it all and the sheer romanticisation of what it must be like to be there *all the time*. The ability to get any kind of takeaway no matter the hour. The constantly opening and closing and shifting and changing exhibitions. The sheer artistry of the place. When I'd first moved to London, I'd been bowled over by how *late* corner shops seemed to be open, too. Imagine being able to get a pint of milk any time you wanted! I'd even said as much to Mum during one of our earliest conversations after I'd left. And she'd flatly answered by saying she got enough milk for one — I noted her emphasis, too — during her weekly shops, so what did it matter? Needless to say, her admiration of the new city was markedly different from my own. In the first months of living away, it sometimes felt, whenever I spoke to Mum, like I was being a disloyal partner. One who had lovingly stayed in the same space, with the same person, for so many years, that neither one of us had ever really believed there might come a time when that place wasn't enough. And yet, as soon as I'd been old enough to ship myself off to brighter pastures, I'd gone; hooked by the dazzling lights and the brilliant opportunities. I'd left country living for a newer, younger, more impressive model.

Now here I was again, leaving.

I was sitting in the waiting room at Lewes station when the weight of it all hit me. I wondered what on earth I thought I was going to achieve by leaving the city at all. It might have been Elza's advice, or it might have been an idle search for the sunny spots in Los Angeles, but that wasn't exactly what I was trading London for. So far, all I'd actually got from the shift was a short stretch on a crammed train, a coffee that cost too much and tasted of too little, and a two-hour delay because my second train was cancelled. That, and a shocking insight into the fact that while London had been warm that morning, despite the season, the rest of the country was decidedly more overcast. From my view out onto Lewes' station, I was already worried that there was a threat of rain. Which, of course, I wasn't dressed for.

I pulled my wrap-around dress a little tighter and fastened the buttons on my cardigan. The overhead announcement confirmed there was still another thirty minutes' wait on the cards, so I ferreted into my bag to pull out my phone. I hadn't updated the Dear Dotty Instagram account in a full three days and now felt like the perfect time to rifle through my Favourites album on my phone and finally put some candid shots to good use. I skimmed through a stream of photographs that was largely populated with mine and the girls' food orders at different restaurants. But eventually I came to one that made me stall: it was a simple square of my window ledge in the apartment, with my laptop open and a steaming cup sitting alongside it; the image was focused enough to actually see the steam, too. Outside, there was a brilliant bright sunshine, and I tried to place what I would have been doing in the moments before or even after the snap was taken. I would have been working, most likely, or I would have been thinking about working at least. I would have been letting the drink cool, and killing time by taking the photograph while I waited. I might have been idly planning dinner, or thinking of calling the girls, or wondering whether Caitlin—

But no, I realised, *Caitlin would have left by then. Only just, but definitely.*

I uploaded the image to my work account and heightened the colouring to make the sunshine pop before I started on the caption: 'Dear Readers . . . '

Dear Readers, what, exactly?

I pulled in a greedy breath that was tainted with vehicle fumes, and I caught myself smiling. Apparently, there were some similarities between Lewes and London that I'd overlooked up until then. I tipped my head back and rested it against the wall behind me. I was enacting the old return and retreat. I was leaving the city to breathe elsewhere. I was leaving to find something I'd lost. And I caught another smile.

> *Dear Readers. Heartbreak hits us all sometimes, doesn't it? And after dishing out some quality advice — if I say so myself — I recently had my own brush with a broken heart. So, I'm taking care and taking time and taking space, and you can expect a healthy dose of countryside snaps while I do so. Rest assured, though, I'll keep writing, and I'll keep giving advice to those who need it. Enjoy the autumn sunshine, and keep London warm for me whilst I'm away. All my love, Dear Dotty xox.*

I hit post before I had the chance to talk myself out of the honesty, and I braced for the berating that might come from Elza, too. The Dear Dotty account had always been beautifully stylised, but I reasoned — or something in me did, at least — that some frank talking mightn't go amiss either. Marissa told me once many years ago that you should never trust a thin chef. It seemed like a strange adage to live by, but I eventually understood what she meant. You should never trust someone who seemingly doesn't try their own meals, enjoy their own innings, or explore their own tastes. This was the same, and I would tell Elza that when her inevitable email came. *How could you advise the broken-hearted if you'd never been one? How could you combat loneliness if you'd never given yourself the chance to be lonely? How could you start over—*

'This is the delayed 3:45 service for Alfriston. Boarding now for Alfriston.'

—if you never let something end?

CHAPTER SIXTEEN

No stranger to blind optimism, I was only too aware that the glass-half-full attitude that I was leaving London with might not last. It was a certainty in life, I'd found, that even when you went into a situation with a glass that was half full, there were still certain things that could come right along and knock the glass over altogether. In my case, my beaker of hope was knocked over the second I arrived home, stepped into my childhood bedroom, and saw the same *Buffy the Vampire Slayer* poster of Willow — it was a formative experience for my sexuality, watching that woman be good, bad, then good again — still hanging in pride of place on the wall adjacent to my bed. My single bed adorned, no less, with a floral bedcover that I felt quietly sure I'd picked out when I was sixteen, thinking it was somehow both demure and chic. Now, in my mid-thirties, it was neither. Mum, clinging to my arm and telling me she was glad, so, so glad that I'd come home, showed me into the room as though she was presenting a shrine. It felt more to me like a relic.

'Nothing has changed,' I announced flatly.

'And isn't that the beauty of home, love?' She stretched up to kiss my cheek. 'I'll go and put the kettle on, leave you to get yourself settled for a minute. I suspect you'll want to shower that London smog off you before we start making plans for the coming weeks, eh?' The final question followed her down the corridor and back towards the stairs, punctuated by the heavy chunk-chunk of her footfalls on the well-trodden carpet. *Another thing that hasn't changed.* And I realised, then, that she wasn't exactly expecting an answer.

In the days that followed I found I was totting up other things that hadn't changed: Mum's offensively bright-eyed morning attitude; the knock of the milkman at all hours; the constant smell of cooking — I was into my second week at home when I discovered the most offensive consistency of them all: my mother's levels of patience.

'Dorothy Ellison!'

I was woken by the rattle of a curtain rail and a sudden glare of sunlight. I cracked my eyes open and saw Mum's silhouette, backlit by the brightness of the outdoors. She stood with her hands on her hips, sturdy and determined. I was glad that I couldn't see the accompanying facial expression that went along with the stance.

'It has been ten days, Dorothy, *ten*, and you have hardly left this pit.'

There's something painstakingly terrifying about hearing your parent use your full name like that, no matter how old you are. And the sound of my own name, twice, made me so tetchy that I almost instantly needed a nervous wee. I tucked my legs up towards my tummy under my mound of duvet, closed my eyes, and groaned.

Mum may have had a fair point. I hadn't exactly been a social butterfly in the time that I'd been at home so far. But that wasn't what I'd gone home for! *So why* did *I come back?* I wondered, in answer to my own internal protests. Apparently not to heal but to wallow — in something. I hadn't been checking Caitlin's Instagram, Facebook or X profiles, nor Lili's. I hadn't even been idly fantasising about their stylised new life together. In fact, there had come a strange sort of relief, with being home, that I *didn't* have a Caitlin to text or a Caitlin to answer to — or a Caitlin to upset. And yet, I couldn't shake the feeling of loss, and of being lost . . .

'Dotty, you're a grown woman now, and I won't stand for this moping.'

'I'm heartbroken,' I managed, muffled, not quite knowing how true it was now.

'*Are* you?'

The question was so pointed, her tone so curt, that I instantly bobbed my head up and cracked my eyes open that bit wider. 'Mum!'

'Love, I don't mean to be brutish now . . .' *Lie*, I thought. 'But I'm not altogether sure that you miss Caitlin as much as you think you miss her.'

'I don't even know what that means.'

'Why don't we talk about this over breakfast, hm?' She leaned forward and cupped a hand around my cheek, which felt like a disconcertingly tender gesture given the forceful address that had come only seconds before it. 'Though it'll be more like brunch.'

I flashed a tight smile at her pointed remark. 'I'll be right down, Mum.'

'Fantastic. 'Atta girl.'

* * *

Mum managed to wait until I was two bites into my bacon sandwich before she started goading me again. Although she looked to be picking up an entirely different conversational thread, it was a change I wasn't altogether sure I welcomed, given that she was listing options for things that we might busy ourselves with that day.

'I really don't feel like doing much, Mum,' I admitted, chewing around a crust of bread as I spoke. 'I'm just . . . I don't know what I am. I'm not in the mood.'

'You don't always have to be in the mood for something to get it done, Dotty.'

103

'That's true,' I agreed, 'if we're talking about deadlines for work. If we're talking about . . .' I scanned down the list — an actual *list* — of options for the day's activities that Mum had placed in front of me along with my breakfast, like an unwanted menu. 'If we're talking about a visit to Follers Manor Farm, then I think you do have to be in the mood.'

'Then pick something else from the list.'

'I think you're missing my point, Mum.'

'And I think you're missing mine.' She dried her hands on a nearby tea towel and came to sit opposite me at the breakfast table. Like muscle memory, I suddenly thought back to the many mornings we'd had together, sitting right there, sharing breakfast before I hurried off to school. And I was only ever in a hurry *because* of those breakfasts, too, though I remembered loving them all the same. 'Dotty, why did you come home?'

I narrowed my eyes at the question.

'It isn't a trick,' she added.

'It sort of feels like one.'

'You have ketchup on your face, love.'

I wiped my mouth on the sleeve of my pyjama top and surveyed the stain as I spoke. 'I came home because I needed to be out of London for a while. I need a change and—'

'Ah' — she held up a finger — 'you needed a change.'

Ah, I echoed, *so this* is *a trick*.

'If you were writing advice to someone who had recently found themselves in a slump, what would you say?'

I was starting to spot this trend in my life now: people asking what advice I would give to someone in my situation or a similar one. But what I think people were very quick to overlook was that it was notoriously easy to give *someone else* advice and notoriously difficult to follow it yourself.

I rolled my eyes. 'I would tell them to try and do something new.'

'And what's newer than' — she paused to cast a glance down her list — 'the Clergy House and Garden?'

'I imagine there are lots of things newer than that, actually.' I went back to my bacon.

'Dorothy.' She huffed. 'I'm trying to help you.'

'And you think taking me out for the day will miraculously help, do you, Mum?' My tone was sharper than I'd meant for it to be. But then, I'd always had my mother's patience. Both of us were wont to only be pushed so far before we began to bend, and I could feel myself starting to give way under her strain. 'Mum, I came home because I've spent the majority of my adult life loving someone who's decided she doesn't love me anymore. I've lost . . . I've lost my evenings at home together, I've lost movie marathons, I've lost meeting each other on our lunch breaks.' I didn't pause there with an interlude about how I couldn't remember the last time Caitlin and I had done some of these things. It didn't seem like it would serve my point. Instead, I only pressed on, incensed. 'I've lost all the comfort of my life and I'm struggling, okay? I'm struggling to know what to do with all of that.'

At some point during my speech I'd dropped my bacon sandwich, and the hand that had been holding it only seconds ago was balled up and knocking against the table with a thump. Mum only frowned at the outburst, and I suddenly felt every bit like the troublesome child I'd been some . . . *Christ, twenty years ago.* A groan fell out of me, and I let my head fall to the table with a final thud. Seconds later, I felt Mum's hand cup the crown of my hair and softly rub.

'My darling, darling, Dotty.' I lifted my head again to look at her. 'I think life has given you more of a gift here than you realise.'

I huffed. 'What's the gift, Mum?'

'Sometimes you don't know that until you start to unwrap it. But you're being given time to know yourself and to *re*-learn yourself. Isn't that a valuable thing? Especially for someone in your line of work? Love, you just described life as *comfortable* . . .' I wasn't sure I'd used that word *exactly* but whatever. 'Doesn't that tell you something about where you are, and perhaps, where you should think about being instead?'

'Are you really going to come at me with that vague, mumbo-jumbo self-improvement stuff and expect me to buy into it?' I flashed her an expression that could only be described as a stink eye.

'I'm afraid so. Now' — she tapped the table softly with her index finger — 'if you don't choose something from my list of maybes, then I'm going to. Wherever we're going, we're leaving in an hour.'

CHAPTER SEVENTEEN

It was in that very moment that I realised my taste for the occasional bit of blind optimism was obviously inherited. While Mum had only too clearly been pining for a churchyard and gardens, I thought that it was only right — given that I was doing this whole thing very much under duress — that she was also forced to meet me somewhere in the middle when it came to where we spent the first day of what my mother, shamefully, came to refer to as 'Project Dotty'.

And that's exactly why, ninety minutes later, I was sipping from a tall glass of Pinot Noir in the centre of Rathfinny Wine Estate — while Mum was swilling and spitting.

'You were right, Mum; this is exactly what I needed.'

She sighed. 'I thought we might end up doing something we'd *both* enjoy, Dotty.'

'But this was on your list,' I said in the most mocking tone I could muster. After three glasses of wine on nothing more than a half-eaten bacon sandwich, it was actually a little *too* mocking. 'Besides, a glass of wine never hurt anyone.'

'You asked for the bottle.'

'I knew I'd like it.'

'Are you ladies ready to try the next wine?' a well-dressed waitress asked, a bottle neatly propped against her arm. 'This is one of our signature—'

'That's great, thank you. Hit me,' I answered, already holding out my glass. My booze cleanse had very much been abandoned, and I couldn't wait to tell Elouise this good news at least.

'You're not a very elegant drunk,' Mum said flatly when we were alone again.

'I'm not sure anyone is,' I sipped, swallowed, and scrunched up my face. 'Not if they're *really* drunk, anyway.' I paused to set my glass down and reach for a glass of water — to swill out the taste, not to dilute anything. 'Plus, some of the advice I'd give to someone in my situation would definitely be to let their hair down and enjoy themselves.'

Mum narrowed her eyes. She was fiddling with her phone by the time she spoke again, which was markedly out of character, but I was tipsy enough not to query it. 'What other advice would you give someone in your situation?'

'Mum,' I whined. 'I'm not even on the clock.'

'I'm being serious, Dotty.' And she was — I could tell by the tone. 'What else?'

I thought about the question for longer than I really needed to. I had, in fact, given advice to lots of people in my situation already. Heartbreak had provided writing material for months on end, with a readership starting in the confines of promiscuous old London before spreading out to a national front. There hadn't been much variety from one broken heart to another, though — they all needed a change, something new, something—

'That they need to get rid of all their old rubbish from their ex.'

'Meaning?'

I shrugged. 'Don't keep their clothes. Don't keep . . . I don't know, pots and pans you bought together. Don't keep the sofa that you watched Netflix on.'

'That sounds like quite an expensive overhaul.'

I sipped my drink at the same time as trying to murmur my agreement. 'Heartbreak doesn't come cheap, I'm afraid. I haven't even started on the self-improvement.'

'And what does that involve?'

'Mum' — I lowered my voice and leaned over to lessen the distance between us — 'are you secretly nursing a broken heart and rinsing me for information here? Because it's starting to feel a little like that's happening. That' — I nodded towards her phone — 'or you're planning on making me a to do list.'

Mum chuckled, a deep and sincere sound.

I was suddenly glad that I'd been able to bring some gentle comedy to an otherwise bleak afternoon. Of course, I explained, the self-improvement stage would involve getting a new haircut — nothing drastic, because I'm a firm believer in making as few mistakes as possible during times of grief, which shouldn't be undermined by lunchtime drinking with my mother at a wine estate. But try out a fringe or highlights — at least cut the dead ends from your hair. There might be a new outfit, or a couple of new outfits. Then there would be trips to places to wear those new outfits: dinner with friends, solo cinema outings, and even a few extra coffee shop dates. Time and again, I have encouraged the broken-hearted to try new things as well: go somewhere and do something that you absolutely wouldn't have done with your ex-partner. Then, once complete, go somewhere and do something that you absolutely wouldn't have done as your ex-self.

'Your ex-self?' Mum queried.

'Heartbreak is transformative, Mum. None of us are the same on the other side as we were in the beginning, so it makes the most sense in the world to embrace that. Harness it, even.' I was gesturing with my wine glass, punctuating my enthusiasm with small splashes of pink wine on the fresh tablecloth. 'There has to be an exciting version of yourself out there that you haven't even met yet. Do you know what I mean?'

She narrowed her eyes. 'I think so.'

'Can I interest you ladies in bread and cheeses to go with your—'

'Hit me,' I interrupted the poor waitress again, and my mother audibly tutted.

'My point is,' I started again while the young woman laid out three different types of bread that made me salivate so much that I was genuinely concerned about dribbling, 'on the other side of a break-up, you know more about yourself than you did in the first instance. You learn, you hurt, you bloody ache with feeling, but you also do a lot, *a lot* of thinking, and a lot of reflecting, which teaches you more about who you are.' I dropped back in my seat and looked wistfully off into the distance, trying to think what song would match this moment in the movie. 'It's a transformative experience, Mum.'

'Did you want butter?' the woman cut across any response that Mum might have had.

'Please,' Mum answered for us both, already reaching for a slice of olive loaf that I wagered she'd probably been eyeing since midway through my lament. 'What else might you tell someone in your situation?'

I laughed. 'Mum, I'm running out of juice here.'

'Nonsense. You're Dear Dotty. You don't run out of juice.' She set the slice of bread down and replaced it with her phone, which I only then realised had been lying between us the entire time. 'In all the years I've known you' — she huffed a laugh — 'which you might remember is quite a few, writing is one of the few things you've done consistently. *Advice* is one of the few things you've done— thank you, dear' — she paused to flash gratitude at the waitress for her plate of offensively thin slices of butter — 'and one of the few things you've done and loved.'

'Mum, it's *all* I've done!'

'Well, surely that proves my point. If you can't write yourself out of this, and advise yourself out of this, then who else in the world is going to help you, hm?' With her free hand, she reached across the table, squeezed my hand, and looked at me with such tenderness that it made me ache. 'My darling Dotty, did you ever consider that maybe *you* are exactly what you need right now?'

'Oh, Mum, I . . .' I stopped as I heard a sharp noise chirp up from her phone. 'What was that?'

'It was me ending the voice note I was recording.' She still looked down at the screen of her phone. 'I'm going to email it to you, just as soon as I work out how. And then when you're feeling doubtful, or like you don't know where to turn, you can turn right back to yourself and remind yourself of this moment, right here, lunchtime drinking with your mother.'

'Mum, I . . . This is . . . That's such a—'

I wanted to be outraged. And I'll admit that a part of me was. But there was a part of me that was also alight suddenly, a low sounding spark in the back of my brain that snapped, crackled, hissed, and caught.

'Mum, have you got a pen?'

Dear Dotty,

I am, in plain blank terms, a bit of a mess. My partner of a hundred years left me. Maybe for another woman, maybe not, but there's definitely another woman now. And of course, she's a much fitter and finer woman than me, whose main use for her gym card is not jimmying open the front door to a London apartment (I can hardly afford) because I've forgotten my keys again, and the person who used to let me in when that happened has since shaped up and exited my life in a cloud of smoke.

She said I'd stopped trying. I'm old enough and ugly enough to know that that's one of those easy reasons to throw at someone. Old enough and ugly enough to know that, in this case, though, she's actually right. I hate writing that. But at some point between twenty-five and thirty, Dotty, I started to settle. I settled for London, I settled for never looking for other work, different work — not that I don't love my job, but hey, there are definitely other ways I could have done it over the years — and I settled for safe. Now, nothing is safe. I feel as though I've lived myself into a corner and I'm faced off with decisions that I never thought about making before — precisely because I was so settled, it never occurred to me that all this might even happen. But maybe that's why it has. Maybe sometimes, we need to be unsettled. Maybe unsettled is where we live for a while, while we're learning how to become brave.

So I'm going to learn, Dotty, slowly. I don't need your advice yet, I don't think. But consider this a placeholder until I do.

Take good care. Don't be dumb. Love and hugs,
Dotty xx

CHAPTER EIGHTEEN

There is something I know to be absolutely true: my mother is an infinite source of wisdom.

The morning after the lunchtime drinking the day before, I woke with a groan of a hangover. It was the type that penetrates body and mind in equal measure. My thoughts were watercolour, and my legs were doing their best impression of Ariel the first time she tried to walk on land.

I managed to get myself upright without upchucking, but I knew that the walk to the bathroom was going to be a risky endeavour. Already, I could hear the clatter of action rising from a room somewhere below that I took to be my mother — basking in the joy of not having a hangover, because she was wise enough to drink sensibly. I wasn't going to give her the satisfaction of shouting downstairs to ask for a bowl — not least because I was an adult now, and therefore there was an expectation that I, too, should know how to drink sensibly. Though the record should note here that I *did* know how to drink sensibly. I just hadn't.

Moving at what can only be described as a glacial pace, I made my way from my bed to the door to the landing. I heard more voices when I started my sluggish journey, and I had to stifle another heartfelt groan at the prospect of Mum having company. Not that it should have mattered, really. I was still at least two litres of water and a power nap away from even tackling the stairs. So I powered on, keeping one hand flat against the wall as though that might steady the rocking that was very much inside me. I was nearly there, too — the bathroom door was within clutching distance. But, I assumed, through years of practice at listening to me shamefully creep from one end of this very corridor to the other, there soon came the sound of my mother, bright-eyed and perky.

'Dotty, sweetheart, is that you?'

'I'm just popping to the loo, Mum.' I clasped my palm flat over my mouth as a soft belch erupted out of me. 'I'm not feeling too good, but I'll be down soon.'

I was certain I heard stifled laughter between her and whoever was brunching with her.

'Bacon sandwich?'

I felt another lurch of my stomach, another belch that threatened to turn into more. And, apparently groaning louder than I'd even realised, Mum took that to be an answer.

'I'll give it half an hour and then bring one up.'

I'd been stashed back in my bed — after a successful and surprisingly vomit-free trip to the bathroom — for ten minutes when a soft knock at my door came. Mum pushed into the room tentatively, as though uncertain what she might find on the other side of the threshold, but when she saw me she only let out a gentle laugh.

'My poor girl.'

Another groan. 'Why did you let me drink so much?'

'Oh, Dotty, you're a fiercely independent young woman. What chance did I have?'

I managed to laugh then, too, and I held my arms out weakly to gratefully take the breakfast tray — though more like an early lunch now — that was offered to me. There was a bacon sandwich (the smell of which seemed to make me hungry and sickly at once), a strong cup of tea, and a neatly folded napkin.

'You've got a friend here?' I asked.

'Only Joan from my book club. She understands you're unwell,' she said with a smirk. 'Take all the time you need. There'll be no excursions today.'

'I love you.'

'Because I'm not dragging you out?'

I smiled. 'Because of everything.'

Mum stood and set a gentle kiss on my forehead. 'Eat up, drink plenty. Use your napkin.'

Wait, what?

'Use my napkin?' I laughed, already reaching for the folded sheet. 'What . . .'

'I'll bring you another cuppa in a bit, love.'

And then she quietly crept out of the room and pulled my door closed behind her, leaving me alone with what I soon saw, was an ex-version of myself . . .

* * *

There is something else I know to be true: in this day and age, nothing good can come from ignoring your social media notifications.

After communing with my past self, and her drunken honesty that had been hastily scribbled on a winery's napkin, I ate my bacon sandwich in utter silence. I drank my tea, read the note, and then read the note a second and third time to be sure. My laptop was within grabbing distance — it always was — and without thinking, as though it were an entirely automatic act, I snatched at it like a greedy child might, opened it, and pulled up a new Word document. Mum appeared after what could have been thirty minutes — though in the mood I was in, it could also have been about three hours — and replaced my empty tea with a full one. She took the remains of my breakfast/lunch away, gave me another kiss on the crown of my head, and disappeared without a word.

Although my focus remained on the document in front of me, where all manner of honesty was spilling from my fingers as though a well had been tapped, I couldn't help but wonder how many times Mum must have seen me like this over the years. To my shame I was backtracking, editing as I went so I could tweak this sentence, add another, put in a caveat here and there, but something like an idea was definitely coming together.

And that's when my phone started to howl.

The longest time had passed without me so much as even thinking about my phone, or the connections to the world beyond this new home life, and I struggled to remember when that had last happened.

I blinked hard to clear the writing fog, reached out to grab the handset and then — I didn't. Instead, my hand hovered for a second or two, the phone still just out of reach, and I resolved to let it go to voicemail. I expelled a hearty sigh as I went back to my typing. It felt like a Dear Diary moment.

Until, of course, the phone started to ring again.

'For goodness—'

The frustration snapped off midway when I leaned over far enough to see the name on the display.

It was Elza.

In the entire time I'd been home with Mum, mine and Elza's contact had been limited to emails alone. A worry passed over me, then, whether this was the dreaded '*When are you coming back to London?*' phone call, whether my time away from the office had finally run out, even though my columns had been turned in on time, to a high enough quality that Elza had only made *slight* edits to their contents — a marked improvement on how they'd been in the weeks immediately after Caitlin.

I sucked in a greedy breath and on the exhale, having decided to be a grown-up, I managed a convincingly happy hello as I answered.

'Do you want to talk me through what happened on your Instagram yesterday?'

A chill moved through me. It crossed my mind that it was the second wave of the hangover. But that would have been far too lucky. No, this, I quickly realised, wasn't the body panic that comes from a hangover at all. It was the brain panic that comes from realising you've acted like an idiot under the influence — and you haven't even been smart enough to cover your tracks and delete the evidence.

'I, ah . . .'

I hesitated for too long. In the seconds' pause between thought and plausible explanation, Elza jumped in to fill the space. She was two sentences in when it occurred to me that the words sounded eerily familiar.

One sentence later, I realised why. I stared down at the open napkin that was lying next to my laptop.

'Elza, I'm so sorry, I—'

'Dotty, it's genius.'

It is?

'It really is,' she answered so promptly that I thought I must have said it aloud. 'I mean, it's a nightmare for the team because we haven't announced anything or prepared literally anyone for this but' — she blew out a dismissive noise — 'we've worked under worse circumstances and quite frankly marketing have been resting recently anyway.'

I have friends in marketing, I thought, feeling a pang of guilt for adding to their workload. I glanced down at the proposal in front of me — three pages of ideas and justifications for why a turn in focus for Dear Dotty could be a good thing. And here Elza was, handing me the opportunity with no need for gentle or forceful persuasion at all. I smiled, and felt like a complete idiot for the day that had drained away in front of me — all the while past and drunken Dotty already had this life development in the bag.

'For now, don't post another letter. We need to think about how we're going to play this . . .' She lingered on the end of the sentence in such a way that I thought it probably wasn't over. I knew Elza all too well, and I could tell when the woman was plotting. 'We won't want to post a letter like this *every* day, because quite frankly you'd be exhausted. How does weekly sound? So we'll go with weekly . . .'

The sentences rolled out without breath, break, or pause, and it soon started to feel a little like having created a monster. At some point, though, Elza actually did pause — there was an interruption on her end of the line when someone came blundering into her office without knocking — and that's when I leapt at my chance.

'I actually have a document,' I hurried out, 'a proposal, I suppose, for how I think the series might look once we get it started, and . . . Would that be helpful?'

There was a long pause on the other end of the line. But when Elza started to speak again I realised the pause had been filled by a smile — it cracked through her response. 'That would be great, Dotty. Send it over and I'll be in touch. In the meantime, keep talking to yourself.'

Elza disconnected the call before I could try for a witty comeback — which was probably a good thing, given how flummoxed I felt by the entire exchange.

No sooner had I dropped the phone from my ear, I was snatching at it again to see the dreaded Instagram post. The one that had seemingly given me away. And with two hasty clicks, there it was: an arty photograph of my empty wine glass, Mum's slightly blurred wine glass in the background of the shot, and a stream of what looked like autumnal sunshine beaming in from somewhere out of shot.

Beneath it sat the very first Dear Dotty letter . . .

CHAPTER NINETEEN

Alongside a surprising and altogether unexpected turn in my career, I soon discovered there was something else I owed to Instagram.

Because apparently Drunken Dotty didn't only spill her emotional innards. No, she also started a poll. A poll that had a frankly overwhelming seventy-eight percent 'in favour of' vote, that was only reinforced when I messaged the girls in our group chat — that I had muted only days ago, owing to their overwhelming concerns about whether I was *ever* coming back to London — and found three yes votes there, too. Though I think Tots may have bullied Marissa and Elouise into it. As much as anyone can ever bully Marissa, that is. Still, there was all-caps encouragement from them all by the end of the conversation. I promised to call Tots later in the day so she could see my new hair — she'd be with the others, so everyone could see the reveal at once. And when Elouise started to ask about my plans to go home, I promptly muted the chat again and started to browse bobs and bangs on Pinterest.

And so it was that Instagram plus best friends plus a new-found bravery and poof: I was in the car on the way to the hairdresser's with Mum.

'And you're *sure* about this?'

I laughed. 'You don't think it will suit me?'

'It isn't that at all, love. I think anything would suit you. You have one of those faces.' A compliment, yet somehow in Mum's nervous-dulcet tones, it sounded more like a judgement. 'But didn't you tell me that you shouldn't make big decisions while you're grieving?'

'Mm,' I murmured in low agreement, 'but I also told you that you might try a fringe.'

'And I've noticed you browsing furniture online?'

I cocked an eyebrow, even though Mum was too busy staring straight ahead, her hands at ten and two, to notice the expression. 'And I . . . shouldn't be?'

'Isn't that a drastic change?'

'Not as drastic as a break-up.' I looked out the passenger window. 'But no one actually asked me about that change; it was just something thrust upon me. And I also said' — I turned back to her and pointed to underscore my argument — 'that you shouldn't keep anything that you shared with your partner.'

'So why not get rid of the whole flat?'

'Now *you're* being extreme.'

'I just think you're starting to make some very big decisions, Dotty.'

'Well, maybe I need to, Mum.'

A loud and grumpy silence elbowed its way into the car with us, squatting on the armrest between our seats. I was suddenly reminded of all the times Mum had driven me to this same hairdresser as a kid, as a teenager, and now as a fully grown woman going through a break-up: splitting up with my partner and, it felt more and more now, like a bit of a separation from myself, too. Something in me softened, then, at the unstoppable flurry of memories — full fringe, side fringe, blonde highlights, bob, charity haircuts — that were tangled up with this one woman, this one place, even, and the welcome reminder that brought with it that even during times of change, there are constants.

I reached over and gave her knee a quick squeeze. 'Besides, you won't be telling me I'm too brave this weekend when you're dragging me into Cuckmere River.'

Mum laughed. 'I think you'll find that was *your* idea.'

'And I think you'll find that my ideas apparently can't be trusted right now.'

Another laugh hiccupped out of her and she reached over to slap playfully at my leg.

She let another minute or two pass before she said, 'I think you're going to look beautiful with a full fringe.'

We pulled up at the hairdresser's minutes later, and I instantly recognised the woman who came rushing out to hug Mum as the same one who had given me this very cut during my teenage years. The salon and Genevieve both looked to be a carbon copy of the space and stylist I remembered from years back: five foot nothing, she was, with a personality loud enough to compensate for it. She wore brash clothing, bold make-up, and I was pretty sure she hadn't aged a day since I'd last seen her, some . . . *fourteen years ago?* I double-checked the maths and tried not to let the shock write itself across my face as Genevieve — 'Call me Genie, babes' — draped a cape around my front and offered me a Diet Coke, regular Coke, tea or coffee, in tones that suggested there was a deep pride in being able to offer me a drink at all. So maybe there had been upgrades to the place in the last decade or so. But I steadfastly believed that Genevieve was the same age now as she'd been then, which left me idly scanning the ceiling space for signs of an attic, perhaps one big enough to stow away a portrait . . .

'Thank you so much,' I said when Genevieve came back. I poked my arms out from under my cloak to take the can that was offered, complete with a glass and ice.

'Now, babes, Mum said a full fringe on the phone?'

'Mhm,' I agreed while I concentrated on pouring my drink, 'if that's okay for you?'

'You're gonna be a stunner with it, I just know it. Now, anything else while you're here?'

'No,' Mum answered flatly before I had the chance, and Genevieve and I both burst into a disproportionate giggle.

'Did you just time travel, too?' Genevieve asked, then, speaking to me through the mirror. 'Mum still having a say in your hairstyles?'

I only nodded before sipping my drink and glancing at Mum over the lip of the glass. She was standing with her arms folded, and I imagined squiggly lines of nervous energy radiating out from her. But the view only lasted a second before Genevieve pulled forward a curtain of thick hair and started to cut . . .

* * *

Two hours later, when I had stared at myself in every reflective surface I came across, I decided to stare at myself through the medium of my laptop screen instead. I scrunched my eyes and covered my face and waited for the WhatsApp call to connect.

'Oh my *days*, Dotty, you look *gorgeous*!'

'Let me see, wait, no, let me see.'

I uncovered my eyes in time to see Tots skid and stop behind Marissa and Elouise, who were sitting side by side on what looked like Marissa's sofa.

'Oh, Dotts, you look amazing. Do you like it?'

'I *do* . . .' I answered in a tone that said otherwise, and I caught myself before one of the girls could catch me. 'No, I do, it's just that weird thing when you do something to your appearance and then . . . you know when you don't recognise yourself for a while?'

Marissa narrowed her eyes. 'I'm pretty sure bereavement does that, too.'

'But in this case it's probably the haircut,' Elouise countered with too much cheer, as though overcompensating. Tots said nothing at all, too busy pouring drinks in the background from what I could gather from the motion and sweep of her arms, and the occasional knock of glasses, and I thought she was better off out of it. Especially when Elouise stretched out her optimism to nearly a full minute, regaling me and Marissa about the psychological benefits of a new do.

'So, you like it?' I leapt in to clarify when Elouise was taking a breath.

'Seriously, Dotty,' Tots knelt behind the sofa and rested her arms on the back of it to position herself in frame between the other two, 'how you're only just doing this to your hair is beyond me. You look like you should have always looked like this.'

I managed a bashful smile. 'Thank you, Dotty's angels.'

'Oh,' Elouise whined, 'we do miss you, Dotty!'

'But we understand you need space,' Marissa rushed to add.

'And we understand that home is a comfort,' Tots chimed in. 'Are you having the best time while you're there? How's your mum?'

'Mum is . . . mothering.' I laughed. 'She definitely likes having me under her roof again, even if she does think I'm stupid for getting a fringe. We're going wild water swimming at the weekend,' I said with a degree of boast. But the gloat didn't land. I saw Elouise throw the other two a look, one that lingered so long I couldn't help but notice it.

'What, what's that look for?'

'I told you,' El spoke out of the side of her mouth, ignoring my question entirely.

'Told them what?'

Marissa rolled her eyes. 'Good grief, Elouise. Dotty, Els thinks you're not coming back to London.'

I spluttered a mocking noise. 'At all, ever?'

'I'm worried about you,' Elouise protested with a whiny tone I'd heard her use on boyfriends before. 'You take off, you fall off the grid, it's like you're becoming . . . country, or something.' She shuddered. 'I wouldn't want that for you.'

'The ways in which that's ridiculous, I can't even . . .' Tots waved her hand in a dismissive gesture and then sipped her cocktail.

'So, you *are* coming back?'

'Elouise, I *live* in London, of course I'm coming back.'

'Just as soon as this crisis is over?'

'It isn't a crisis,' Marissa and I said in unison.

And even though this was, by our standards, a spat among friends, I found the whole thing quite suddenly warming me. We were miles apart — they were drinking gin cocktails while I was drinking tea. Any one of them could have walked into a London bar without being spot-checked for their outfit, while I was all ready for bed. But they were still the best women I knew. And listening to them thrash it out amongst themselves about whether, when, or if I would come home, I soon found made me want to go home that bit more.

'Elouise,' I said softly, to call their bickering to an end, or *try* to anyway. 'I hand on heart promise you that I will definitely be back in London. There are just a few things I need to sort out first.'

She frowned. 'Like?'

'Myself,' I said without missing a beat, and the three of them broke out laughing.

Tots was first to speak once the eruption had died down. 'Okay, beaut, we get that, we genuinely do. Is there anything we can be helping with though? Talking more, talking less? Smack-talking Caitlin all around London?' She paused to sip her drink. 'Whatever you need, we're here for you, I swear it.'

'Apart from smack-talking,' Marissa added. 'Actually, ladies, don't do that.'

'Okay, well I'm not a lady so I'm good,' Tots answered in a notably confrontational tone.

I spoke before Tots could think of a way to show Marissa just how much of a lady she wasn't. 'Actually, it's a bit of an ask, so don't feel that you have to, but there is one thing I could use some help with? And it would be really good to get it sorted before I come home, if any of you think you can manage it.'

'Name it, what do you need?' Elouise's answer was tinged with eagerness.

I started to click about on my laptop. 'Let me just share my screen…'

CHAPTER TWENTY

With all the excitement of the fringe and the flurry of emails I was receiving from Elza every day, it would have been easy to overlook the so-called Project Dotty that Mum had been busy planning. But she didn't let me forget for long, though.

The morning after the haircut I found her list of places to visit pinned to the fridge in the kitchen. In the days after that, Mum spent an inordinate amount of effort dragging me to Every. Single. Place. We started the trips with a jaunt out to Clergy House, Garden and Shop which, to my utter dismay, I heartily enjoyed. After a thorough walk around the house, a 15th-century build that the blessed National Trust had managed to save, Mum wooed me even further with tea, cake, and the reveal of a second-hand bookshop stashed on-site.

'You know if you'd led with the bookshop this would have probably been my first place to visit as well,' I joked as I squatted to scan the bottom row of books. 'Let me buy you something,' I said, still browsing, 'it'll be a little memory.'

'Shouldn't I be buying you something to remember the trip by, for when you're back in—'

'Don't say it,' I cautioned her. I was getting enough of that, still, from Elouise in particular. After taking up my request of a favour, which I was tremendously thankful for, Elouise took every opportunity to remind me that I would have to go back to the Big Smoke at some point. Although every time she did this, she somehow managed to do it under the guise of contacting me about the favour instead. She was nowhere near as smooth as she thought.

'Just let me treat you,' I pushed.

'Okay,' Mum answered, giving in far too easily, 'I'd like this.'

I stood up to catch sight of her with a well-thumbed copy of *Eat, Pray, Love*, and I huffed a laugh. 'I'll buy you a pizza and a new pair of jeans, and you'll basically get the gist of the book.'

We left with our arms linked and two worn out copies of *Jane Eyre* instead. It was Mum's favourite book, and I'd long since lost my own copy, having discarded everything from my A-levels with a flurry of haste and excitement several years ago.

And so I fell into bed that night with a heart full of quiet and a good book to read. The calm of a National Trust property had even topped the excitement of the fringe. But the early morning call for Drusillas Park the following day had me groaning like a pre-teen all over again. It felt like *Groundhog Day*, a carbon copy of the groan and protest that had come the day before.

Mum set a cup of tea heavily on my nightstand. 'You moaned yesterday, too.'

'So you know my process,' I answered from beneath the covers.

'And you *enjoyed* yesterday, too.'

'So you know my process,' I repeated.

Only this time, instead of answering with a too truthful reply, Mum resorted to outright warfare. There came a violent shower of tickles — her hands scurried about between the folds of my duvet to reach my ribs and *tickle, tickle, tickle* at me until I was writhing like a toddler rather than a thirty-something year-old who might know better than to show such a reaction.

'Okay, okay,' I admitted defeat, 'you win. We'll go to your sodding zoo.'

'The best small zoo in Europe, I'll have you know.'

I struggled upright. 'Oh, well, now that I know that, shut up and take my money.'

'Sarcasm doesn't suit you, Dotty.'

I reached around to grab my tea. 'But it's all I have.'

Mum leaned over me and set a damp kiss on my forehead that made my face scrunch up, then looked hard into my eyes and cupped my cheek as she spoke. 'You, my girl, have so much more, if only you realised it.'

* * *

The park, which was really a zoo and therefore a watering hole for parents and their loud children, kept Mum and me busy for the entire day — and it was joyous. Much like the day before, Mum managed to play to every weakness I had, thereby ensuring that despite my moans, we actually had a beautiful time. Not least because it turns out I really am a sucker for a red panda!

By Thursday of that week I had given in entirely to Mum's plans for busyness and mayhem, not least because Wednesday was pitched to me as Shopping Day. Playing to my weaknesses once again, Mum started the itinerary with a trip to Much Ado About Books, closely followed by — some two hours later — a visit to the Dressing Room across the way, where both of us played fancy dress with things that suited us and, counter to that, things that made the other howl with laughter and disbelief. I was only the tiniest bit gutted that Mum thought my choice of flower-embroidered jeans fell into the latter of those, especially when I'd tried them on with the utmost sincerity. But apparently embroidery was not part of Dear Dotty's future.

By Friday evening I was exhausted and not at all ready for the wild water swimming that was to come the following morning.

127

After Mum had made such an effort for the entire week to remind me of everything that Alfriston had to offer, I thought it was about time that I took my turn to do something kind. *I owe her*, I thought with a smile as I shut the kitchen door behind me, firmly locking my mother out of cooking endeavours. I'd briefly flirted with the idea of trying something new, fancy and altogether impressive, to show Mum that I really, truly could be an adult when I tried, really and truly, hard to be. The threat of imminent failure was enough to put me off any wistful attempts at barbequed oysters or roasted squash and pepper pie with a homemade crust, though. Honestly, it was like my search engine results didn't know me at all and had therefore vastly overshot the results for fancy and impressive home-cooked meals. *Who even makes this stuff at home?* I wondered as I grated mature cheddar, before putting the block of cheese back in the fridge, then promptly getting it back out to grate more. I left the pasta and broccoli to cook through while I picked at pieces of cheese that were dotted around the edge of the chopping board, before eventually remembering that I'd forgotten perhaps the most important part of the recipe. I yanked a garlic baguette out of the freezer, took the wrapping off, and set it to one side to pop in ten minutes before serving. I admired this last addition as though I'd personally baked the bread myself.

'So how long does this signature dish take to cook?' Mum asked when the pasta bake was safely stashed in the oven. The potential for any cooking mishaps was now radically minimised by the fact that I'd gotten this far in the process.

'I wouldn't call it *signature*,' I answered, 'but it'll be another fifteen minutes or so.'

'I'll set the table, shall I?'

'Already taken care of.' I winked. 'Everything is in hand, Mum, seriously.' *Garlic bread!* 'I'll be right back, there's just one more thing.'

Twenty minutes later Mum and I were sitting down to eat a feast of broccoli cheese pasta with a breadcrumb topping complete with shop-bought garlic bread that I had lovingly coated with grated cheese before popping it into the oven. It wasn't a dish I'd made often, but I had learned some years ago that anything can be thrown in with pasta to make a 'pasta bake', and this was one fine example of it.

Mum poured us both moderate — but by no means generous — glasses of wine, then dropped back into her seat with what sounded like a contented sigh.

'I would have poured more, but I can't have you doing tomorrow on a hangover.'

I laughed. 'Mum, it's wild water swimming, I'm going to be fine.'

The biggest concern I had was how shamefully ridiculous I was going to look in what I had lovingly been referring to as the seal costume. Mum had made me buy it two days ago: an all-in-one swimwear look complete with a cap that did nothing for my fringe. Apparently this swimming was something Mum had started doing often, who knows when. In amongst telling me about the village gossip every other day, it had somehow slipped her mind to mention this. But she'd suggested it as part of our Intense Week of Trying New Things — so intense that I thought of it with capital letters every time Mum mentioned a new phase of the plan. The wild water swimming had come as a surprise, but it also felt like it had great potential to be hilarious writing material — and the fact that I had even thought that was a surefire sign that I was a more Dotty version of myself than I had been three weeks ago when I had first arrived back home.

'You *are* going to be fine,' she answered. The sentence was doing such heavy lifting that I looked up from the table to catch her expression. It was soft, aglow in the early evening light of the dining room, and she looked . . . *Proud?* I wondered whether that was right and rolled the word around my mind like a pair of jeans I couldn't *quite* get the button to close on. But there was definitely something like pride in her expression.

'It's going to be weird,' I said. 'Not being here again.'

'It's going to be weird not having you here again!'

'Maybe I shouldn't go back.' I said it jokingly, but there was a vein of serious thinking running through the comment.

Life back at home hadn't quite been the horror show people might have expected it to be. For the longest time, Mum and I had been best friends and flatmates. Because of that, living with her again hadn't felt like a step backwards. Or if it was, it was a step back into the known, which I firmly believe everyone needs from time to time. But waking up every morning to the clatter of cups and the whistle of a freshly boiled kettle downstairs hadn't done me any harm. And neither had all the sightseeing, despite my ardent protests. I wondered, then, whether *not* going back to London would be the worst thing after all . . .

'Don't even think it.' I'd been wistfully gazing out of the window, just behind Mum's head, when her comment snapped me back into the room. 'I know what you're thinking, and don't.'

'You mean to tell me,' I started as I leaned over the table to score a free spoonful of cheese-soaked pasta, 'that you *wouldn't* want me to be living with you full time again? Am I going to cramp your single lady style, is that it?'

She laughed. 'Shut up, you bloody idiot.'

I carefully lowered the food down onto Mum's plate. 'Second spoonful?'

'Please, love. It smells' — she leaned over the steam of the food — 'genuinely beautiful.'

'See, if I was here all the time, I could even cook for you.'

'Dotty, we both know you aren't going to stay, just like we both know I'd love it if you did. But London is your home. You have business to take care of there.'

'I do?' I was dishing up my own serving of food by then, taking great care to scrape the burnt cheese from the outer edges of the serving tray to scoop it up with my portion.

'Unfinished business.'

130

I let out a curt 'Ha'. 'You make it sound like I'm a ghost.'

Mum cut through the cheese that had hardened on the garlic bread. 'Part of you is. Isn't that what you were saying the other day? Your ex-self, or ghost-self, or something. There are some things you can't get over or away from by running from them.' She flashed me a sad smile when I looked at her. 'Yes, I speak from bitter and crusty experience.'

I rested the serving spoon back in the bowl and Mum quickly grabbed my hand.

'But you will always have a home here, my darling Dotty, if you decide that.'

'Thanks, Mum.' I swallowed hard and felt something thump in my throat. 'And thank you for, you know . . . nursing me back to being something like an adult.'

She brushed the comment away with a wave of the hand and then collected her cutlery from the table. 'Now, are we going to eat this thing or what?'

I spread my arms out, as though displaying a feast. 'I give you, broccoli cheese pasta with breadcrumb topping and accompanying garlic bread that I absolutely did not make. I promise that as part of the big self-improvement kick that's going to happen when I'm back in the Big Smoke, one of the first things I'll do is learn how to cook bread.'

Mum laughed as she took her first mouthful. I watched her bite down, and chew, and chew and—

'God, love, I'm sorry.' She grabbed a nearby paper napkin that I'd laid out when I was setting the table. I'd only done it for the aesthetics — because *obviously* I took a picture of the dining room all made up in its finest — but I hadn't imagined Mum might actually *use* the napkins for anything, at least not this.

Looking every bit as embarrassed as I felt in that moment, Mum demurely spat out what turned out to be the hardest piece of broccoli known to man — before erupting into laughter befitting of a school girl. Mum laughed until her face was red and her breath was caught in her throat. Her amusement was *so* enthusiastic that within seconds I was laughing, too, and we both fed off the other's ridiculous facial expressions and accompanying noises to drag the hilarity out that bit further. It was something we'd always done, engaged with and encouraged these contagious giggling fits, where seeing the other one happy was enough to bring it out in ourselves.

Mum finally caught her breath. 'Sweetheart . . .' She leaned over the table with an open palm that I placed my own hand inside. 'Promise me something?'

I wiped at the corner of one eye. 'Anything.'

'Promise me you'll also learn how to cook broccoli.'

Somehow, I managed to answer with an entirely straight face. 'You should probably try the pasta first, too, in case we need to bake that into the big promises I'm making.'

Mum huffed and spluttered a laugh before braving a second mouthful. And it was all fine, as it turned out it was only a stray piece of broccoli that hadn't quite cooked through.

'It's normal,' Mum said as she wiped her plate clean of sauce with one final slice of garlic bread. 'Every now and then in life you'll be doing something or making something, building something even, and there'll be a little bit of hardness along the way.'

I sensed she was trying to turn this into a teaching moment. 'When that happens in life, what's the best thing to do?'

Mum picked up her napkin from earlier, dropped it on her plate and smiled. 'Sometimes you just have to grab yourself a tissue and spit the hardness out.'

PART THREE

Dear Dotty,

I ran away from life recently. Well, 'ran away' might be an overstatement. I went home for a while, to see my mum and to sleep in my childhood room, which might seem like running away but that wasn't the intention behind it. The intention was more to take time and to heal, and not to run into my ex-partner and her new partner every time I turned a corner in London (it literally happened one time and I have no idea whether it was a new partner, really, but it certainly looked like a new partner and frankly that was all reason enough to leave the city for a while). But now I'm coming home. London is calling me back — and I'm a bit scared.

When I was at home, I had all these small epiphanies and big conversations about me, and my relationship, and the spaces between those two things. I had all these grand ideas for self-improvement, the type of self-improvement that I'd built so much of my work life on, too! But now it's come to it, I'm less than steady about it all. It isn't the self-improvement that bothers me, Dotty. It's a lack of self-improvement. I suppose what I'm really worried about here is, what if I go home and instead of finding ways to improve and change and shake myself up, everything just goes back to normal? Is there any way of making sure that doesn't happen?

Don't let me be ordinary, Dotty. Let's aim for extra.

Love and hugs,
Dotty xx

CHAPTER TWENTY-ONE

One month later . . .

Admittedly, it took a little longer than planned for me to build up enough courage to leave the comfort of home. Mum and I visited various landmarks in the area, we went wild water swimming, and we enjoyed home-cooked meals together — home-cooked by Mum, that is. But after another month of being blissfully detached from my old life, I realised the season for a new one was beckoning; from a distance, but beckoning, nevertheless.

'We'll see each other over Christmas?' Mum asked.

I groaned at the mere mention of it, and she laughed.

'I know your feelings about Christmas, Dotty, don't worry. But we'll get a visit in over the holidays, won't we?'

I was already overwhelmed by the sheer thought of everything I would need to get in over the holidays: the work Christmas photo; the *Dear Dotty* Christmas column; the holiday parties. *Groan, again.*

'Of course we'll get a visit in,' I answered brightly, though I felt a tug of sadness that this visit was ending.

So I kissed Mum goodbye, boarded a train, then boarded another train, and waited out the journey. On the other side,

I struggled free with a suitcase that felt much fuller than it had been when I left London, crammed now with secret Christmas presents that I'd been organised enough to start buying for the girls already. And that spoke nothing to the books that were precariously wedged inside the tote bag slung over my arm, too.

The visit home had been fruitful in plenty of ways. But as I started to fight my way through the beginnings of the London crowd, I realised how divorced from the city I'd become in such a short space of time. There was pushing and shoving and jostling, and tuts and huffs galore when all of these physical manoeuvres failed in making me move any faster because — go figure — there was someone walking in front of me, struggling to move at exactly the same pace I was already moving at.

By the time the mass of travellers was ejecting me out into the open air, I was gasping like a fish who had barely escaped the net. I heaved and chugged fumes back into my lungs and, mid-panic and deciding the fastest way home, which I reasoned to be a taxi, there they were: the most gorgeous thirty-something-year-old women I'd seen in my life, holding up an embarrassingly large banner that read:

'Welcome home, Dotty!'

They shouted in unison as I settled my eyes on them, and I wondered how long it had taken them to choreograph that.

'You guys!' I rushed towards them with my suitcase knocking awkwardly against the pavement and my tote bag knocking just as awkwardly against my ribs. I threw myself open-armed to them, despite the limited space I had at my disposal, and tried to envelop them as they enveloped me: three pairs of arms wrapped around me so tightly that I wasn't sure which of them I was hugging and which I wasn't, or where I stopped, and they started. There were squeals of excitement that can only be likened to the sounds that birds make in nature documentaries.

In the time it took for the four of us to get back to my flat, I could have had an entire trip out somewhere in Alfriston. *One of the beauties of being back in the big city*, I reminded myself, as we pulled to a stop outside the building I'd once shared with the woman I'd once loved. I felt a stab of something in my belly as I realised the thought had emerged in the past tense.

'You okay, babe?' Tots caught my elbow to steady me. I hadn't realised my one free hand had gravitated to my stomach, as though the pain were a physical one. 'I know you're going to be nervous,' she said in a lowered voice, 'but I promise it's going to be fine.'

'Come on, it's getting bloody chilly out here.' Marissa grabbed the handle of my suitcase to free it from me. 'And I didn't take a day's holiday so we could stand around on the pavement all day. We've got cocktails to sink.'

'Oh, girls, I really don't know that I'm up to going out right away,' I protested.

'Out?' Elouise repeated as she fumbled with the spare key to the apartment building — the one I'd told Marissa to give her, so Project Favour could be enacted before I got back to the city. She held the door open for me to enter the building ahead of her. 'When you take a foot in here, you aren't going to want to go *anywhere*.'

'Oh boy . . .' I groaned as I hit the button to call the lift down.

When we were on my floor, Elouise actually went through the shameful task of blindfolding me before I was allowed through my own front door. It would make the surprise that bit more impactful, she promised me, and that, shockingly, did nothing for my nerves. Elouise wandered in ahead of us; Marissa took charge of my suitcase and then my tote bag; meanwhile Tots stayed behind me, a hand on either side of my waist to guide me forwards.

'Okay, okay, two steps further in,' Elouise announced.

'It's my own flat, El, how different can it be?'

'You might regret asking that,' Tots answered, and even though her tone was jovial, I somehow took her as being serious.

'Right, blindfold off!'

With a flourish, Tots pulled the handkerchief away from my eyes. It was the warmth of the room that hit me first. I hadn't realised how cold London had grown in the time I was away, until it was compared against the cosiness of home. I scanned the space around me, and my jaw promptly landed on my freshly polished laminated floor. The living room was a haven of brilliant white and jungle greens. There were houseplants; there was a new sofa; there was an actual window seat! With what looked, from this vantage point, like a padded cushion for me to perch on, for all those whimsical afternoons spent looking out into the distance of the city. The television, Elouise proudly told me, was tucked away behind a brand-new entertainment unit, because she knew I hated the big screen being on show. Either side of that entertainment unit there were bookshelves already populated with my books. She caught me looking and said, 'And before you ask, they're already alphabetised.' I could have kissed her.

Elouise led me through to the open plan of my kitchen, where my once old and drab cupboard fronts had been repainted in a green that matched the living room. The breakfast bar had been fixed up, too, with stools on either side and a for-show fruit bowl perched in the middle of it.

'She says, "for show",' Marissa explained, 'because none of that fruit is actually real.'

'Oh shush,' I answered as I grabbed an apple and— 'Boy, that really is plastic, huh?'

'Come on, there's more!' Elouise tried to tug me along, but I yanked her back.

'El, I asked you to get rid of some furniture and scout some thrift shops. This is . . .' I petered out and, finding that words really had failed me in that moment, I only threw my arms up to gesture to the remade space that I could see. 'This is too much,' I managed to finish.

'Too much?' Elouise asked. She looked genuinely perplexed.

'Was it too much when you helped Elouise pack up Colin's clothes after the break-up of the century?' Tots asked then.

'And when you took them back to his house, so she didn't have to see him?' Marissa added.

'Or, or,' Tots said excitedly with a click of her fingers, 'was it too much when you pretended to be Marissa's plus one for an entire year of work events, so she didn't have to go to them alone?'

'And let's not forget the time you let Tots crash with you and Caitlin for three months when her old landlord gave her the boot.'

I felt myself blush as Tots tucked an arm around me. 'Maybe it's just our turn to look after you; you ever think about that, lovely Dotty?'

I opened my mouth to answer but soon realised I didn't have much of a defence. Of course we looked after each other; that's *the point* of friendships. So I only said, in a tone befitting my mother's own mouth, 'Well, this must have gone well over my budget and you absolutely have to let me pay you back, when I can afford it.'

'That's the best bit,' Tots chimed in, and Elouise shot her a dagger look. 'Sorry' — she threw her hands up in surrender — 'your thunder. Have at it.'

'That's the best bit,' Elouise parroted, then. 'I reached out to agencies and designers that I'd worked with and told them I was part of *the* Dear Dotty relaunch—'

'It isn't a relaunch,' I interrupted.

'*The* Dear Dotty relaunch,' she repeated as though I hadn't spoken, 'and they were throwing free things at me left and right. You have literally no idea how famous you are right now, Dots, especially since that first Instagram post with the letter and all, but let me tell you, when I say that they were handing me free stuff, they were *handing* me free stuff. The only part of the deal you have to come good on is making sure you take pictures, post them online, and tag the designers. I've got a list of them, so don't worry. Now' — she tugged at me again — 'can we *please* all go and jump on your new bed? Because it feels like a cloud and I need for you to love it.'

* * *

139

Elouise was right — the bed did feel like a cloud. The floors felt like an ice rink, such was their finish; the cocktail bar that was hidden in my kitchen cupboard felt like a dream, and my office — that now actually *looked* like an office — seemed like a space that I might never want to leave, not least because of the perfect organisation of my books that sent a wave of relief crashing through me so hard that I could have wept a little.

Thankfully, I managed to save any emotional outpourings for when we were two Cosmopolitans in and waiting for the pizza delivery. My hair was tied up, I was in my biggest jumper and my oldest joggers, and I absolutely was not photo ready. And yet, I somehow had enough liquid courage to ask Tots to take a picture of me standing in my sparkly new kitchen, with a cocktail in one hand and a plastic banana in the other. That's when the tears started.

'Whoa, what did we miss?' Elouise asked from where she was slumped on my new beanbag chair. 'There'll be no tears in the happy apartment.'

I laughed, and tugged Tots a little closer to me. She already had her arms around me by that point. 'She's right, babe, what's this for?'

Marissa joined us and cuddled me from the other side. 'Happy tears, right?'

I nodded against her. 'Such happy tears.'

'Come on, let's get you settled.' Tots led me back to the living room, set my drink on the coffee table ahead of me, and squeezed us both into the corner of my green velvet L-shaped sofa that framed the room so perfectly that I wondered how I'd gone this long without owning it. 'We knew that it would be a lot, but Elouise really got stuck in and—'

'I didn't mean for it to be too much, hon.' She held her arms out to me. 'Come, cuddle.'

'You go to Dotty if you want a cuddle,' Marissa said to her. That's when I noticed the look between the two of them.

I inched forward on the sofa. 'El, are you stuck in the beanbag chair?'

'Oh sweet heavens . . .' Tots was on the edge of her seat then, too. 'Are you actually?'

'No, Dotty, I am *not* stuck in the chair.'

'Okay' — Marissa sipped her drink — 'then get up and give Dotty a hug.'

Elouise dropped even further into the seat, which seconds ago I wouldn't have thought was even possible. 'Whatever, you all suck.' No sooner had she said it than she threw a hand in the air to stop any rebuttals. 'That's not true, I shouldn't have said that. Marissa, Tots, you suck. Dotty, you're welcome to join me on the beanbag for a cuddle if you'd like, but if you don't, then that's cool, too.' She fidgeted and then added, 'And it might actually be the more sensible decision.'

Tots tucked an arm around my shoulder. 'Now, aren't you glad you came back?'

The downstairs buzzer to my flat rang, a noise so sharp that it made my shoulders bunch. But for Elouise it stirred what can only be described as a Pavlovian response. At the promise of pizza, she immediately set her drink down on the floor, a safe distance from her seat, and wiggled and thrashed until, somehow, through sheer willpower, she managed to get onto her knees before bursting up into a standing position. She smoothed down her clothes and collected her drink to sip on.

'I'll get the door.'

We managed to wait until she was out of the room before erupting into schoolgirl laughter.

Yes, I realised. *I'm glad to be home . . .*

141

CHAPTER TWENTY-TWO

Even though I was glad to be home, I still waited three days before I confessed to Elza that I was back in the city. I wanted to enjoy the luxury of writing from my new desk, leaving the flat in the middle of the day to reacquaint myself with the local coffee shop and emailing my column in whenever it was ready — such had been our agreement while I was away — rather than sticking to anyone's time schedule. Not least because I knew that when she did know that I was back, her first response to the news would be—

'Can we do tomorrow for a meeting, then? First thing? I'll get coffee.'

'Your first thing, or everyone else's first thing?' I asked as I wandered through the gloriously open space of my home, from kitchen to living room with a cup of tea in tow. Elza's work-life schedule knew no bounds; it was important to check what I was getting myself into here. I could hear her clicking through her diary as I curled up on the window seat with my steaming mug and pulled my legs neatly beneath me. Second to my office, this was my favourite space in the flat, which should be a startling indicator of just how much I loved the office since Elouise worked her magic.

'Does 10.00 am suit you?'

'I can do that.'

'Wear something photogenic.'

'Why do I— *Oh*.' I broke off before the question was fully formed, realising how ridiculous it would be to even ask it. 'Of course, I'll wear something from my pre-approved pile of Elza clothes.'

'You're a peach,' she answered as though she hadn't detected the sarcasm. 'I'll see you tomorrow.' She disconnected the call without waiting for a goodbye.

I allowed myself one cup of tea — a standardised measurement of time — before starting to worry about what the hell I was going to wear . . .

* * *

By the time I fell into one of Elza's comfy chairs the next morning, I was already overwhelmed. Everyone and their dog had wanted to say hello to me on my way through the open plan office that morning. Not only that, though, they said hello with the Sympathetic Head Tilt — the one true giveaway that someone *knows* you've been through a hard time, and they're trying to ask about it without asking about it.

I chanted, 'I'm fine, glad to be back,' to everyone who asked, but my enthusiasm was dipping by the time the last colleague spoke to me.

I was relieved to make it to Elza's door on the other end of the corridor, but I was immediately whisked away to the floor where the Marketing People live. Their level of importance was so pronounced in my head that I always thought of them with capital letters.

In their on-site photobooth — a ridiculously large office that they reserved for so-called emergency photoshoots, which apparently, this was — there was a stuffy man who looked my outfit up and down, narrowed his eyes and humphed, before taking what felt like thirty-eight million pictures of me. He and

Elza manoeuvred me around the space, posing here with my laptop and there with a reusable coffee mug. 'Everyone loves sustainability,' the photographer had said when he handed me the prop. 'Do you think you can do something with your hair?'

'My hair? It was raining on the walk here, but what's, I mean, what's so—'

'It always looks like that; it isn't the rain,' Elza interrupted, and the man shot her a quizzical glance as though he couldn't quite believe what she'd said. Elza only shrugged, and the rigmarole started again — this time with my laptop *and* the coffee cup.

'I'll spend some time with these, talk to Jen and Elsbeth—' *Who the heck are Jen and Elsbeth?* '—and I should have something with you before the end of the week.'

Elza narrowed her eyes at him. 'The end of the day.'

A high-pitched noise hiccupped out of the man but I didn't hear him say no.

Then, and only then, was I allowed to step into the quiet of Elza's office, fall into one of her comfy armchairs — rather than the uncomfortably hard visitor's chair — and welcome the strong black coffee that was soon brought to me with open arms. I thanked the young woman — a face I didn't recognise, who must have crept in while I'd been licking my wounds elsewhere — and wrapped my hands tightly around the mug. She also set down a plate of pastries and I tried and failed not to be too eager about eating them.

There came a snap-crack from the other side of the room and I turned to see Elza opening a Diet Coke. 'I upgraded,' she explained, nodding to the fridge behind her. 'If you ever need gin, go right to the back of the top shelf.'

I laughed. 'Noted.'

'Do you want me to ask how you are, or shall we cut right to it?'

'I feel like we've already cut right to it,' I said with a smile. 'So let's get this over with.'

Elza took a seat opposite me, set her drink down, and grabbed a croissant to replace it with. She pulled the crusted end of the pastry free, tucked it into her mouth, and spoke around it. 'You make it sound like I'm about to pull a tooth. We'd like one Dear Dotty letter, to yourself, every week. Manageable?'

'Just once a week?'

Elza nodded and took a second bite of pastry.

'And the rest of the content stays the same?'

'Your Instagram needs tweaking, if we're talking content broadly. But for the column itself, you keep up with the website stuff on the daily, we'll keep publishing a small amount in the print copy, but we'll also have a full-page spread reserved for your personal Dear Dotty letters in every print issue from now on, too.'

I swallowed hard. 'It's a full-page feature?'

'Mm. Is that a problem?' Before I could answer Elza held a finger up to stop me, and my mouth snapped shut. 'There's only one response to that question that I think is appropriate at the moment.'

'No, it isn't a problem.'

'Good girl.'

'What needs to change about my Instagram?'

Elza smiled. 'Brace yourself because this may be the most surprising change of them all. I want, and this is me, not marketing, so if there's a problem take it up with me directly, because they're already shaky on this, but I want more authentic content.'

I lingered over her phrasing for a second. 'I . . . I'm not sure I understand.'

'What do you wear when you're writing at home?'

I huffed a laugh. 'Am I meant to give an entirely honest answer to that?'

'So honest that I expect to cringe.'

'I wear joggers and an oversized jumper, unless it's the summer, in which case I'm probably wearing dungarees.'

Elza actually shuddered. 'Okay,' she said as though trying to collect herself. '*That* is what I want to see on your social media. I don't want swearing or heavy drinking, or anything *worse* than heavy drinking. But I want more than cocktails and flat lays of expensive brunches. I want to know what your home looks like, what your writing routine looks like, all the things in between. I don't want something . . . tailored.'

I inched forwards, suddenly uncomfortable even in the comfy chair. 'Elza, where is this coming from?'

'Dotty, when did you last check that first Instagram post? The first letter, I mean?'

Elza clearly had no idea that she was asking me to look back on the antics of a very Drunken Dotty, and I was determined to make sure she never found out the truth of how that first letter was posted, either. But I wasn't in the habit of backtracking through social media posts that I'd shared while under the influence. I didn't delete them because what was the point? Someone, somewhere, probably already had a screenshot of the post that I was about to delete. Or it might already have done the rounds in a group chat. It might already be on a forum. Deleting anything in this day and age was a wasted effort. But so was looking back. It felt like a good ethos to live by, and I wondered whether I might integrate it into a letter somewhere.

'I haven't, at all.' I huffed a laugh. 'It wasn't really about views or shares to me.'

'Of course, of course.' Elza waved my comment away as though it wasn't something openly sentimental. 'It's been shared over ten thousand times now, Dotty.'

'I'm sorry, *over*—'

'Over ten thousand times. Dotty, that letter caused such a whirring that there are people writing articles about you right now. There are people researching *you*, your life, your relationship history—'

'My God in heaven . . .' I groaned and rubbed at my forehead.

'It's okay; the worst of it is Caitlin and she's being very tight-lipped.'

146

'The *worst of it*?' I parroted with a high-pitched emphasis. 'What do you mean, Caitlin is being . . . Is she *involved* in all of this somehow?'

Again, Elza waved a magic hand as if that might make all of this a bit less terrifying. 'Honestly, Dotty, it's nothing to concern yourself with. As soon as we saw the beginnings of interest, we set aside a couple of researchers to dig into your background a bit. Really, there's nothing there to cause a problem' — it felt wrong that I was offended by that — 'and I reached out to Caitlin myself and spoke to her directly.'

'You did?' That was the biggest slap in the face so far. I was so completely over the idea that my relationship history was a dead end with nothing worth writing about. Everything now was Caitlin, and the sudden white noise that rushed about my ears at the thought of Elza having spoken to her. 'How . . . I mean, is she okay?'

Elza narrowed her eyes at me and then dropped what was left of her croissant onto a napkin. 'Dotty, this is going to hurt.'

Oh, please no . . .

'I told Caitlin that you'd cracked something big, and she laughed. I asked whether she was going to make herself available, should anyone want a comment, and she said she had nothing to say. I told Caitlin there might be money thrown her way, by other publications, and she said' — Elza drew in what sounded like a shaky breath — 'there was nothing of your relationship that was worth buying.'

The white noise stopped. Instead, everything went uncomfortably muffled, cotton-balls in your ears muffled, and there was a stab followed by a throb of pain across my forehead. My hand cupped the space where the sensation was spreading, and I tried hard not to groan aloud with it. But then I felt the press of four fingers tapping at my knee. Elza was leaning across the table, tapping first, but then softly shaking my leg.

'Come back to me, kid. There's nothing worth worrying about wherever your head just sent you.' She smiled, and I tried to mirror the gesture, but the movement of my cheeks made my face ache. 'You're onto something big here, Dotty, and she isn't a part of it.'

'She is if I write about her.'

But Elza shook her head. 'You aren't writing about her anymore. You're writing about *you*.' She rubbed my knee more firmly, then, before she dropped back into the bucket of her seat. 'Have a croissant, it'll make you feel better.'

I ummed and ahhed over my only follow-up question. But eventually I pulled in a deep breath and averted my eyes. 'Elza, for future reference, just so I know . . . were you serious about having gin in your fridge?'

CHAPTER TWENTY-THREE

Though it might be a less than conventional thing to praise London for, the city had some fine and luscious parks. My mother would have anyone believe that there was nothing green left within these city limits. Contrary to that, though, two days after my meeting with Elza, and determined to take a break from snapping pictures of my now beautiful home, I vowed to take myself to one of those very green spaces for a little Dotty to Dotty time — and I was overwhelmed by choice. There was Holland Park and Brockwell Park, Clapham Common and, the somewhat unimaginatively titled, London Fields. In the end, I let my phone's navigation system decide for me, and apparently that day Siri was leaning in favour of Regent's Park.

The irony wasn't lost on me that the decision of finding somewhere to relax and unwind had in fact made me feel *more* stressed. But it seemed to be a theme for that day, too. Dressed in ripped jeans, a white T-shirt, and a mustard cardigan that was as old as the hills themselves — an outfit that had taken me nearly an hour to throw together, not that anyone would have known — I ventured out with a genuine relief that I knew where I was going. And I hadn't accidentally tasked myself with the job of aimlessly walking around the city for a few hours until I wound up at Marissa's office, which was precisely what I *had* done *after* that meeting with Elza. Marissa had been uncharacteristically gentle and supportive — with minimal interludes of tough love — to such an extent that it felt like she was handling me with kid gloves. But it had been exactly what I'd needed then, and in the days since. Far from basking in my newfound career status, and the plans to make that status even more pronounced, I'd found the entire meeting with Elza to be utterly . . . terrifying. Everything felt enormous in scale, even my luxurious flat, a space that I had managed to convince myself I didn't even deserve! It was a horrid mental backlash of the sudden rush of good things, but I couldn't control it. Everything in me was screaming, 'This isn't for me! This isn't for me!', and stopping the noise felt impossible.

Hence, an afternoon in the open air.

On my way to Regent's Park I walked past no fewer than four express something-or-others where I could have stopped to grab lunch. I also lingered outside the doors of a fancy-looking deli place that I hadn't tried before and therefore one that I could definitely get Instagram content out of. And yet, the sheer sight of their menu was too much, not least because there were definitely ingredients listed that I'd never heard of before and . . . *Gosh, what if I pick something I hate?* I also couldn't disguise my alarm that they were offering something called a 'Seasonal Sub', that seemed to be all the trimmings of Christmas stuffed into a sandwich — even though Christmas still felt like it was years away!

A young woman with beautifully blonde hair stepped around me and held the door open. 'Are you heading inside?'

I felt my cheeks flush. 'Oh, no, I'm just browsing. Thanks, though.'

She shrugged and went in ahead of me. It rattled around my head that she was exactly the type of woman this place was aimed at: young, fashionable, and confident. By inference,

I realised that I was brandishing myself as *not* being any of those things. The insult stung, perhaps even more so because it was self-administered, and I skulked off in the direction of the park again, comfortable with the knowledge that I would never discover what Cajun aioli tasted like on a sandwich.

I carried on the walk and decided that, to minimise decisions entirely, I would simply step into the next foodie place I found — which happened to be a mini Tesco. *Good enough for me*, I thought as I ducked beneath lunchtime suits who were out for their own meal deals. I bought myself a tuna and sweetcorn sandwich, a Pepsi Max, and a tub of pineapple chunks, and I left the store with a ridiculous weight lifted. The rest of the walk to the park felt easy after that — or rather, easier.

Once there, after what felt like an epic journey through London town (though it really hadn't been), I settled myself on a bench and took the greediest breath imaginable. Then I took another. The air was cool but crisp, an in-between of seasons. I suddenly wondered where the best part of the year had gone; how we'd ended up here, with winter warming its toes by the fire, and me hardly realising time had been moving. And so, to ease the panic that prickled in response to that, I took another slow breath. Like a meditative practice, I spent a few minutes feeling my body expand and deflate, expand and deflate, accompanied by a blissful rendition of Lorde's 'Supercut' that a guitarist was playing within earshot. There was a huddle of teenagers on some nearby grass that looked to be taking it in turns to play acoustic covers that I thought, somewhat depressingly, they likely remembered from their *child*hoods, while I remembered the same songs from my twenties. But still, the sounds were welcome, and when one Lorde track faded into another — 'Royals' was up next, to no real surprise — I allowed myself another few of those deep belly breaths to steady the nerves.

And then I looked at my nerves head-on.

Elza's meeting had been huge and massive and brilliant. So I couldn't work out why, exactly, it had been living rent-free in my head as a source of anxiety for the last however many days. I decided to take my own advice for a second and reached into my tote bag to pull out my notebook. I'd deliberately left my laptop at home, having taken a picture of it sitting on my beautifully neat desk and uploaded it to my Insta story with a caption that read: *Out of office*. I wanted the OG of writing instead that day — the slow scratch of pen against paper, the inevitable disintegration of handwriting as the ideas came thicker and faster. At the top of the page I wrote: *Dear Dotty* . . . and the words that poured out afterwards might have been the easiest I've ever written.

I was scared of the new normal. Despite my lip service about self-improvement, the actual act of it, I was starting to see, took guts the size of an island. Self-improvement wasn't just about making yourself that bit better — it was about believing that you *deserved* to be that bit better. And something in me didn't have that conviction. The same part of me, perhaps, that thought I didn't deserve the gorgeous home I was now living in, or didn't deserve the support I was getting for that bright spark of an idea in my work life. I didn't deserve my friends being so kind, or my mother being so generous, or Elza being so encouraging, and believing in me so much. *I didn't deserve it, I didn't deserve it* . . . I wrote it over and over again until a full three pages were populated with a mess of things that I truly seemed to believe I was undeserving of. And then I tore the pages out of the notebook. I scrunched them up until they were a messy ball of badness and I took aim at the nearest bin — and missed.

A laugh belched out of me that was so loud I caught the attention of the nearby teens. I held my hand up in apology and they only smiled in return and went back to their collaborations on the single guitar shared between seven of them.

Then I started the Dear Dotty letter all over again, ignoring the voice of the imposter who'd written the previous one. Instead, I thought about me and what I might want for myself, and when I struggled with the boldness of that, I thought of what I might want for a friend. It was age-old advice that I'd given a thousand times or more: *What would you say to a friend in this situation? Would you want a friend to be treated like this? Would you want a friend to feel so undeserving of goodness?* I wrote the last question out and put a box around it in the corner of the page. Underneath that, I drew another box that, inside, read: *No*.

I replaced the notebook in my bag and grabbed my pineapple chunks in replacement. The sting of the juices was something beautiful. The freshness seemed to pierce my mouth and bring things into focus, and I swallowed greedy chunk after greedy chunk until the box was gone. Then I started on the sandwich, pulling away the crust and eating that separately from the main bulk of the bread — a habit that Caitlin had always found inexplicably irritating but now, I found, I could embrace the habit with the quiet indifference it deserved. Somewhere between the first and second half of the sandwich, though, I paused my hungry intake to actually look around and digest everything, including that first half of my lunch. The teenagers were still there, the suits were still hurriedly eating their wraps and sandwiches while on the move from Point A to Point B, and the couples were still wandering with their hands wrapped around each other as though time were only an abstract concept. There was, I realised in that moment, a lot of stillness in London, and a lot of things that from day to day went unchanged.

Not you, though . . .

The thought occurred to me as I looked up at the trees that lined this row of the park. They bristled in the wind, and I imagined that I could see them, slowly, leaf by leaf, moving from green to orange to red to brown.

With a strange but welcome sigh of contentment, I thought that must mean something, somewhere in the world, was starting to shift.

Dear Dotty,

Funny, the last time I wrote one of these I was terrified of nothing changing. Now, I'm writing with the opposite concern. I've been able to acknowledge the opportunities but, Dotty, let me tell you something about them: they're only opportunities if you do something in the face of them. And it seems my go-to response in the face of them has actually been to freeze or flee. The latter of which means that I've eaten a delightful array of meal deals at various London locations over the last two weeks, including Regent's Park, Hyde Park, and the window seat in my flat. 10/10 feel that pineapple pots are my new true love, closely followed by anything that involves tuna and sweetcorn.

You probably don't want to know about my lunch choices though, and I probably shouldn't want to tell you, given that that's another area of life where I've been resisting change. It's tuna and sweetcorn, every day, and I tell myself I'm doing something different because one day it might be a salad and the next it might be a wrap, or a sandwich, or an open sandwich (if I've only got one piece of bread left in my kitchen because I cannot stand the idea of making a sandwich with the crust of a loaf). But it isn't change, it's the same old comfort every day. And isn't that what got me into this mess?

But tell me, Dotty, is there any way to go easily into change? Before I ask this of you, or of anyone reading, maybe I should be questioning whether what I'm asking is even a thing, or whether I'm looking for a Holy Grail of self-improvement here. Maybe the whole point of change isn't to find a way to go easily into it; maybe it's just to go into it anyway, even when it bites.

Less a question and more a thought dump. But thank you for the space. (That said, if anyone reading this does happen to know any answers then you're fully encouraged to slide into my DMs and share your life hacks with me, okay?)

Be kind to yourself Dotty, and dear readers, and I heartily promise to do the same.

Love and good things,
Dotty xx

CHAPTER TWENTY-FOUR

When Elouise made my home shiny and new, she insisted on placing a full-length mirror in the corner of my bedroom. I'd questioned her on it endlessly and in response heard only variations of the comment that now more than ever it was important that I knew what I looked like naked. She'd said something about being single, something about how that changed things. The comment had irked me to such an extent that even the sight of the mirror made me want to smash the thing — hindered only by the thought of having to clean it up after myself once the deed was done. But my newfound bravery, prescribed by myself in my last Dear Dotty letter — that had since gone to print, and earned me just over nine hundred new Instagram followers and an insane flurry of emails — meant that staring down the barrel of myself felt something like a necessity now.

Because I knew the experience was unlikely to be a joyous or easy one, I treated myself to a morning bath first. I shaved my legs and other essentials, soaked in the bubbles, and read the first thirty-eight pages of a fresh Agatha Christie novel that I'd pulled from my perfectly organised shelves that morning. It felt *a little* like I was trying to woo myself, which I suppose

I was. I wrapped a brilliantly white towel around me after my soak, determined to make the most of these new linens before I inevitably put them in the wash with a black sock or a dark blue pair of jeans, and I trod back into my bedroom feeling disproportionately happy that there was no one there to tell me off for leaving wet footprints across the floor. But once there, my mood shifted. I stood in front of the mirror with my towel still tucked around me, and I sucked in the biggest breath I could manage given the constraint of the fabric.

'Good grief, Dotts,' I spoke firmly, 'it's just your body.'

In a swift motion I let the towel fall and, quite without realising I'd done it, I scrunched my eyes closed. It was only when I thought, *Hm, this isn't so bad*, that it occurred to me something hadn't quite gone to plan. So, one eye at a time, I actually peeked a look at the mirror.

'Good grief, Dotts!'

I wish I could say that it was a quiet moment of elation. I *wish* I could say that I saw my body and marvelled at the brilliance of it, at the way this curved or that wobbled or they still perked upright rather than downwards. But for those first few ugly seconds, the only thought I was capable of hearing was: *Well, that doesn't look how it used to*. Because, of course, it had been years since I'd last practised looking at myself — and even then, it hadn't been *like this*. It had been pulling on clothes in a hurry before a night out, or it had been drunkenly experimenting with an ex-girlfriend, or it had been craning around awkwardly to check how an abscess was healing. I shuddered at that final memory. But in none of those recollections could I tell anyone of a time when I'd really looked at myself like this. And boy, was looking at myself *hard*.

When Caitlin and I had first got together, we were hardly out of our teens. My metabolism was fuelled by energy drinks, black coffee, and whatever groceries we could afford between us, after humbly declining the offer of help from Caitlin's parents, convinced we were equipped to go it alone. It was in the years after that our tastes began to differ, literally, and pizza, Diet Coke, and cocktails became the flavour of the decade instead. My movements changed, from rushing around in my early twenties to a job that mostly meant I could sit comfortably at home in my early thirties. Pizza and takeaways became brunches with the girls. Although admittedly, the Diet Coke and cocktail combination looked much the same if my bank transactions were anything to go by. And my body showed every one of those changes, I realised, now, for the first time. There *were* curves that I hadn't seen before! My stomach was softer and, though I'm a little pained to admit, somewhat more jiggly than I had perhaps thought it would be. My legs were better, my boobs were bigger, and my body was mapped by thin memory lines — stretch marks, my nan would have called them — that documented these cycles we'd been through together. I ran a finger along one of them, that curved up along my side stretching almost from hip to midriff, in a not-at-all linear trajectory. The line seemed to fracture and break so there were times when it was quite hard to tell exactly how the skin had stretched at all. But the longer I looked at it, the more enamoured I became at the sight of the thing. There was a purplish tinge in some parts, but it was mostly white now, and I wondered how long it must have been there without my noticing it for it to have faded like that.

Why didn't Caitlin tell me it was there?

The thought shot into my head without exposition, and I frowned at it like an intruder on an intimate moment — which I suppose, in some ways, is exactly what it was.

I sighed and stepped back from this newly discovered version of myself. Caitlin hadn't told me a lot of things; I was coming to accept now. She hadn't told me she was unhappy; she hadn't told me she felt alone; she hadn't told me what I wasn't doing, what she needed me to be. In fact, there were so many needs that had gone unmet, and I realised that I carried the weight of that right there — I drew a line along my reflection — right in the well of my belly. I wondered how many pounds I might shed if I could find a way to let that guilt go.

157

Eurgh . . .

I shook my shoulders as though freeing myself from an ill-fitting shirt. The point of this exercise, I reminded myself, hadn't been about finding things — finding *physical* things — that I needed to change. It had been to acknowledge things that already *had* changed, quite without my realising it somehow. So I cupped my boobs and laughed like a schoolgirl seeing herself in a nice bra for the first time. I pinched both of my hip dips softly, so as not to cause hurt, and I turned around to get a good hard look at my bum that, from this angle, had an unexpectedly neat curve to it. And another giggle emerged from me.

'Good grief, Dotts,' I said in an altogether different tone. 'Look at how you've changed!'

All in all, I managed to stare at myself for six minutes before the discomfort won out and I moved away from the mirror. But I didn't get dressed. Instead, I decided to tackle one of the many areas in life that I had recently decided was in need of a change: my wardrobe.

During the great flat renovation, Elouise had taken it upon herself to 'organise my clothes', which I had since discovered was code for 'colour-code everything I own'. It was a kind gesture, but an utterly wasted one. My wardrobe was made up of items I didn't wear anymore, items that definitely didn't fit anymore, and items that certainly didn't belong to me. I plodded — butt naked, still — into my office to get my stack of Post-it notes, and I wrote out one for *Keep*, one for *Charity*, and one for *Return to Original Owner*, and I laid them out a decent distance from each other on my bedroom floor. Then I got stuck in.

I was *stunned* to my absolute core to learn just how much rubbish I had managed to hang on to over the years, including the white T-shirt I'd worn to my very first T-shirt party at university, that still boasted the hastily drawn on boobs my flatmate had scribbled on me at the start of the evening. It didn't feel right to keep it, but it certainly didn't feel right to donate the thing either, so I threw it in the corner of my bedroom to mark the beginnings of what became the Rubbish pile. It took two and a half hours in total, but by the time I was finished I had four distinct piles dotted around the bedroom and a streamlined wardrobe that Elouise would insist on coordinating all over again.

I texted her with a snapshot of my Keep pile: *I've got a job for you.*

Fantastic!! We can prep for the winter wardrobe. The first of two replies came through almost immediately. *Is now good?*

I caught sight of my naked self in the mirror again and asked Elouise to give me an hour. From the Keep pile I pulled free my cosiest jogging bottoms and a too-big jumper that I couldn't bring myself to throw away. Then I crouched down on my knees to start folding the Return to Original Owner pile. I'd been kidding myself in calling it that, though. What it really should have been called was the Return to Caitlin pile. There was the first jumper I'd ever bought her, thread-bare and pulled all over, but it didn't feel like mine to throw away. Alongside that, there were a pair of ripped jeans — ripped only because she had spilled lip gloss on them and couldn't get the stain out, so she'd decided to get creative — and a pair of penguin print pyjamas that I'd bought her for our first Christmas living together.

There were things of less sentimental value, too: a hoodie for a sports team she didn't support but she liked their colours; emo band T-shirts galore from the time she went through her grunge phase; a bra that I thought didn't look big enough, but I had no idea whether she'd want it anyway. I wasn't heartless enough to throw everything in bin liners, but once the items were folded away in a neat stack I realised I didn't really know what to do with them either. I pulled an overnight bag from the bottom of the wardrobe and tried to wedge everything in as neatly as I could, though it somewhat ruined the effect of the folding, and then I set it at the bottom of the bed. The rest of the returns process was, I decided, something that could wait for another day.

Having used up any bravery I might have had for the morning, I fetched bin liners for the Rubbish pile and bags for life for the Charity pile and shoved, wedged, and pushed until there was no evidence whatsoever of the changes I'd made left inside the bedroom. *Apart from that bloody overnight bag* I thought, casting another side-eye towards it as I left the room. I was grateful when the front door buzzer pulled my attention around and I rushed to let in who I assumed would be Elouise.

Seconds later, footsteps came pounding up to the front door, and I opened it to find Elouise with Tots lingering behind her.

'I bought pastries.' Tots gestured with two brown bags as she spoke. 'Do you have milk?'

I laughed. 'Of course I have milk.'

'Good because this one' — she shoved her way round Elouise as she spoke — 'has had me shopping for dresses all morning and I need the strongest brew you can muster.'

I moved out of their way so Tots could make a beeline for my kitchen while Elouise headed for the bedroom. 'Why have you been shopping for dresses, exactly?' I directed the question at Tots, but it was Elouise who shouted an answer.

'Because Tots has a date tomorrow night that she didn't tell any of us about!'

I wandered into the kitchen after Tots. 'Do you actually?' I asked in a low voice.

She rolled her eyes. 'Yes, I do actually.'

I snatched the pastry bags from her. 'Brilliant. Sit your butt down. I have questions!'

CHAPTER TWENTY-FIVE

Given the one-on-one time I was allowing myself with my body these days, and my new taste for radical acts of change, I spent an entire morning researching exercise classes that I might attend somewhere in my area.

Once I'd determined that I wasn't looking to tone, shape, or flex my way into a happier me, (a promise made by many establishments, even though I thought it bordered on false advertising), my options became more limited. Yoga seemed to be the most tempting option of the ones left, not least because swimming would mean a never-ending battle with my hair for three days afterwards while the chemicals worked their way out. That, and I never would have got one of the girls to agree to go along with me if they thought there was a pool involved — unless there was also sunshine and a jug of pina colada, which I wasn't sure my local leisure centre would stretch to.

I texted the group chat to ask who would be interested in a girls' date for some gentle exercise. There was an uncharacteristic stretch of silence that followed, whilst I imagined one of them calling the other to make custody arrangements for me. The girls had been amazing since I came back to London.

But it hadn't escaped my attention that they were beginning to hang out with me on rotational shifts. We still had our times together: brunches, lunches, and general lazing about. But we also had Dotty and Elouise time, and Dotty and Tots time, and Dotty and—

I'd love some. Can we make it a lunchbreak thing? Marissa was the first to reply, and I wagered she must have drawn the short straw.

Maybe I shouldn't have offered, I thought, as I tried to work out an appropriately enthusiastic response for her. I *had* asked whether someone wanted to come, but did that mean I was *facilitating* their shared custody of my free time? I rested my head on my desk and let out a sigh. Then I grabbed another Post-it note, wrote down *Do more things alone*, and stuck it to the top right corner of my laptop. I was starting to see that once someone starts making changes to their life, it became a domino effect whereby one change would always lead to five more. That Post-it note, I already knew, would inevitably end up tucked into the centrefold of my notebook where I had so lovingly stashed the others, all of them boasting a to-do list of further changes. And I recovered from that stark moment of personal clarity by spending the following forty-five minutes researching yoga classes — who knew there were *so* many flavours — before texting Marissa the details for a class the following day. I still wasn't altogether sure what yoga we were signing up for, but the fact that the class had *beginners* in the title gave me a glimmer of hope.

* * *

The following day Marissa met me outside of the yoga studio that I'd texted her the address to. I fidgeted from one foot to the other, feeling every bit exposed in my Gymshark attire that I only usually wore for the promo. When a sharp gust of wind caught my bare legs, I realised the errors of my ways; this was not the season of skimpy shorts. But when I turned around and caught sight of Marissa coming around the corner at the end of the street, I burst into such a ferocious belly laugh that I could feel the beginnings of a stitch.

'You're wearing a suit?' I managed through bubbles of laughter.

'Oh, Dotty, don't be an arse.' She gestured to her back-pack which, in my defence, had been stashed out of sight on her walk towards me. 'I have joggers and stuff in here. Am I meant to be wearing what you're wearing?' She looked me up and down as she said it.

'Excuse me, what's wrong with what I'm wearing?'

'Oh, there's nothing *wrong* with it. I just don't *own* any of it.'

I linked my arm through hers. 'Thanks for doing this with me.'

'Don't be daft. I need to do more exercise. This is good for me.'

I huffed a laugh as we climbed the steps to the studio. 'You hate exercise.'

'Which is exactly why I should do more of it.'

'Marissa' — I came to a halt on the landing — 'I know you angels are trying to make sure I don't feel lonely. And,' I rushed to add, because I could see that she was eager to inter-rupt, 'I know that I've been leaning on you, too. Like today, I *asked* one of you to be here when I could have just come on my own. I get that. But, maybe after this' — I pushed out a big breath — 'maybe I do just need to start doing a bit more stuff on my own.'

Marissa leaned forward to give me a brief squeeze and a peck on the cheek. For her, it was disarmingly sentimen-tal behaviour. 'Whatever you want, Dotts, okay? We're with you.' She laughed. 'Though not *literally* with you, perhaps.'

'Come on then, let's see what all this yoga business is about.'

With linked arms again, Marissa and I tentatively walked into the studio to find that, at a glance, it seemed to be pop-ulated with anything but beginners. Admittedly, most people there were dressed like me but they made it look an awful lot more natural than I did. There was stretching and chatting and yet more stretching. A disconcertingly beautiful woman sat at the front. She looked like exactly the type of person who spent most of her life exercising, *and* like the type to tell you that ladies don't sweat. 'They perspire,' I could hear my mother finish the sentence in my head. The woman — the teacher, it turned out — rounded everyone up to their mats whilst Marissa had snuck off to get changed, so I grabbed two free spaces right at the back of the room. From every tutorial I'd watched online, yoga seemed to involve an awful lot of sticking your backside in the air, and I didn't really want a total stranger behind me while I was doing that.

'Right, my loves, welcome, welcome, I'm Adeena,' she spoke in a voice that was so soft I thought it must have been tailor-made for the setting, 'and a special welcome to those who haven't been here before. Welcome.'

Marissa awkwardly raised her hand in hello as she skulked from the changing room to her mat, and I had to stifle a laugh at the firm blush that was moving through her cheeks. She softly slapped my arm before dropping her bag on the floor and turning attention to the front. This was, I imagined, how recruits must feel during some sort of drill, and I wondered then whether I would have done just as well signing up for one of the body bootcamps after all.

Of course, while idly comparing our yoga teacher to a drill sergeant within the first five minutes of meeting her, I'd also managed to miss the instructions for the first pose we were meant to be doing. Looking at Marissa gave me absolutely no clues, given that she seemed to be standing with her arms by her sides, doing nothing at all but staring.

'Have you been brainwashed?' I asked in a stage whisper. 'Blink twice if you're here against your will.'

She slapped my arm again. '*You* wanted to come to this. Now do the stupid pose.'

'What pose, Marissa? You're literally—'

'Mountain pose,' the teacher's voice bellowed with a greater force than it had done before, and I couldn't help but feel it had been a targeted gesture, 'can help with balance and strengthen your muscles to prepare them for more advanced yoga positions as you progress throughout this process. Good,' she said to one student then another as she completed a lap of the room, 'alright, very good. Now we're going to move into Downward Facing Dog. Remember to keep those toes pointed towards the front of your mats, very good.'

'It's okay,' I whispered to Marissa, 'I know this one.'

After that, I managed to awkwardly sink myself forward onto my hands and nearly lose my balance in the process. Marissa snorted next to me, and then she glanced around at the others, quietly consulting them for guidance. The women around us were at various different angles, but the basic idea of it seemed to be the same: make a triangle with the floor. So I leaned forward again, placed my palms flat against my mat, and sucked my core in.

'Do you mind if I touch you?'

'I'm sorry?' My head snapped around to Marissa, because I wasn't sure where else to look for the source of the question. But my view of her was blocked by a new pair of legs standing between us.

She laughed. 'It's Adeena. Do you mind?'

'Ah, no, I guess, not, I—'

I tried not to flinch as her hands wrapped around my stomach from behind.

'These muscles are loose.'

In part, I was pained by her observation. But I was also dying to laugh at the absolute absurdity of the situation, too. And that wasn't at all helped by Marissa, back in my side-eye sightline now, who looked to be barely holding herself together, with the odd splutter of laughter escaping while she tried to hold her pose.

'Now, I'm going to line these hips up a little easier,' Adeena said as she shifted her body weight against my own, 'then we're going to have another feel of this core, right here.' I murmured in agreement because I needed *something* to do. But I wagered any difference in core muscles she might be feeling right now would be the barely controlled belly laughter that was building inside me. 'Concentrate all your strength on your core in this moment, that's right, and now I really want to feel you tighten against me.'

And that was the fatal blow.

Marissa collapsed onto her mat with a *gumph* and a howl of laughter, her face red, her hair wild, and her core — much to Adeena's dismay — entirely unposed.

CHAPTER TWENTY-SIX

Days later, after recovering from the hilarity of yoga, and
wondering if running might be the exercise for me instead,
I was being prepped and primed by an excited Elza, whose
enthusiasm was doing nothing for my nerves. As part of the
Dear Dotty Self-Improvement Scheme, the latest name for
my character turnaround, Elza had arranged for me to be
interviewed on Radio London — and she'd made no secret
of the fact that this was a Big Deal, not least because it gave
her ample opportunity to trot out my fancy new headshot. Its
importance was only further evidenced by her having offered
to come along with me to the interview, despite my passionate
protests. So, when I say offered to come, what I mean to say
is she *insisted* on coming. I'd *just* about managed to convince
Elouise that I didn't need her company — Elza was quite
enough — nor her styling tips, given that it was a *radio* interview. And yet, I still found myself tugging at the waistband of
my ripped jeans, tucking and re-tucking my T-shirt, pulling
and shoving at the sleeves of my blazer, hoping that this was a
good enough outfit for the day. I'd gone for a low energy style,
something I actually felt comfortable wearing, in the hope that
it might lessen the shock of the whole ordeal, but the glittering

lights of the studio were too much for my young heart, and the nerves remained.

I took another sip of water and set my cup on the table in front of me with a shaky hand.

'You're going to be fine,' Elza said from behind her iPad screen.

'I know,' I answered. But my tone suggested I didn't know that at all. 'I just don't want to say the wrong thing.'

'You couldn't possibly.' Then she paused, lifted her head, and glanced upwards for a second. 'Well, I suppose you could. But you're not going to.'

Thanks, I thought, *that's the support I need . . .*

'You and Candice are going to make a great pairing.'

'I'm sorry?' My head snapped around with the force of whiplash. 'Who's Candice?'

'Candice Egan. You're being interviewed together.'

Elza said this like it was a throwaway remark, something I should already know, even. But I absolutely, undoubtedly, one hundred percent did *not* know. And the sound of that name alone set my heart racing to the point that I wondered whether there was a tidal wave coursing through my ears.

Candice Egan was *the* name in self-help publishing. She'd set up her own company nearly twenty years ago, and in those two short decades she had paved the way for a catalogue of authors covering everything from romantic breakdowns to how to grow a garden for the mind — though given that her publishing company was based in London, where very few people could afford a garden, I had some reservations about the market viability for that last one.

'Dotty, you're flapping.'

I forced out a breath before answering. 'Yes, I believe I am.'

'Dotty?' An alien voice caught my attention from the doorway. 'We're ready for you now.'

'All the best,' Elza said, still from behind her screen. I made a mental note to write her a thank-you note for the invaluable support she'd offered through this experience . . .

Two rooms away I was seated with a fresh glass of water and a microphone. I was introduced to the host, a charming woman called Jessica, who was doing her utmost to ease my obvious nerves. Unfortunately, I couldn't hear much of what she said through the blood that was still rushing about between my ears. So I smiled and nodded like I understood an ounce of what was going on, and I waited for Candice's inevitable appearance.

When she did arrive, she entered the room with the confidence and grace expected from someone of her standing. She was wearing a linen pantsuit, which made my own outfit feel that bit more tardy, and she said hello and thank you to everyone with a perfectly lined bright red smile. Her lipstick shade was gorgeous, and if I'd had the courage I would have told her so. In place of that compliment, all I actually managed was a weak handshake and a noise that resembled something along the lines of 'Hmmphfr'.

'The infamous Dotty,' she answered with a wink as she took the seat next to me. Something inside me sank. 'I have been following your work, lady, and you are doing something *exciting* with this new column of yours, aren't you? Well, not *new*, I know you've been going for some time now, but this whole turn you're taking is fabulous on you.' She leaned closer and lowered her voice a little, 'I especially like seeing more of your actual life on the old Instagram feed. The old you was . . .' She slapped her lips while looking for the right word. 'Too tailored. You're much more real now, and people like real.'

'Ladies!' Jessica saved me the hassle of thinking of an appropriate reply, short of making the same idiotic noise for a second time over. 'Let's save this for when we're recording, shall we?'

Candice threw her hands up in defeat. 'I know my place.' Her tone was jovial, easy, and I thought I might be in love with her. I imagined myself as the literal embodiment of the heart-eyed emoji. 'So, this is a pre-record?' Candice asked, and my attention snapped back.

169

'It is, so if you say anything you're not happy about, then there's no need to worry,' Jessica said with a smirk, and I spotted Candice roll her eyes. It seemed like an inside joke, like the easy familiarity of friends who went way back, and I felt the imposter syndrome roar inside me.

'Dotty, are you ready?'

'As I'll ever be,' I managed.

The lights changed from dark to light and we were away. Jessica made her opening announcements for the show with a gentle but confident tone, followed by the impressive and seemingly never-ending biographical introduction of Candice — which made her feign a blush, but I wasn't buying it. *Candice must have these introductions all the time*, I thought, *alongside outbursts of adoration and endless praise from heathens like me.*

'But before we talk to Candice,' Jessica continued, 'today we're also going to be hearing from the fabulous Dear Dotty herself who is causing a storm with her own self-help venture. Now, Dear Dotty, for anyone who's lived under a rock these past few years, am I right, ladies?' I managed a gentle laugh, but the implied praise only made me feel more awkward. 'Dear Dotty is one of the city's, no, scratch that, one of the *country's*, I feel justified in saying, best-read advice columns. But earlier this year, our Dear Dotty started a brand-new venture which she's going to tell us more about today. Dotty, welcome to the show.'

'Thanks so much for having me. Honestly, it's a real pleasure to be here.'

'Oh, the pleasure is ours, my lovely, all ours. So, I want to start off by talking a little about your journey here, if that's okay? For anyone who hasn't followed your story to date. Now, a celebrated advice columnist, that much we already know. But these days you're . . . writing advice to yourself; is that the best way of explaining what's happening?'

There was a long pause that seemed to stretch out for an eternity before I managed, 'That's exactly right.' Elza hadn't coached me on what to say exactly, but she had endlessly encouraged me to be honest — and to be myself. I glanced from Jessica to Candice and back again, and decided that honest Dotty was exactly who I was going to be. 'I got my own heart broken, which is a horrid thing for anyone to go through, but it actually happened *after* giving my partner advice, and so—'

'Woah, be kind and rewind,' Jessica interrupted me. 'This is new?'

I forced out a laugh, or an awkward noise, depending on your perspective. 'Yeah, that's the part of this story that I'm *slightly* more bashful about. My partner, well, my *ex*-partner, wrote into my column asking for advice about our relationship, and off the back of that advice, she left me. And that's really where the new Dear Dotty sequence started.'

Candice was obviously taken aback but still smiling widely at me. She gave me another wink but this time it magically settled my stomach into soft butterflies rather than angry moths, so I carried on with the bravery that I'd started with.

'She wrote in to say her relationship had gone stale, her partner was complacent.' My bravery wavered for a beat. 'But anyway, that's her stuff to share with who she wants, whenever she's ready to. The crux of it was that she wasn't happy, but that she'd reached a point of not knowing what to do.'

'And you told her?'

I shrugged. 'I told her to leave.'

Surprised sounds erupted from the pair of them.

'I imagine that's advice you kicked yourself for?' Jessica asked after she recovered her composure a little.

'Not really,' I admitted. 'Obviously I was heartbroken, that goes without saying, because I really did think she was my forever person.' I felt a dip of sadness admitting it aloud, and I noticed a slight frown from Candice, as though she shared some knowing in that admission. 'But, look at where I am now. I do yoga, terribly, but I *try* yoga admirably. I have a new wardrobe and a new home; I've spent time with my mum, which I always treasure; I've . . . started to heal.'

'Amen to that, my girl, amen,' Candice said as she reached over and grabbed my hand to squeeze. I felt bolstered by the gesture.

'Besides which, that partner is, I hope, happier, and I hope she's doing things that she felt she couldn't do with me for whatever reason. Whether it's because I wasn't in a place for it, or she wasn't in a place to nudge me towards it, maybe because she was simply tired of all the nudging and—'

'So, you admit that you were taking some nudging?' Jessica interrupted.

'Of course I was taking some nudging! Hi, I'm a thirty-something living in London, and I've devoted my life to my work, and my brand. My *twenties* were for devoting myself to a relationship. Yes, I absolutely admit that after *years* together I was taking some nudging. And, do you know something, there were times when she was, too, and that's okay, I'm sure she owns that.'

'Honestly, Dotty,' Candice leapt in, 'it's just refreshing to hear someone actually take their share of the responsibility in this sort of break-up because you're absolutely right, people do change their priorities, and they do have peaks and dips in life. Owning those experiences is how we learn from them and grow from them and, well, how we do what you're doing.'

'But you're obviously doing it very publicly?' Jessica highlighted.

'I am, happily,' I lied. It wasn't always happy. I was writing letters to myself most days, with only a few going to print — the few I was comfortable sharing. Because there were some things that you just couldn't openly admit to a nation full of people, which I thought was reasonable. But this, I realised, in this moment, I was only too happy to share. 'Of all the things I trust in the world, ladies,' I took on a tone that made me sound that bit more confident, too, 'it's my ability to give advice. I stand by the advice I gave to my ex-partner when she wrote to me that week. And I'll stand by the advice I give to myself.'

Candice threw her head back and made a joyous noise. 'You, young lady, are a triumph.'

And two hours later, with Elza hanging onto my arm and promising me a rich and expensive lunch, I felt a bit like a triumph as well.

Dear Dotty,

The worst thing about trying to make yourself a better person is that you begin to realise what a shoddy one you were to begin with.

Dotty, I have made some terrible mistakes. My friends have shown up for me more than I have for them lately. I let my partner down when I stopped turning up for our relationship for whole weeks at a time. And I definitely ignore my mother's calls sometimes, simply because I don't always have the energy to answer — or, sometimes, even to call back. There are certain things I can't change. I can definitely answer the phone more, for instance. But on the relationship side of things, the more time I spend with myself the more I realise that this is what I was doing when I was with my ex — I was spending time with myself. And I'm not taking all the blame, because no one is totally blameless. But in my quest to be better, I am certainly taking a decent slice of blame pie, complete with whipped cream and a glazed cherry.

I suppose what I'm trying to say, Dotty, is that I've done things so, so wrong over the years. How do I own that now? How do I make good?

Please send advice for a reformed sinner.

All my love, for what it's worth,
Dotty xxx

CHAPTER TWENTY-SEVEN

Though I was talking a good talk about self-improvement, like any great renovation project, there were issues. For three days after the radio interview, I found that I couldn't get out of my jogging bottoms, and that was most definitely *not* owing to any new exercise regime. The interview aired only hours after we recorded it and after that, the messages started to flood in. Excited fans — because apparently, yes, I had real-life fans — were contacting me on social media to exclaim their joy and interest in hearing from Dear Dotty in the flesh. The girls were spamming the group chat with their own excited chatter. And Elza was fencing phone calls from radio hosts and podcast producers, all of whom seemed to want a piece of Dear Dotty for their latest self-help, romance, you-name-it centred shows. Even our lunch together was punctuated by calls from the marketing team at work, who were busying themselves with graphics and pictures and teasers from upcoming letters to stagger the release of them across the magazine's website and social media feeds to further promote the interview. I found that by the time I got home that day, I was ready to curl firmly into myself and ignore the world for an undetermined period of time, preferably while curled up in front of an open fire

— or at least, one of those videos you can find on YouTube that turns your television into a roaring fire. And that feeling didn't really go away. My social battery was whittled down, and I was thoroughly overwhelmed.

On the fourth day of that, I decided it was time to get proactive. I called Mum and spent my first cup of tea of the day listening to her tell me the latest news about village life, peppered with details of people that I was sure I'd never heard her mention before. I stayed perched in my window seat, too, to soak in the sights that my own London street had to offer. It felt a little like the city was living in an in-between, one season grappling with another for dominance. The street was made up of those desperately hanging onto early autumn — cardigans only — and those ready to rush into winter — I caught sight of a beanie hat and gloves. There was even one person wearing what looked like a Christmas jumper, though it could have just been a particularly bold red and white stripe. When the time eventually came to hang up — 'I've got to head off, love, they're doing basket weaving today at the community hub and I thought I might try my hand' — I made two executive decisions.

The first, I would have to call Mum that evening to get more clarity around this whole basket weaving situation. The second, I would have to call in reinforcements for this unexpected slump in the great Dear Dotty makeover.

That's how, two days later, I found myself sat in front of Lola. She was, at a guess, a forty-something year-old woman with a fantastic dress sense — there was no guessing about that part. She was wearing tailored black trousers with a thin white pinstripe and a loose-fitting white blouse to match. Her hair, streaked with natural silver, was wavy and unruly despite her efforts to tame it with an oversized hair clip. And she was looking at me from over the tops of her gold-trimmed glasses when she asked, 'So you've *never* been to a relationship counsellor before?'

I huffed a laugh. 'Is it so hard to believe?'

She smiled. 'Well, you give good advice. I would have thought there was some sort of counselling experience behind it. Not that it's necessary, I suppose.' She made a note of something on the pad that was balanced on her knee and I immediately felt nervous. 'If you give good advice, you give good advice.' She looked back up at me. 'And you clearly do.'

'Thank you, that's . . . thank you.'

Lola narrowed her eyes. 'But that's not why you're here.'

'No.' I fidgeted with my hands in my lap. 'No, it isn't. I'm here because . . .' I blew out a long puff of air and tried to find the end of the sentence. 'I'm here because I've arrived at a point of knowing what I've done wrong, but not knowing how to fix it.'

Lola narrowed her eyes. 'Your relationship?'

'Relationships.' I leaned hard on the plural. 'The more I think about things I've done, the more I'm wondering whether I've just *always* been letting people down without realising it.'

'How do you feel that you're letting people down?'

I answered in a low voice. 'Well, my girlfriend left me, so I must have done something.'

'Did she tell you that you'd done something?'

'Oh yes, she wrote a very carefully worded letter to my own advice column to tell me exactly what I'd done.' It was the first time I'd relayed Caitlin's behaviour with such a note of bitterness. I didn't like the shade on me, but there was no denying it was there. 'I stopped investing in the relationship. Time, effort, everything, apparently, and she felt stuck, and like life was passing her by.'

'And you told her?'

'To leave,' I snapped. 'I told her to leave.'

'Do you wish you hadn't told her that?'

'Not really.' I answered too quickly and my eyes widened at the admission. 'I mean, it was solid advice, and I stand by it. That's what I mean.'

Lola narrowed her eyes at me again. 'That isn't what you mean.' She shifted forwards in her seat, set her notepad down, and rested her forearms on her knees. 'Dotty, you came here for a reason. You booked a double slot, for a reason. Now, my opening gambit for a bit of advice, is that you need to cut through your own bullshit, worry less about how you're saying things, and think a bit more about the things you came here to say. Can you do that?'

Even though I felt as though Lola had leaned forward and slapped me hard across the face, I managed to determine two things in that moment. The first being that I really did like Lola. The second, Lola was absolutely right . . .

There was still a box of Caitlin's things living rent-free in my home. By the time the first sixty minutes of my session with Lola was over, we'd established that needed to change. We also established that *feeling* like I'd let people down and actually *having* let people down were very different things. There was a fleeting mention of my parents' relationship, and the resultant *lack* of relationship with my dad, which seemed an obvious bear to poke at, but still, one that might have contributed to my desperate need for *comfort* with Caitlin, above anything else. Oh, and I might have been grappling with some low relationship self-esteem; we established that, too. In short: Lola was good at her job.

She handed me a sheet of paper from her own notepad, passed me her pen, and told me to write down the first of my intentions. I smiled and thought of Mum and her endless lists, and I realised there might be something to it. While Lola stepped out to make us a midway cup of tea, I wrote down: *Buy a box*. Underneath that I wrote: *Parcel up Caitlin's things*. Following that: *Send them to her office*. I didn't know where Caitlin was living now. For all I knew she might have shacked up permanently with Lili from The Gym. But I wasn't in the headspace to find out whether that was the case and Lola had, gently but firmly, told me that that was more than okay. I gratefully took my cup of tea from her when it was offered, and I took note of the fact that she glanced at my three-point list before she sat down opposite me again with her own drink.

'Next.'

I smiled. 'I'm worried I haven't shown up enough for my friends.'

'You're worried you haven't, or you know you haven't? Quick fire answer.'

'I know I haven't.'

Lola snapped her fingers and pointed to my list. 'Point four: Show up more.'

I made an awkward noise that was meant to be derogatory but instead just came out disbelieving. 'It isn't that simple! What about all the times I feel like I've let them down?'

'Dotty, what can you do about that?' She gesticulated with one hand as she spoke, keeping the other cupped around her mug of tea. 'People let others down all the time and more often than not we're not doing it deliberately, or consciously. We get swept up, we get busy, we get life. If you feel bad for having not shown up that's great, that's growth, but you can't *do* anything about those times now, can you?' I narrowed my eyes as though searching for an answer and she smiled. 'No is the answer you're looking for. Do you know what you *can* do something about?'

Oh, oh, I know this one!

'The times when they're going to need me in the future?'

'Put it on the list.'

By the time I left my appointment, my list was thirteen points strong, and my head was that bit clearer for it. Lola and I had decided that we'd see each other again at some point, but it was open-ended. I was, she told me, welcome to call for a follow-up session whenever I felt like I might need one. *Any day now*, I thought but didn't say out loud, because that was the type of grumpy thinking that Lola had absolutely no time for.

Even though I'd just invested a staggering amount of money on my brain — *seriously, who can actually afford a therapist in London, which is ironic, considering most people must need one* — I decided a further investment was called for.

I treated myself to a cinnamon bun and a strong cup of tea at the nearest coffee shop, and I grabbed a seat outside. It wasn't until I looked through the camera lens of my phone, to catch content of busy London life complete with the outrageously big bun I was about to eat, that I noticed more and more of the world shifting.

The street was peppered with trees in their seasonal change, and when I pulled in a greedy breath of appreciation I felt the bite of autumn in my lungs. It was that delicious burnt smell that comes with cold air sometimes, as though someone, somewhere nearby, was stoking a fire. It was a stark and much-needed reminder that time moves. We move.

I took an aerial shot of my bun and my tea, then pocketed my phone for the rest of my visit. It was just after lunchtime by the time I left. I had a deadline to meet for a fresh column that was calling me home.

But I decided to 'Buy a box' on the way, not least because it would give me the satisfaction of ticking something off the list.

CHAPTER TWENTY-EIGHT

'Okay, everybody, if you could head over to your assigned cooking stations.'

I'd be lying if I said that Caitlin always thinking I was incapable of cooking a decent meal wasn't a thorn in my side. Spag bol? I'm all over it. Freshly made Diane sauce to go with the steak she brought home? Maybe less all over that. Still, it felt like there were a few pit stops along the way between those two points on the map, and I was sure enough of my skills to think I might be able to rest comfortably in those pit stops — if someone were only to hand me a recipe and a bag of ingredients. My wounded pride aside, whether I *could* cook or not was less of an issue against whether I *had* cooked, and I most definitely hadn't. And whether it was for a partner, friends, or future Dotty, I couldn't be sure, but my cooking skills suddenly felt like something that I needed to brush some extra oil over and pop in the oven to brown.

Of course, what I hadn't banked on was that broadening my cooking skills would also mean sharing them with a stranger. Because while I'd optimistically signed up for a *singles'* intermediate cooking class, I stepped into the room to find workstations set up for *two* people.

'Are you okay working together? Fantastic. Are you okay . . . Fantastic.'

Edward, who was the leading chef-tutor for the course, was in the process of making laps around the room and randomly allocating workstations for people. He'd paired the middle-aged men together, while the lovestruck twenty-somethings who were obviously here together stayed together. The oldest man in the room had been paired with a thirty-something-year-old woman, who tucked her arm around him and led him to their station like she did it for a living. Which left—

'Are you two okay working together?'

—me and the most attractive woman the human world has ever known, working together.

'I'm Alia.' She held out a hand in greeting. She was the type of beautiful where you can't work out whether you're instantly, wildly attracted to her or instantly, wildly jealous. But the ease with which she carried herself from the introduction through to the workstation, doing up her complementary apron like it was the sort of thing she wore at home on the daily, made me think I'd probably landed in the latter of the two camps.

'The dish we'll be cooking today,' Edward announced from his worktop at the front of the room, 'is seafood and saffron pasta. The meal is designed for two which is why you're working in teams today, and we're looking at about fifty minutes in total. That's twenty-five for prep and twenty-five for arguing it out over who does the washing up.'

Alia nudged me softly with her elbow. 'I'm great at washing up, don't worry.'

My jealousy turned to an eye roll of annoyance that I hoped she hadn't noticed.

Edward served out his opening instructions and left it to the attendees to divide and conquer the jobs. My opening confidence was bolstered by the beginner's task of bringing a large pan of water to a boil and getting a bowl of cold water ready.

Meanwhile, Alia cut crosses into our cluster of tomatoes and seemed blissfully ignorant of the fact that juice was squirting across her with every other score. She dropped them into the pot carefully and said, 'Fifteen seconds, right?' to double-check the instructions. No sooner had she asked and I heard her counting under her breath.

'Could you hand me a spoon, please?'

I passed over the nearest wooden spoon to hand and she laughed.

'No, the deep metal one, for the scooping.'

'Oh, sorry, of course.' I replaced one spoon with another and, still holding the wooden one, I idly wondered how many times exactly I'd need to bang myself on the head with it before this situation felt in any way bearable.

'You're looking at me like you've never seen someone cut tomatoes before,' Alia commented. Her tone was light and friendly, as though we already knew each other. I was fascinated by the way her hands moved, yanking out seeds and gunk — 'It's called membrane,' Edward informed the room — like she was a pro at executing the action. I couldn't help but wonder whether she was secretly far beyond the level of an intermediate cook, or whether I was just well below it. 'This is nearly done now, if you want to add that pasta to the water?'

I was grateful for an action that I could perform with a moderate level of confidence. Meanwhile, Alia took control of heating oil in a frying pan and then, once heated through, she added garlic, which she stirred until it started to turn a light brown. I seemed to be owning the pasta situation at least; a fundamental, albeit entirely unimpressive, part of the task list.

'Right, folks, you should be at a point of adding prawns and scallops to your frying pans,' Edward announced.

There was a fluster of noise that echoed around the space. I wondered how the other stations were getting along — or rather, how the other cooks were getting along. Alia hadn't done anything wrong, exactly — at all, in fact. And yet I couldn't settle into a rhythm with her. I couldn't navigate her body well enough to find a way for us both to occupy the space, and it left me fidgeting with the awkwardness of a teenager buying their first bra; I just couldn't make things fit.

'Do you want to take the lead on this?' Alia asked.

I nodded. I'd never cooked prawns before in my life, but sure, there was no time like the present. I threw in prawns and scallops, and felt a deep sense of satisfaction when I heard the hiss of the pan as they made contact. The smell was instantly satisfying, too, enough to make my stomach turn over in hunger, and it must have been audible.

Alia laughed. 'I always get hungry the minute I start cooking, especially when it's something wholesome like this. I swear as soon as winter hits all I want is pasta and warm colours. Well that, and things that are coated in cinnamon. I'm quite a fan of that at this time of year, too.' She stood close to me, inhaling over my shoulder. 'Jesus. I hope we actually get just to sit and eat this on the other side of the cooking.'

There was no denying it: Alia was gorgeous. She had long, thick hair that snaked in curls down past her chest, with make-up that was drawn on to perfection and an easy clothing style that showed off the fact she was slim without boasting it too unashamedly. She was wearing loose-fit jeans and a long-sleeved T-shirt that I guessed was a bodysuit, tucked neatly into her waistband. It didn't shift an inch as she leaned over the front of the cooking station and watched what I was doing with the ingredients.

Things finally felt a little easier to navigate. Although whether that was because I actually had something important to do, or because there was some physical distance between me and the blindingly beautiful woman, it was hard to say.

When the scallops were golden brown I scooped them and the prawns free from the pan and set them to one side. Alia made a deep sound of appreciation that did something to my stomach. She handed me the mussels to drop into the pan while she added white wine.

'Do you think he'd notice if there were two glasses' worth of wine missing from this bottle? That's part of the cooking process, surely?'

'I dunno,' I answered. I was still trying to focus all of my attention on the food and none of my attention on the rising heat that was emanating from my belly. 'It isn't listed in the instructions.'

She laughed, a curt, hard but somehow utterly pleasing sound, and I gave myself a proverbial pat on the back.

Jesus, Dotty, what is happening right now . . .

'So what brings you to a cooking class?' she asked.

'What brings *you* to a cooking class? You seem to know what you're doing already.'

She shrugged. 'I like to try new things. There's something to be said for getting out of the old comfort zone now and then, isn't there?' I moved away from the pan to make way for her to cover it with the lid. 'Which I guess is why you're here, too . . .' she said, throwing a lemon into the air before catching it. I shot her a quizzical look. 'I read your column.'

Of course you do . . .

'I didn't want you to think I was some weird creepy fangirl.'

'So you thought you'd wait until we were halfway through making a meal together to mention it?' I managed to sound jokey rather than judgy. I imagined my face to be flushed red with embarrassment already. It was the least I could do to try to keep my voice free of the feeling though. 'I'm trying to . . . I don't know, work on myself, I guess. Although you know that already.' I took the cream from her when it was offered and poured it into the sauce. 'Which means you must also know that cooking is a weak spot for me.'

It was something that had cropped up in my Dear Dotty letters. Not that I didn't know *how* to cook but rather, I'd hardly ever cooked for Caitlin. I felt discomfort weave itself through me knowing, now, that this woman already knew that.

Alia stood next to me with her shoulder pressed neatly against my own. 'You seem to be doing just fine to me.'

The rest of Edward's instructions came thick and fast as we neared the end of the cooking time. The entire room was a box of heat, a blend of focused attention and high-energy hobs, and I was grateful that these final minutes seemed to have forced me and Alia into a stretch of silence, too. She signalled for me to give everything a final mix together and then topped the food with parsley and pine nuts.

'And presto!' Edward shouted, as though *he* were the one revealing something. 'Underneath your cooking stations you'll find two dishes and two wine glasses, that's assuming there's any wine left.' I glanced up to see Alia wink at me.

'Good job we waited,' she said.

'Serve up and I'll start making my way around the room to sample your delights.'

'I can't help but think he has the easiest job out of the lot of us,' Alia said as she scooped our efforts into the two bowls. I was busy eyeing the wine like it was a mortal enemy. I'd spent the last three-quarters of an hour being batted between flirtation and awkwardness, attraction and mild resentment. I wasn't sure that drizzling with wine and leaving it to simmer was the best of ideas. 'Do you want to pour?' Alia asked as she pushed a dish to my side of the counter.

'I'll just have water.'

She shrugged. 'Suit yourself.'

It took Edward ten minutes to make his way around to our station. 'Mhm, something smells good over in this corner. How did we do?'

Alia passed him a small sample bowl that she'd been conscientious enough to set to one side for him. Which was wise, given that both of us had been so quietly pleased with our efforts that we'd nearly demolished our own meals. I worried that the 'leftovers' Alia had put aside might not actually make it out of the building with us. Though admittedly, while I'd enjoyed the food, I'd been just as thankful for something that kept our mouths otherwise engaged for ten minutes as well. I'd managed to fence the occasional comment from Alia during that time, mostly about how well we'd done, with nothing more than noises of enjoyment.

'You two are quite the team,' Edward announced through a mouthful of prawns and pasta. 'Nicely done, ladies, nicely done.' He disappeared to the front of the room and started to make his plug for the next of his cooking classes — which I absolutely wouldn't be attending.

'Pleasure doing business with you,' Alia said, her tone still friendly. 'It's been really nice to, oh—' She looked at me. 'You have a little something.' Alia leaned forward as though to wipe my mouth with her thumb and I recoiled. The tiniest jerk backwards, but she noticed. It hadn't been conscious; I hadn't deliberately moved away from the nice lady but . . . *Jesus, Dotty, what are you doing!* 'My bad,' she said, handing me a napkin instead, 'you have a little something on your face.'

Prawn, I imagined. Prawn and blind embarrassment was what I had on my face.

'Thanks,' I managed, before I wiped my mouth clean of it all.

I was tugging my coat on when Alia caught my attention again. 'Where are you heading after this?'

Oh, home, to berate myself for recoiling from the pretty girl. I swallowed my thoughts and managed a much more normal answer. 'I thought I'd cleanse my nose of all these gorgeous smells by heading to the Tube and then home.'

Alia laughed. 'Fancy that, I'm heading to the Tube, too. Want some company?' When I hesitated to answer she added, 'Literally just to the Tube, I'm not going to follow you home or anything weird. I'm not *that* much of a Dear Dotty follower.'

My stomach was gripped with nerves again though I couldn't work out why, and I hardly had the time to think it through. Alia was gathering up her things while I was keeping her waiting. Suddenly the tick-tick-tick of the wall clock at the front of the room was deafening.

'Sure, some company would be nice.'

'Alright then,' she said, smiling, and pointed. 'Don't forget your food.'

CHAPTER TWENTY-NINE

Because apparently I am a stickler for unimportant details when faced with a beautiful woman, I spent the first two minutes of our walk guesstimating exactly how long it would take for us to get to the Tube station. Thankfully, Alia had been talking for those two minutes. She'd told me how much she loved cooking — something she inherited from her nan — but she was getting complacent when it came to making meals for one. Something about work, something about not making the time. I wondered whether we might have more in common than I first thought.

'I know I could have just grabbed a recipe book and made it all from the comfort of my own home. But' — she hesitated — 'well, I wouldn't have met you then, would I?'

An awkward noise fell out of me. 'Sorry' — I coughed — 'dry throat.'

Alia pulled up to a stop. 'Do you want to grab a drink?' She nodded somewhere behind me and when I followed her look I spotted a quiet bistro. There were strings of fairy lights dangling from the windows, as though the manager had wanted to get a jump on the festive season. Each pane of glass was coated with whisps of sprayed on snow. 'I'll treat you to something fizzy and sugary to wash down the pasta.'

'Sure, that would be nice.'

Argh, Dotty, things can be something other than nice! I berated myself, remembering my lukewarm 'sure, that'd be nice' that had got us here to start with.

'My treat though,' I added for colour, flair, and hopefully something flirty. 'It's the least I can do after you carried me through that whole cooking class.'

'I did not carry you!' Alia knocked my arm playfully and I blushed at the contact. 'You're better than you think you are. Though, fair enough, you didn't exactly seem . . . comfortable.' She held the door to the bistro open and gestured for me to go inside. 'Ladies first.'

I ducked in ahead of her, grateful that the change of scenery had given me the perfect opportunity to avoid explaining that my discomfort was only one part due to the cooking itself. The other nine parts of discomfort that made up the perfect whole were due to the fact that I'd spent most of it trying to work out whether I was attracted to or intimidated by my cooking partner. Both was the quick answer to that. But now, as I watched the easy way Alia moved through the space as though London bistros were her natural habitat, I realised it was most definitely the former — still a bit the latter, but *definitely* more the former.

'As the drinks are on you,' Alia said, as she rested her bag of leftovers on a barstool, 'I'm just going to nip to the loo while you order.'

'What can I get you?'

She shrugged. 'I'll have whatever you're having.'

'Great.' *That's just great.* What I actually wanted was a Diet Coke packed with ice that I could guzzle at speed. But that didn't exactly scream sophistication now, did it? While I was waiting for the bartender to make his way around to me, I wondered whether I could order the soft drink, down it, and have two tall gin and tonics waiting by the time Alia got back.

'What can I get for you?'

I hesitated. 'Can I get two gin and tonics, please?'

'Ice?'

'Perfect, thanks so much.'

Now all I needed was not to neck the gin by the time Alia was back and we'd be fine . . .

'Think your friend will mind if I keep her seat warm?'

The voice caught me off guard and I flinched. I turned around to find a tall hunk of a man, by anyone's standards, leaning over the back of Alia's barstool. He wore glasses and what I guessed was two-day-old stubble. It was hard to tell exactly from his slumped stature, but he looked well over six feet tall, with broad shoulders and blonde hair that would have had Elouise swooning and making bad decisions all over the place. If I'd been so inclined, I probably would have made a bad decision or two with him myself. But, as it was—

'Oh, my friend won't be long, sorry.'

'Come on,' he pushed, 'you don't want a little company until then?' He moved as though to pull out Alia's stool to sit down. 'Besides, I'm sure your friend won't begrudge you making another friend, will she?'

'Really, she's not going to be long.' I hoped that by saying it again I might somehow make it true, and that Alia would reappear in seconds.

'Can I get you anything else?' the bartender interrupted us.

A get-out-of-jail-free card, I wanted to say — but didn't. Because it didn't seem likely to help the situation.

'Just those two are great, thank you.' I tapped my phone against the card machine and felt a tug of hopelessness when the bartender left me to the clutches of the man who was still propped up next to me.

'You know, I love a gin and tonic myself,' he said then.

'Well, I'm sure the bartender will make you one if you ask nicely.'

He laughed. 'Okay, spicy, I like that. I'm Elliot.' He held out his hand towards me and I made a point of not taking it.

'I'm Dotty.'

'And I'm Alia.'

There must have been another entry-exit to the toilets because Alia literally appeared out of nowhere. While I'd seen her walk away minutes ago in one direction, now she was standing behind me, and I felt the firmness of her body pressed against my back as she tucked an arm around my shoulders. She leaned in and kissed my cheek, and I was sure she lingered there for a second longer than absolutely necessary, too — of course, that could have been a part of the show, but either way, I certainly wasn't sad about it.

'Sorry, babe, got distracted brushing the wind out of my hair.'

'Oh, that's no trouble. Elliot here was just keeping me company while I waited for you.'

I'd be lying if I said I didn't look a little smug.

'Well, thanks, Elliot, you're a pal.' Alia moved from behind me then and set her hand on the back of her stool. She pulled it out and nudged Elliot out of the way in the process, moving him as though he wasn't a big hunk of male muscle at all. 'You have yourself a nice day now.' Alia smiled pointedly before turning her back on the man. She moved her bag of leftovers onto the bar itself, hopped onto her seat, and eyed up the drinks. 'Gin and tonic, you always know my favourites, D. Thanks so much.' She squeezed my knee and then reached for one of the tall glasses. Meanwhile Elliot — *oh, poor Elliot* — retreated in slow motion, unsteady, and apparently entirely unsure of what had just happened.

'Mm.' Alia made a noise of appreciation after taking her first mouthful. 'Gin and tonic really is my favourite. I know this amazing recipe for muffins that involves gin, if you're ever interested in branching out from sensible pasta-making to slightly reckless baking instead.'

I sat there agog for a handful of seconds before I managed to speak. 'We're really not going to talk about you absolutely serving that man a slice of embarrassment just there?'

Alia spluttered a laugh as she tried to take another sip. 'Did I make you uncomfortable? My friends say I can be a little . . .' She waved her free hand around to pluck a word from thin air. 'Over-friendly.'

'Do you often pose as the girlfriend to get your friends out of trouble?' I asked playfully. Though inwardly I chanted, *Please say no, please say no.* I wanted the moment to have meant something — even though I wasn't altogether sure what it could have meant, other than Alia had much more experience getting rid of pushy men than I did.

'I'm not gonna lie to you, Dotty, no.' She laughed. 'But I thought this situation called for special measures.'

I didn't ask why. I only smiled and took a blissful mouthful of my own drink then, too. The glass was cool in my palm, heavy with condensation running down the length of it, and I resisted the urge to press it to my forehead, chest, wrists, anything to cool myself down in what suddenly felt like a heated situation.

'I'm just going to grab the bartender for a second.' Alia raised her hand to try to signal the server from the opposite end of the bar. 'Then you can tell me all about why you enrolled in the cooking class.'

Because I nearly broke my mum's tooth with frozen broccoli.

'Did you want a different drink?'

'Yes and no,' Alia answered me as she ferreted free her phone, ready to pay before she'd even ordered. 'The gin is lovely, a little too lovely.' She laughed. 'But I'm bloody parched and I could just do with something I can down in one go. You know, without making myself tipsy in the process.'

'Is everything okay over here?' the bartender asked, clocking our nearly full glasses.

'Oh, absolutely. But could I get a Diet Coke? With plenty of ice in the glass, too. Thanks so much. Dotty, did you want anything else?'

For the second time, I was painfully aware of my mouth hanging open.

'Dotty, are you . . .'

'Yes, sorry, yes.' I snapped out of my haze and smiled. 'A Diet Coke would be great as well, thank you.'

'Ice?' the server asked.

I was all too aware of the heat creeping up my neck, past my jumper and into my cheeks. I managed a dry swallow before answering. 'Loads of it, please, absolutely.'

And then, slowly and somewhat begrudgingly, I told Alia about the fish and chips incident — though I wasn't altogether forthcoming about Caitlin's involvement in the story. And I told her about Tots telling me I was caring, in a non-home-cooked meal sort of way. And then, and only then, when she was already pink with laughter, did I tell her about the frozen broccoli.

CHAPTER THIRTY

Given that it was the first time Elouise had visited the flat in a while, I decided that careful measures needed to be taken. I gave myself an entire afternoon away from reading letters and emails that were piling up by the hour, which included the first e-invite to a Christmas party that a colleague was throwing, and cleaned my home from top to bottom. I even buffed the windows in the living room, and by the late afternoon they were letting in such a glorious winter sunshine that I wondered why I didn't clean them more often. The new season was most definitely coming, and when I cracked the window open — because I didn't know how else I might possibly get rid of the smell of bleach that had wafted in from the kitchen — I realised that while the sun may have *implied* warmth, the cold air rushing was winter right the way through.

I lit three chunky (cinnamon-scented, no less) candles across my coffee table in the lounge, rearranged a bunch of bright and burnt orange flowers, and then took the longest shower known to man.

For the first time in living memory, I had invited the girls over for a homemade dinner. Only, the homemade part was a surprise. I chopped peppers, sliced carrots, and wedged onions, and while they started to bake through I made a valiant effort at only using eight chipolatas — but had a mild panic when I inevitably lost count of how many I'd chopped.

'I hope they're hungry,' I said aloud as I eyed the mound of meat on the chopping board. I added the sausages and decided there was still time to answer another couple of Dear Dotty emails.

I wasn't quite at the point of cooking confidence where I could leave anything unattended, though, so I fetched my laptop into the kitchen and perched myself at the breakfast bar while I read through the subject lines. I'd been truly sucked in by 'Having my best friend's baby?' when the oven timer sounded, and I had to stop what I was doing to add tomatoes, beans, and stock. I was barely into the fine details of the best friend's baby situation — a request from one lifelong friend to another to be a surrogate — when Tots texted to say they were nearly at mine, and I breathed a hearty sigh. The letter was interesting and all, but I hadn't a clue where to start in writing a response. I only knew Elza would lap it up for a magazine piece.

By then the flat was a gorgeous mess of smells. I lined up four wine glasses on the breakfast bar, pulled a chilled bottle of pink from the fridge, and started to top up each glass in turn. I'd only just texted Tots back to say the door was open when I heard—

'Oh my word, what is that smell?'

I craned round the corner to see Elouise, Tots, and Marissa queued up together in the doorway to the living room. They looked stunned, and I'd be lying if I said I wasn't pleased with myself for prompting the reaction.

'Come in, come in.' I ushered them through. 'I've got wine waiting.'

'I bought . . .' Marissa gestured with a bottle of white but her sentence died out. 'Seriously, Dotty, what is that smell?'

My stomach sank. 'Oh. Bad smell?'

'Ah, gorgeous smell.' Elouise rounded past me and made a beeline for the oven. 'You're actually *cooking* for us?'

I slapped her arm. 'Don't sound so surprised. I cook now, every day.' Tots narrowed her eyes and I caved. 'Okay not *every* day but some days. Most days, I would go as far to say.'

'These cooking classes have really taken off,' Marissa answered as she accepted her glass.

'Actually, I only went to the one,' I admitted with some shame, 'but I've been reading recipes online in my free time and, I thought, I don't know, I just . . .' I suddenly felt awkward, bashful, as though these weren't women I'd openly made an arse out of myself in front of for years now. 'I just wanted to make an effort for you all.'

'Babe!' Tots wrapped an arm around my shoulder. 'You are the limit.'

'In a good way?'

She kissed my temple. 'In the best way.'

'Seriously, what are we eating?' Elouise asked.

'We are having sausage and white bean casserole,' I announced proudly, 'and I've got some boiled rice on the go for anyone who wants it, but I also popped to that bakery down the road, you know the one? And I bought us some fresh ciabatta. I wasn't sure whether it would go but I figured bread never made anything . . .' I petered out when I clocked the three of them staring at me. 'What?'

'Who are you?' Marissa asked, her expression suspicious.

'This is nothing,' I answered. 'Just you wait until I tell you about my masterplan for a homemade Christmas dinner for us all this year.'

Marissa looked as though I'd slapped her. 'Seriously, who *are* you?'

I laughed. 'I just wanted to do something kind, to remind you all that I love you and I appreciate you, and we don't always have to order a takeaway when we're eating here.' I raised my glass. 'Cheers to that?'

'I'll cheers to anything that gets me fed.' Elouise was peering into the oven as she spoke.

I reached out and closed the door. 'You'll let the heat out. Living room, everyone? Not least to get Els away from dinner

196

before it's actually ready. We've got' — I peered at the timer to check — 'probably another fifteen minutes or so.'

Marissa and Tots were the first to wander through, taking their places on the sofa and in an armchair respectively. Elouise loitered behind me — still watching the food, I assumed — in the kitchen. It wasn't until I was comfortably perched on the other side of the sofa from Marissa, my legs tucked beneath me and the first swill of wine in my mouth, that I heard Elouise say, 'Who's Alia and why is her number pinned to your fridge?'

I winced. *Bugger.*

The napkin had been tacked to my fridge with a red dot magnet since the cooking class three weeks ago. Even though I'd had no intention of using it, I hadn't been able to force myself to throw it out either. Alia and I had a great time over gin, tonic, and my cooking failures but neither of us had actioned anything further. Frankly, I hadn't had the confidence or the know-how to even ask for her number. And when she didn't ask for mine, I assumed the drink had been just that: a drink, and some idle flirting for good measure. Little did I know, then, that she'd readily given me her number half an hour before we'd even set foot in the bistro. I'd thought nothing more of our shared leftovers — carefully packaged by Alia at the end of the cooking class — until I'd arrived home at the end of the night and tucked the storage box of food into the fridge. I'd found the napkin at the bottom of the bag, and there, behold, was Alia's phone number. For a while I'd sat at the breakfast bar and stared at it as though it were likely to launch an attack if I didn't watch it carefully. Then, I'd put it in a kitchen drawer. Then, I'd moved it to the fridge. It had taken up such a permanent residence there that I didn't even notice it from one day to the next. Though that, of course, had been a sizeable error . . .

'She's someone I need to call for work,' I lied. I glanced around to Marissa who was staring at me through slitted eyes, while Tots only wore a smirk. 'What?'

'Liar,' Tots answered.

Marissa nudged my knee. 'Who is she? Did something happen?'

'Nothing has happened, she's someone from work.'

'The more you say it, the less convincing it is,' Tots said, laughing to herself as she took another sip of wine. 'But whatever, if you don't want to tell your *best friends* who Alia is, that's fine. I guess we all know where we stand.'

'I cooked for you!' I gestured wildly to the kitchen.

Elouise finally wandered through to where the rest of us were sitting. 'You can't count that as a kindness when we haven't eaten yet.' She pulled the window closed and made a show of shuddering slightly against the cold — though I would have welcomed it to cool the flush on my cheeks. 'Is she someone you like?'

'She's just someone I met; it's not even a thing.'

'So why did she give you her number?' Marissa pushed.

I let out a dramatic sigh and dropped my head back against the sofa cushion. 'She's from the cooking class I went to. She wrote her number on a napkin and put it in my bag of leftovers. I didn't know it was there until I got home.'

'But that class was what, three weeks ago?' Elouise asked. 'Have you called?'

Tots snapped her fingers and pointed at me. 'That's why you didn't go back.'

'Oh, you *don't* like her?' Marissa picked up the thread.

'You three are relentless. I didn't go back because I didn't enjoy it.'

'Because you were getting hit on?'

'Tots, I was not getting hit on.'

'So she gave you her number because . . .' Elouise added in what could only be described as a patronising tone.

'Do you lot want feeding or not?' I snapped.

Tots held up a hand in defeat. 'Okay, okay. How about you feed us, we drink some more wine, then *maybe* we swing back to this Alia situation later?'

'I don't have a choice, do I?'

'No.' Marissa squeezed my knee. 'I'm afraid it looks like you don't.'

'Great.' I raised my wine glass. 'Cheers to that, then.' I inched forward in my seat while the girls were taking their own sips, and I waited until they'd finished before I picked up something altogether more serious. 'Wildly different tone, so strap in,' I warned them, 'you all know I've been doing a lot of . . .'

'Soul-searching?'

'Growth?'

'Introspection?'

'That. You all know I've been doing a lot of that, and as part of it, I've been thinking about my relationships, and that doesn't just mean romantic ones. I've been thinking about us, as a friendship group, and the times you've shown up for me, and the times for one reason or another I mightn't have shown up for you recently. Firstly, I'm sorry for that, but more than that, I'm just thankful. You've all been amazing, not just through this but always and that's . . . well, that's why I wanted to cook something, to show a little more effort, and to tell you, seriously' — I looked at them all in turn — 'to tell you that I seriously love you, and I value you all for the many, *many* things you bring to my life.'

There was a long and full silence that made me fidget a little.

'Bloody hell, Dotts.' Marissa closed the distance between us on the sofa. 'We love you, too, you know?'

Elouise was wearing her thinking face. 'I honestly can't think of a time when you haven't shown up for me, and I'm really trying.'

Tots crossed the room and lowered to a crouch in front of me. 'You're a bit of a babe, Dotty. We love you, and we value you, and we also value the journey you're going through right now, and any changes that involves. We're here for it, because, again, we love you, but also because you'd be here for us.' She reached up and guided my chin upwards so we were

eye to eye. 'Any thoughts you've had about letting us down or
. . . anything, it's nonsense. We're all just in it together, babe.'
She shrugged. 'We got on that bus a long time ago.'

Elouise came to join our huddle then. 'There's an old
adage that I like to think on when I'm worrying about this
sort of thing. Do you mind if I share it with you, now?' She
set a hand on my knee as she spoke. I was already tearing up
and I was low-key concerned that whatever came next might
tip me over the edge of feeling, but I managed a nod. 'If you
love someone' — she pulled in a big breath and smiled —
'feed them.'

Dear Dotty,

I'd be lying if I said that self-improvement came easy to me, Dotty. There are some days when curling up on the sofa and being a slug for the duration is a much more appealing option. But I've been making a concerted effort to avoid doing that. On days when exercise feels too much, I might clean. On days when cleaning feels too much, I might call my mum so she can encourage me to clean. Humour aside, I suppose what I'm trying to say here is that I'm trying, and I've been trying, to learn and know myself better, and that's included trying things that my former self wouldn't have given the time of day to.

But the thing I'm starting to wonder, the thing I'm starting to worry about, is how do I know when I'm done? If I'm taking all these steps to grow and be a better, shinier Dotty 2.0, how do I know when I get there? Or, the more terrifying sibling thought to that, do I never know? Is life one constant journey of self-improvement and/or change, somehow, and do we just have to keep rolling with that until we're eighty (if we're lucky), at which point we might finally say that we've found ourselves? Existentialism at its finest.

Maybe I don't need an answer to this one, Dotty. Putting the thoughts into the ether might be enough. (That said, if you do happen to have an answer, write soon, because there are only so many times I can clean the kitchen sink before the dust under the sofa starts to grab my attention and I actually have to break out the Hoover.)

With love and only mild panic,
Dotty xxx

CHAPTER THIRTY-ONE

I bounced about between Underground stations on what turned out to be a hideously busy London morning. Luckily, it was also a very beautiful one. Even though some shops were lagging behind — with outlandish window displays to denote fireworks still — the majority of shop fronts were clambering onto the Christmas bus. There were small and sparkling lights appearing everywhere; empty boxes designed to look like presents, haphazardly stacked in shop windows ready for arrangement; and stick-on snowflakes being carefully applied to windowpanes. It was a little *too* early for the Christmas spirit to have coursed through me. But it did give me something pretty and distracting to admire on my way into the office, for yet another meeting that Elza had popped into my diary without any forewarning.

There had been a flurry of these meetings when the Dear Dotty Self-Improvement Scheme was launched earlier in the year, but they'd died out as the weeks went on — and the marketing department had come to trust me with my own Instagram account again. It was nowhere near as stylised as it used to be, with messy hair days and high-end brunches logged in equal measure to show that *yes, Dear Dotty was a real human* and *no, she didn't look like one all the time.*

I gave myself a minute outside the office for two big belly breaths — because of course, any unscheduled meeting was enough to unsettle even the most professional of workers, which I was most certainly not — and then I powered through. Elza's secretary-cum-armoured guard told me that Elza was already waiting for me in her office, and I checked my watch — *five minutes early* — to make sure I hadn't made my second mistake of the day (the first being that I very nearly left the flat wearing one black Converse pump and one white).

'Morning El — Ahh . . .'

The cheery greeting died out when I spotted that Elza wasn't alone in her office.

She stood to greet me with an arm outstretched. 'Dotty, love, you remember Candice.'

Candice Egan was sitting in one of Elza's guest armchairs by the window. She was wearing the same shade of lipstick as when I'd last seen her, and I wondered whether the blood red cupid's bow of her mouth was part of her brand. This time, she was wearing drainpipe tailored black trousers and a fitted blouse, pale pink, with fine white pinstripes running through it. Her hair was blow-dried to perfection and I instantly felt envious. My own was clustered into a messy bun hanging low at the back of my head — a style I told myself was befitting of the writer in me, though in reality it was a lazy effort at taming my hair after forgetting to dry it post-bath the night before.

'Candice, how lovely to see you again,' I managed, hoping that the quiver in my tone was only audible to me. 'This is such a surprise.'

The other woman stood from her window-side view and shook my hand when I offered it. There were two empty tea-cups on the table already, and I wondered what time their pre-meeting had started. That's when the loud buzzing of panic hit my ears, and I entirely missed what Elza was saying. But given that she was guiding me towards one of the free armchairs as she said it, I had to hope she was only asking me to take a seat.

'Dotty?'

'Hm?' I turned my attention to my boss. 'Sorry?'

'I said, do you want tea or coffee?'

'Oh, tea, please' — I gestured to the pot on the table — 'if there's some left.'

'We'll get fresh in.'

Elza busied herself calling through to the armoured guard for more refreshments while Candice said a forthright hello. 'She didn't tell you I'd be here.'

I laughed. 'Elza likes to keep me on my toes.'

Candice leaned back in her chair and laced her fingers together. 'She should take good care of you. You're quite the USP these days.'

Thank you? I smiled and followed her glance out of the window.

'Sophie will be in with fresh tea in a second or two,' Elza announced as she joined us. She had a look about her that suggested she'd just pulled off a master bank heist. Her smile was wider than I'd ever seen it, and she looked between us like a mother hen orchestrating a playdate between her prized child and the most popular girl in school. 'Now, Dotty, you're probably wondering what this meeting is all about.' She paid no attention to Sophie, who came in just then carrying a tea tray with a basket of muffins in tow. 'Candice reached out to me after your interview all those weeks back. How long ago was it, now?'

'*Weeks*! Really I left it far too long,' Candice answered. 'Thank you, Sophie,' she added, just as the other woman was about to leave the room. I thought there was something pointed in the way she said it. I stifled a smirk and tried to wear my best listening expression instead — though of course, I made a point of thanking Sophie, too.

'Candice got in touch with me after that and asked what my plans, well, what *our* plans were for the Dear Dotty letter series. Not the whole series, you understand, but the letters you've been writing, well, to yourself.' I murmured my understanding and she carried on. 'Candice reached out to me first, as your existing editor, because obviously we at the magazine have certain . . . rights, I suppose, over the column.'

'I would have come straight to you, Dotty,' Candice leapt in, 'but there's so much red tape to cut through these days I thought it was best to go to the mechanics of the operation before I targeted the heart of it. You understand?' I murmured again, though this time my understanding was less certain. 'Tea, Dotty?' she asked, her hand already on the pot.

'Please, absolutely, thank you.'

'Candice wanted to run an idea by me for the future of the column, to see whether it aligned with our vision for where Dear Dotty is going.'

I wanted to ask what exactly that vision was. I hadn't thought beyond Christmas — and even that, honestly, felt a bit far-reaching — so to think *beyond* that was a grasp.

Elza took a cup from Candice when it was offered. 'Anyway, the rest is best left to Candice to explain. Thanks ever so much, Candice.' She sipped at her drink, signalling the end of her opening spiel.

'Dotty, you probably already know a bit about Bright Ideas' — *The country's biggest publishing house for self-help books? I was loosely familiar with it* — 'but just to fill in any blanks. We currently represent over eighty authors, covering a range of topics that fall under the exceptionally broad heading of self-help. It's a vague title that we can't quite shake, but it helps people to know what we're about, I suppose. We're always looking for new authors to represent and support, and we're always looking for new angles to explore in terms of how we can help readers, emotionally, intellectually, philosophically' — she waved her hand around while searching for more words — 'you get the idea.'

Candice paused to take a sip of her drink, and I used the opening for a non-committal response. 'Of course, absolutely. I know your work.'

'Do you mind if I grab a muffin, Elza?' she asked. The turn made me jerk. 'I'm absolutely starving. Too much work and not enough time for the finer things.'

'Goodness, take two! Treat yourself.'

Hello! Can we not focus on the muffins? If there had been subtitles for this moment, they would have read '*Internal screaming*'. But instead, I sipped my drink and took a blueberry muffin when the basket was offered to me.

Candice spoke around a demure mouthful of sponge. 'Anyway, look, I absolutely love the work you're doing with the new Dear Dotty thread. I think it's fresh, bold, interesting, and I think you discuss it *so* well when you're given a platform for it. Honestly, I was so taken with how you handled yourself during that interview those weeks back.'

I managed a smile. 'Thank you, I . . . It was a lot, obviously, to be that honest. But I don't see the point in not being honest these days.' I shrugged. 'The letters are being published, so people may as well know the whole story behind them.'

'Yes, exactly that, yes,' she answered.

Elza echoed her with, 'Yes, yes.'

'That's why I approached Elza with this idea.'

The idea that no one had told me about yet . . .

'I see,' I said, even though I didn't.

Candice brushed her hands free of crumbs. 'Now, tell me, how many Dear Dotty letters do you think you have that have never seen the light of day?'

I threw a questioning glance towards Elza who gave me an encouraging nod. 'As in, letters that other people have written, or letters from my new Dear Dotty . . . thing?'

Candice shrugged. 'Let's say both.'

'Okay, well' — I tried to do some fast maths — 'the Dear Dotty inbox is periodically backed up and cleared out, but everything is stored *somewhere*, you'd have to talk to the computer folks, tech, whoever for that, though,' I fumbled with my words, every one of them weighing awkwardly in my mouth. 'But at a very, very rough guess, into the ten thousands that probably haven't been and won't be published now,' I admitted with some shame. I'd spent so long trying to get through every letter, but the more steam and popularity the column had gained, the more impossible a task it became to make sure everything saw the light of day. It stopped being feasible soon after the Dear Dotty reveal for the magazine, and though that was a good thing in so many ways — to know the column had so much attention — it did mean that not every reader saw their troubles in print. 'As for my own letters, I tend to write maybe between one and three every week and, well, you know that only one of those gets cherry-picked and published.'

'So that's probably what, another twenty letters, since this all started?'

'I would guess so?'

Candice laughed. 'Dotty, don't look so suspicious! Honestly, nothing that is said here today will be set in stone and you'll absolutely have time to think through these plans and amend them as you see fit before anything is concrete. Does that sound okay?'

I looked to Elza again, hoping for support, or clarity, or both. But she just bunched her shoulders and gave me a smile that can only be described as somewhat unsettling: forced and awkward and definitely not an expression she wore easily.

I swallowed hard and tried to ignore the hard knock of it in my throat, and then I decided to be brave. 'Okay' — I nodded — 'that all sounds fine and reasonable.' I looked from Candice to Elza and back again. 'But you realise that neither of you have actually told me what the idea is?'

That's when Candice winked — that same disarming wink from when I'd met her the first time — and she reached into her bag to pull out a planner. It was brown leather and tabbed to within an inch of its life with sticky notes. She unfolded it a handful of pages in, her fingers knowing exactly where to find what she was looking for, and then she placed the open book on the table between us.

'This, Dotty. *This* is the idea.'

The next thing I knew, Candice was nudging a muffin towards me and saying something about my blood sugar . . .

CHAPTER THIRTY-TWO

It was three days later when I managed to pin Tots down for a coffee. We were meeting at Serpentine Bar and Kitchen in Hyde Park, which at least meant I had some easy views while I waited for her. The weather outside had turned bitter, a sharp wind that seemed to come out of nowhere and at random intervals, too, but it was the cleanse I needed from the stuffiness of the flat, where the central heating had been in overdrive for the last week. Here, now, it blew my mind the tiniest bit that so many people were able to go about their business like there was nothing else happening, like my life wasn't blowing up in front of me, like . . . *Like the world doesn't revolve around you*, I thought somewhat callously. I wasn't taking the easiest of tones with myself since the meeting with Candice and Elza, where an early Christmas-present-cum-wild-opportunity had landed in my lap and I'd responded by panic-eating three mini muffins in front of one of London's biggest and best publishing names. Candice had been very understanding about the whole thing, but I had to wonder if even that might only be a part of her brand.

I was oscillating between sickness and extreme hunger. But when the couple at the table next to me sat down with their wood-fired pizzas, I was fiercely tempted to climb over the chairs that separated us and tuck in. It was probably a good thing that Tots arrived when she did, setting a hand on my shoulder that made me jump a clear inch out of my chair.

She kissed my cheek and took the chair opposite mine. 'Wow, testy much? Thanks for agreeing to meet here, sorry if it's a drag for you. Well, a drag, and a bloody freezing lunch venue.' She audibly shivered and bunched her coat collar up tighter against the cold. 'Where are the girls?' she asked then, noticing the two empty place settings at the table.

'They aren't coming. Can I get you a coffee?'

Tots narrowed her eyes. 'How much coffee have you had already? Because you seem . . .'

'It's peppermint tea' — I gestured with my cup — 'but I promised you a coffee.'

'Why aren't the girls coming?'

I shrugged. 'I thought it might be nice, just us. How about that coffee?'

'Dotty, seriously, I'll get my own coffee. What's happening?'

I sucked in a greedy breath and spoke into my drink because I found that was easier than breaking the news directly to her face. 'Candice Egan offered me a book deal.'

A string of expletives followed. 'I'm sorry,' she said to a nearby mother who was shooting her a death stare. 'I'm sorry, my friend just had some really good news and . . . sorry.' The death stare ceased and Tots managed to regain some of her everyday vernacular, said now in a hurried whisper rather than an excited shout. 'Dotty, this is bloody fantastic news. Isn't it fantastic news? Why are you looking at me like this isn't—'

'Fantastic news?'

She shrugged. 'Well, yeah! Seriously' — she reached across the table to grab my hand — 'babe, this is next level stuff and you're acting like you're delivering news of a death. What's the deal? Tell me everything. Wait,' she interrupted my flow before it started, 'let me get that coffee and then tell me everything. I'm just bloody delighted for you' — she paused to kiss my head on her way past — 'can I get you anything?'

I glanced to the table next to ours. 'Do you want to share a pizza?'

* * *

Tots and I were full of meat feast wood-fired goodness, and I had to admit, the food had at least helped to calm my nerves and warm me through.

While we were eating, I explained the deal: a Dear Dotty collection. It would be a book containing *all* the letters I'd written to myself since the new project started, peppered with unanswered letters from 'The Vault', as Candice referred to it. Her editorial team would contact the original letter writers to ask whether their write-ins could be featured as part of the collection. The whole thing would be annotated with diary entries and field notes from an advice columnist, and it would, in the end, amount to a real-life, hardback publication initially, with paperback to follow.

Tots wiped her mouth clean of pizza grease and dropped the napkin on the table. 'Well, bugger me. Hey, did you ever call that woman from the cooking class?'

I groaned and dropped my head back. 'Tots! Can we focus?'

'What? I saw the napkin and it reminded me. Did you?'

'No, no I didn't,' I answered flatly.

'Okay, well we'll swing back to that.'

Of course we will.

I leaned an elbow on the table and propped my forehead against my palm. With my free hand I half-heartedly picked at the slice of pizza I had abandoned on my plate. 'I realise I must seem like the most ungrateful writer on the face of the earth, because someone has literally walked into my life and dropped a dream on me, and here I am . . .'

'Being sad about it?' Tots finished my sentence.

210

'Not sad, just . . . overwhelmed.'

'About the book deal itself, or about . . . everything?'

I shrugged. 'Everything, I suppose. Good grief, just look at this year. I started it as an advice columnist with a semi-decent following, a relatively private social life, thanks to a carefully tailored social media presence, a nice home, and a good girlfriend. And now I'm—'

'An even more successful columnist?' Tots interrupted. Although I kept my head firmly propped in my hand, I managed an awkward glance her way. 'With a greater following, a *real* social media presence that you don't have to tailor, a nicer home? The only thing you're missing is the girlfriend, really, and given that you've replaced that with a book deal from a leading publisher, I'm struggling to see the problem here, Dotty.'

I covered my face with both hands. 'Am I an ungrateful cow?'

'No, silly.' Tots waited until I peered at her through my fingers. 'I would never call you a cow.'

I spluttered a laugh. 'Thank you. I think.'

Tots looked out over the surrounding area and stayed quiet for a minute or two. When I followed her stare, I realised that, if I looked hard enough, I could still see frosted patches of grass left over from the morning, yet to thaw out. I tried to make the most of this break in our big talk and took a few deep breaths. If nothing else, I was glad to have aired the problem — *the non-problem, should that be?* — with someone whose views I valued and trusted, even though the problem was very much still there, flitting about London, minding its own business, waiting for an email from me.

'Do you know,' Tots started again, startling me out of my self-pity, 'I thought when you started all of this, the Dear Dotty letters to yourself or whatever, I thought you really wanted to change. Like, drastic, substantial change. But I think the real issue here is that you don't' — she shrugged and turned back to face me — 'and that's fine. There's nothing wrong with wanting to stay the same and be the same, yada-yada.' She waved a hand around like there was more there to add but she didn't embellish it. 'It's totally fine if that's the life you want for yourself. You might run out of advice to give eventually' — she shrugged again — 'but I guess that's okay, too. The important thing is you know I love you, and I support you. You know that, right?'

'Right . . .' I answered, though there was uncertainty snaked through the response.

'So, that's your answer.'

'What's my answer, sorry?' I wasn't altogether sure I understood — or maybe I just didn't *like* it — a word that Tots had said.

She sipped her drink, which must have been cold by then, and I wondered whether she was doing it to delay some sort of reveal. 'You stay as you are. You turn down the book deal, you don't call What's-her-name, you keep up Dear Dotty until . . . I don't know, you get bored, or you run out of advice to give your-self or whatever, and this can all just have been a nice backlash to Caitlin leaving you that helped to distract you for a while.'

'Tots!' My voice was high-pitched, blistering with sudden outrage. There were at least three other tables looking in our direction, but I didn't have the capacity to care or apologise for my squeal. 'I can't believe you would even say that. These past months have been major, *major* for me; I've changed so much already and I've worked really bloody hard, I'll have you know, not least cooking you lot casseroles at every turn and trying not to burn the bloody sausages while I was at it, but I've tried really hard at other things, too, and I've completely overhauled entire chunks of my life and . . .' My steam died as sharply as it had risen. Tots sipped her drink again and winked at me over the rim. 'And I'm scared of more change.'

Tots looked far too satisfied with herself. 'I know.'

I nodded slowly and looked out over our surroundings again. 'I'm not ready for more changes after the changes I've already made.'

'I know.'

I turned to face my beautiful, clever, sneaky friend. 'How did you get to be so wise?'

Tots shrugged. 'It's a gift.'

'What on earth am I going to do, Tots?'

'Well' — she looked at the emptied plates and cups between us — 'you can buy me a coffee after all, given the sage wisdom I've just served you. But you can listen to this next piece of wisdom and listen good, okay? I know I don't do this for a living or whatever but, babe, I'm about to serve you some gold.' I tried to take her seriously, even though a welcome smile was breaking out over my face. Tots reached across the table to take my hand and I matched the gesture. 'I know that change is the scariest thing in the entire world' — she pulled my hand to her mouth and gave it a quick kiss — 'but no one is ever ready for it.'

CHAPTER THIRTY-THREE

Climbing five hundred and twenty-eight steps to get a bird's-eye view of London wasn't exactly my idea of a good time. But I had long ago discovered that the best and easiest way to get my mother to visit was by luring her there with an attraction she hadn't seen yet.

Thank goodness the city was forever changing, or we might one day run out of things to do. That day hadn't arrived just yet, though, because when I was setting my carefully constructed trap for her I discovered the gem that is St Paul's Cathedral. I had an entire spreadsheet of things that we had and hadn't done, and this entry still remained unhighlighted. I had to assume it was because the sheer number of steps involved had always encouraged me to find something, *anything* else for us to do. I'd been hurried when I decided to invite Mum up, though, and a quick decision had been called for.

Of course, now I was sitting at the front of the cathedral, tucking into my smoked ham and mustard sandwich, I couldn't help but wonder whether Mum had vastly underestimated the fuel we were going to need for the journey up — and down. Mum's idea of a nice lunch in London had always been a quiet spot — which we could never truly find because, hello, it's London — with a sandwich. And that day, I'd foolishly left her in charge of deciding where those sandwiches came from.

'I don't think there's anything wrong with a Tesco meal deal,' she announced before taking another bite of her Ploughman's.

'There isn't, Mum,' I reassured her, 'but I told you that I'd treat us to something. We could have eaten indoors. You know, somewhere *warm*.'

'I know your idea of something.' She paused to undo the awkward lid on her Coke Zero. 'Why are these lids all attached these days? That's what I really want to know.'

I smiled. 'That's a really good question, Mum.'

'Right' — she folded up her sandwich box — 'are we ready for this?'

I eyed the structure in front of us. Beautiful and intimidating as it was, yes, I was ready.

After the first hundred steps or so, I felt less ready. Despite Mum's promises — 'I'm sure we just need to get into a rhythm of climbing' — I didn't seem to be finding her assured rhythm. She spent the next one hundred and fifty steps telling me the latest goings-on in the village, which I listened to determinedly, not least because it meant that I didn't have to juggle climbing, talking, *and* breathing, which I think would have been a stretch.

'Nine, eight, seven . . .' Mum insisted on ringing out her own countdown the closer we got to our first pitstop. 'Oh, Dotty, it's . . .' She obviously couldn't find the right word to encapsulate her awe so instead she settled for a wistful sigh. I gave myself a proverbial pat on the back for finding a tourist attraction that had actually rendered my mother speechless — which was something I thought The Whispering Gallery might like to have listed in its brochure.

'Apparently when the architect designed this space he wasn't even thinking about acoustics,' I parroted from the webpages I'd read six hours ago, 'it was just something that

215

visitors noticed as more and more people started to spend time here, that if you whispered something on one side then you could hear it on the other.'

'No!'

'Honestly' — I laughed — 'that's what I've been told anyway. Even thirty-three metres away' I pointed, 'all the way to the other side.'

Mum turned to face me with the excitement of a child in her eyes. 'Shall we try it?'

I nodded. 'I think it would be rude not to. I'll go—'

'I'll go to the other side,' she interrupted, already hurrying away.

'Okay, sure, that works, too.'

I hadn't told Mum my news yet. She thought she'd been invited to London for an easy day out — mammoth step-climbing endeavours included — rather than a big reveal of any kind. But I hadn't wanted to bait her with the news. There was nothing more unsettling, as far as I was concerned, than an 'I've got something to tell you' phone call or text, so I'd wanted to save the announcement until I could deliver it in person, even though I was still strangely nervous about saying it aloud.

I watched as she continued to hurry all the way to the opposite side of the dome and smiled as I thought back over what Tots had said. It had been a week since our talk about change, about accepting change, and I'd continued to play soundbites of it like affirmations in my head since: 'No one is ever ready for it.'

But somehow, I felt like I was.

Mum waved her arms from the other side of the space to signal that she was in position, still beaming at me all the while, too. I gave her a thumbs up, lowered my mouth close to the wall on my side, and said, 'I've signed a contract for a book deal.'

'What!'

Mum had forgotten to abide by the whispering rule . . .

'Dotty, that's—'

'Ssh!'

'—brilliant,' Mum dropped to a whisper for the final word. I definitely heard it, though, all the way around the dome.

No longer concerned by architecture and whispering, Mum rushed back to greet me, faster than she'd left me only moments ago, and she threw her arms around me with such force that it knocked me unsteady. She was whispering something but between the acoustics and the happy tears it was anyone's guess what she might have been mumbling.

'Oh, my darling, darling Dotty' — she held me at arm's length by the shoulders, and it was only then that I realised I was crying the tiniest bit — 'this is just fantastic news. What on earth has been happening in your life?' She threw her head back and laughed.

That's a mighty fine question, Mum . . .

From one gallery to the next, I told Mum about Candice's offer and Elza's support. It would be a Dear Dotty collection featuring the life and letters of yours truly, punctuated by letters from readers that I'd be able to choose myself — the bits that, regrettably, there hadn't been space for the first time around.

Two days after my talk with Tots, I'd asked Elza for a meeting, and she and I had called Candice together. In that time, there had been a flurry of draft contracts and tweaks that had made me realise just how much Candice's team valued the book already, if the speed at which they got contracts sorted was anything to go by. They were giving me twelve months to put the book together, which also gave me a solid year to work out who I was and what I was doing with my life. I work better with a deadline — though I was under no disillusions about the impracticalities of 'finding myself' in a year either. I'd told Candice, 'I might still be a mess in a year, you know?' She'd laughed and answered, 'Marvellous, we'll get a sequel.'

'My lovely Dotty.' The open air was whipping my hair around by then and Mum reached up and tucked a few strands behind my ear. 'You aren't a mess. You're something . . . wonderful.' She let out the same wistful sigh I'd heard earlier, and

I gave myself another proverbial pat on the back for being able to elicit the same response from her that she'd given to one of the city's best-loved pieces of architecture.

At the top of the climb — *at last!* — we were greeted with views that stunned us both into silence, without so much as a wistful noise. The top of the cathedral gave off a bird's-eye view of the River Thames, the Shard, the Tate Modern, and a wealth of other places that Mum and I had either been to or planned to go to — though we'd never quite seen them from this angle. We were packed in close together by then, as other tourists had overtaken us to the top. Mum made the most of the proximity and wrapped an arm around my shoulders to pull me in for a squeeze. In doing so she forced a deep and hearty breath out of me.

'You will never know, Dotty, how desperately proud I am of you.'

'Not as proud as I am of you,' I answered.

She unleashed me and went back to admiring the city. 'Don't be daft. I haven't done anything for you to be proud of.'

I smiled. I had a feeling she wouldn't remember…

'When I was thirteen,' I started, 'I told you that I wanted to be a surgeon.'

A curt laugh hiccupped out of her. 'Grief, that's right, you did.'

'Do you remember what you said, when I told you that?'

Mum turned and gave me a raised eyebrow. 'Was it something horrible?'

'You've never said anything horrible to me, Mum, apart from that time I came home with my lip pierced.'

She tutted. 'Well really, Dotty, that was awful on you.'

I grabbed her hand and laced my fingers through hers, before leaning forward to set a kiss on her cheek. 'You told me that I hated blood too much to be a surgeon.' Mum threw me a quizzical glance. 'And then you said . . .'

I watched her face lighten as the memory clicked into place. 'You're going to be a writer.'

Dear Dotty,

Life has changed again! I'm starting to think the only constant thing in life is its total inability to stay the same for any period of time. Though I suppose that's part of the journey, isn't it? I signed a book deal — and this is my way of announcing it to the world — and I'm terrified and excited in equal measure. I am still trying, desperately, achingly trying, to do something new and bold and brave whenever the opportunity presents itself — though the book deal feels so big I think it could easily be counted as those three things, if not more. But there's an opportunity that I missed, over a month ago now, that I wanted to write in about.

I've been a single pringle since my partner and I broke up. Somehow, it's been months. As far as I know, she's moved on with another partner, and I'm genuinely happy for her — as long as she's happy. Recently though, for the first time since the break-up, a woman gave me her number. She was gorgeous and funny and, from what I saw, a very good cook. But I didn't call. Instead, I tacked the number to my fridge — where it still is now — so I could periodically eye it suspiciously as though it's something that's about to bite. I wasn't, and haven't been, brave enough, Dotty. And it's been weeks since this happened. Did I miss my shot? Will she have met some other tortured writer with a deep love of seafood pastas by now? Is it worth asking, just in case?

So many questions, Dotty, so many questions . . .

With love and thanks (& questions),
Dotty xxx

CHAPTER THIRTY-FOUR

And just like that, I was shopping for Christmas ornaments. Of course I'd celebrated Christmas in the flat before. But as part of the great clear-out, one of the many things marked To Go was the box of ornaments that Caitlin and I used to decorate our first ever Christmas tree together. Incidentally, the Christmas tree also went.

So. I foolishly decided that my brave thing for the day would be to take myself out into London at Christmas — which was essentially Christmas on steroids by anyone's standards — to find a tree that I could stomach having in the flat.

It has never been an insider secret that I am something of a Grinch at this time of year. Caitlin hated that about me. Nothing bad ever happened around Christmastime, apart from the enforced cheer and the fact that you can't go anywhere without someone offering you food — which, admittedly, would be a good thing at any other time of the year. But *themed* food — eggnog, mince pies, other . . . Christmassy things — was another type of food altogether. There were too many social events, too many jobs to get through, and too many reasons not to be in the comfort of my own home.

But the girls had been insistent. *I* was hosting Christmas this year, and they'd told me in no uncertain terms that they simply wouldn't attend unless there was a tree. I'd thought of using that as my get-out-of-jail card and taking Mum up on her offer of a Women's Institute Christmas retreat — but buying a tree seemed like the lesser evil of the two.

The city — which had been drip-feeding me Christmas for *weeks* already now — had been entirely made over with trees and fake snow every which way you turned. The first hard task of the day turned out to be finding a coffee that didn't have cinnamon either in or on it. In the end, I ordered a breakfast tea to go and then launched myself back into the wilds of London — or, as I was now coming to think of it, Christmas-town.

And, of course, the added bonus of Christmas joy was that there were couples, loved up and blissful couples, everywhere. I dodged a husband and wife arguing over gift vouchers, two teenagers taking a selfie in front of a glowing tree and two women who were definitely my age, definitely having a heated discussion over whether to go ice-skating or not, and definitely making me unexpectedly jealous in the process.

'Grumpy, grumpy Dotty,' I mumbled to myself as I wandered into one of my go-to homeware shops. It was another landscape that had been attacked by spray-on snow, fairy lights, and Wham!'s 'Last Christmas' — shortly to give way to Mariah Carey, I was sure — but at least it was a haven from the outside world for a minute.

It wasn't that I resented the couples, only—

Actually, that might be a partial lie.

I was a week on from having shared the Dear Dotty letter where I'd spilled my proverbial innards over my lack of bravery with Alia. Elza had lapped it up. 'Everyone loves a budding romance,' she'd told me, and she'd only shushed me when I'd corrected her and said that, *actually, it wasn't a romance at all.* Candice had called me about the letter, too — called me, directly, which was still a wild thing to get my head around — and congratulated me on 'a triumphant bit of bravery and smart thinking'. It didn't particularly feel like either of those things, though, not least because I still hadn't coaxed myself into calling Alia.

But what I had done was turn my social media into a hotbed of 'Have you called the girl yet?' comments that were scattered across literally every photo that I'd posted since the letter went out. The marketing team at work had gone as far to suggest I make an Instagram story that featured a poll: *Do I call the girl or not? Vote yes or no below.* The thought alone had been enough to make me want to throw my phone out of the nearest window — and for someone who uses their phone as much as I do, that was quite the threat.

'Do you need any help today, Miss?' a chirpy young woman — dressed like an elf — stopped me to ask.

'I'm all good, thank you.' I smiled and kept moving so I couldn't ask if *she* needed help, to escape the green and red mess that she'd been forced to wear to work.

'You just give one of us elves a call if you change your mind.'

I picked up a snow globe that showed two people standing close together. They were looking longingly into each other's eyes and one of them was doing a Hollywood foot-pop that I thought was intended to make the scene that bit more romantic. I grimaced, groaned, and put it straight back on the shelf.

I was glad when my phone started to hum in my pocket and gave me a distraction from what I was meant to be doing.

'Hi, Mum.'

'Hi, love. Have I caught you at a bad time?'

I assessed my surroundings. 'It's actually a great time. I'm Christmas ornament shopping.'

'Oh, I . . . Dotty, that doesn't sound like you at all.'

'Funny that' — I pinched a bauble between finger and thumb — 'it doesn't feel much like me.'

'Why are you doing that?'

I sighed. 'Because I need to decorate the flat for Christmas. For the girls.'

There was a short pause. 'Love, there's still space on the WI retreat if you want to change your mind. The cottages aren't all fully booked, and I know my girls would be more than happy to host an extra mouth. Gwen is on cooking duty and she's mad about having as many people to feed as possible.'

Gwen sounds like my kind of person, I thought. 'That's really kind, Mum, but it'll be fine. Nice,' I corrected my downbeat tone, 'it'll be nice. The girls and I will have a great time and I'll be drunk by the time lunch is served.'

'And you feel okay about the cooking?'

'Why was it you called, Mum?' I was keen to change the subject. I'd watched far too many YouTube videos about preparing a turkey, and it was something that haunted my dreams enough already without Mum offering me a tutorial.

'Well, it's a funny thing, actually, when you look at it.'

I paused my browsing. Historically, when Mum described something as 'a funny thing', it usually meant that it wasn't funny at all . . .

'Mm?' I encouraged her.

'I was at the library the other day picking up my book club read for the month. We're reading that book, you know the one I mentioned . . . Gosh, I can't even think of the name of it now, by that woman, the one who does all the interviews.' She continued to add a string of details that didn't get either of us any closer to knowing the name of the book she was referring to. 'Anyway, I was in the library picking up my book, and they hadn't got it ready for me even though I'd reserved it, which was a bit of a nightmare' — I loved Mum's definition of a nightmare — 'so I said it was no trouble, as long as they had a copy on a shelf, which they did. So, they wrote down the shelf number for me and Suzie; you know Suzie, you went to school together. Do you remember her? Elaine's daughter? She works at the library now and—'

'Mum, is Suzie relevant to the wider plot?'

She seemed to hesitate before admitting, 'Well no, I don't suppose she is. Suzie offered to get it for me but I said it was no bother, I could get it myself. And I must have been so busy studying this piece of paper, the one with the shelf number on it, that I completely lost sight of myself and went crashing straight into someone.'

'Mm?' I encouraged her again, given that she seemed to have taken a strategic pause.

'Well, it was a man.'

Oh no . . .

'And long story short . . .' I nearly snorted at the fact that, so far, there had been nothing short about Mum's short story. 'He asked for my telephone number.'

'He what?'

I heard a crunch under my foot as I asked the question. When I lifted my boot I found the remains of a red bauble beneath it.

'I'm so sorry,' I hurried to apologise to the staff member who appeared out of nowhere, 'so sorry. I'll take the tag, I'm more than happy to pay for it on the way out.'

'Dotty, are you okay?'

'Honestly, it happens all the time, hon, don't even worry,' the elf — not to be confused with the first elf — reassured me.

'Dotty?'

'Sorry, Mum — you said he asked for your number?'

'He did.' She giggled girlishly. 'And, well, I gave it to him.'

'You did.'

'And we're going for a cup of tea later today.'

'You are?'

'Dotty, why are you being strange?'

'I am?'

I steadied myself with a deep breath. 'I am being strange. Sorry, Mum. This is . . . really exciting,' I managed, not least because I knew it was what Mum needed, but secondly, because it *was* really exciting. In living memory I couldn't actually recall Mum having a single date with a man, or even claiming interest in such a thing. But given that it had been over twenty years since her failed marriage, I thought she was owed at least *some* romance in her life by now. She'd sworn off men after Dad, understandably so. By the time Mum found out about the affair, it had already been going on for at least a year. Dad had actually seemed *relieved* when it was all out in the open and he could finally get away from us. So, this, an easy encounter with a nice man, was well overdue. 'This is brilliant, Mum. What do you know about him?'

'You're not going to look him up on social media, are you?'

Damn it. 'I mean, I'm not going to do that *now*, no.'

Mum laughed and then launched into a long and winding explanation about Phil, the retired risk analyst who'd moved to Mum's area recently. He had two grown daughters and one granddaughter — 'He's a *grandad*, can you believe it?' — who he saw as often as possible. Beyond that he filled his time with golf, although he hadn't managed to find a good course since moving, and he enjoyed reading in his spare time, too. Phil was so funny and charming, tall and quite dashing, especially for an older man, and he . . .

The details continued and I continued to listen as I walked around the shop. But somewhere between baubles and fibre optic Christmas trees, my rapt attention turned to the wailing of a winter storm rushing through my ears.

It took two hard blinks for me to convince myself that what I *thought* I was seeing was what I was *actually* seeing but yes, there she was. There *they* were. Caitlin and Lili from The Gym. Lili from The Gym was running her hands through her hair in what looked like frustration. She dropped her hands to her sides but then pointed to a tree. Caitlin shrugged, a non-committal, not-having-a-good-time shrug that I recognised only too well from parties, nights out, and nights in alike. They couldn't decide which tree to get. But they were *buying a tree*.

'Mum, I'm so sorry, I'm about to be interrupted,' I lied. 'Can I call you back when I'm home? I'll only be about half an hour.'

'Of course, love, absolutely. Love you.'

'Love you.'

After that, I had never navigated London so quickly before in my life. I dodged couples, ducked Christmas decorations, and hailed a taxi home as quickly as humanly possible. Then I ordered a tree online and spent half a month's worth of rent on decorations that I had absolutely no interest in buying.

But I was home — hyperventilating, but home — and the tree would arrive the next day. Until then, there was my duvet.

CHAPTER THIRTY-FIVE

My Christmas tree came with some assembly required, which, coincidentally, was how I felt for about three days after my attempt at Christmas ornament shopping.

My bravery had withered into a much quieter version of what it had been. I did a heinous amount of online shopping for things I didn't need, worked through the Dear Dotty inbox, cleaned the flat from top to bottom, and then set about making the place into a veritable winter wonderland, complete with Christmas hits playing through my speakers. The sudden urge to decorate could be easily explained by the fact that I simply didn't want to leave the flat, and this, of all things, gave me something to do. Besides which, the jingle bells, winter wonderlands, and blue Christmases blasting through my home did actually seem to be helping. I wasn't sure whether it was hermit mode, or something like it, or whether I was just deathly afraid of running into Caitlin and Lili from The Gym for a third time. Not that I'd managed to work out why I was afraid of that, exactly. Was it meeting them as Single Dotty? Meeting them as Dotty with a Book Deal? I oscillated between the discomfort of the former and the confidence of the latter, even though the former hadn't been a problem at all until I'd seen Caitlin and what was very, very clearly her actual girlfriend, rather than someone she'd just gone out for a flirty brunch with that one time.

I let out an almighty groan and rested my head against the window frame behind me. I'd been sitting in the window seat for the past three hours — and two cups of tea — but I was mindful of the time.

The girls, as though sensing that I needed a distraction from something, even though I'd told them nothing of the Caitlin spot yet, had suggested that they come over and help me decorate the flat. It felt like a double-edged offer: I was desperate to see them, but when I looked around at the Christmas tree, the fairy lights, and the cotton wool wadding that was meant to act as snow, tucked neatly around photo frames and side lamps, I felt as though this, now, was quite enough, without their Christmas spirit invading too.

Not that Elouise was giving me much choice: *We'll bring food and gin. Do you have fancy glasses and fruit? Xoxo*

Fancy glasses had been one of my online purchases. They'd arrived, big and bulbous and ready to be filled with pink grapefruit gin, slimline tonic, and an array of fruit that thankfully I hadn't even had to leave the flat for either. There really wasn't much that you couldn't get delivered in London.

I can cook for us? I'd posted into the group chat, offering a generosity that I didn't feel, but I reasoned it would keep me busy — busier still — if nothing else.

Take a break from cooking! Marissa had replied. *We'll bring takeaway. Xx*

I managed to drag myself from the living room to the bedroom to change out of my jogging bottoms and hoodie, and into drainpipe jeans and a white jumper with bell-shaped sleeves that made me feel that bit more like myself. I decided I could keep the slipper socks though — they were one of the many perks of a night in.

I'd just pulled my hair into an updo that looked like one of those deliciously messy styles that takes ages to complete, even though it actually took a solid thirty seconds when the buzzer to the flat sounded.

I checked my watch. The girls were never early. I could only assume their need for gin was as great as mine.

I unlocked the downstairs door. 'Come on up. I'll leave the front door open.'

I was in the kitchen testing out my new measurement glass — a neat, squat little thing that made my drink-making that bit more professional, rather than sloshing in any given amount and judging by eye whether it was a single or a double. I'd measured out the first of the shots and poured them into glasses when I heard the door click open.

'Am I doing singles or doubles?' I shouted.

There came a hesitant noise from behind me. 'Ah. I'll just take a water, if that's okay?'

The voice was enough to scold me. I shot around, measuring glass in one hand and gin bottle in the other, and there she was, standing in what used to be our living room.

'Caitlin, I—'

'You're expecting company.' She smiled and nodded at the glasses. 'I won't stay long.'

'Why are you— I mean, what are you— Is this . . .'

She laughed. 'For a woman with a book deal under her belt you're not doing so good with your words.'

I shook my head as though loosening myself from a trance, then I turned to set down the bottle and measurer. Quite frankly, I was amazed I hadn't dropped them, such was the shock coursing through me.

When I turned back around to face her I found that she was assessing the living room, studying one spot, then another.

'This looks like a completely different flat.'

'I've been decorating. The girls and I are doing Christmas here.'

'I see that.' She looked bewildered. 'I mean, it's generally different though. Not just the Christmas stuff.'

'Yeah, well, it had a bit of a makeover.'

'You both did' — she turned to face me — 'in a good way, obviously.'

Back-handed kind of compliment, but okay . . .

'Caitlin, don't think me rude or anything, but what the hell are you doing here?'

She took a step closer and without thinking I recoiled, only to back up against the kitchen work surface. I was literally cornered.

'I saw you the other day,' she admitted sheepishly. 'Christmas shopping?'

Arses.

'Right.'

'You scarpered before I got the chance to say hello.' She stopped speaking as though just that was an entire explanation for her being here now.

'So, you thought you'd stop in to say hi?'

'No, I . . .' It was Caitlin's turn to shake her head, but it looked like a gesture of confusion on her. She lifted a bag from by her side that I hadn't even noticed. 'I wanted to drop this off. I've finally settled into my new place and I found, well, it's some stuff of yours that you might want. I must have taken it with me by accident. I know you boxed up mine, but I don't know, I thought we might be at a place where' — she shook her head again — 'where we could tolerate seeing each other.'

I narrowed my eyes at her phrasing. 'I've never not been able to tolerate seeing you.'

'Then why did you scarper?'

I turned to grab a glass from an open cupboard. 'Oh, I don't know, maybe because I didn't feel like running into you buying Christmas decorations with your new girlfriend.' I slid a glass of water across the counter. 'Did you want ice with that?'

She laughed, but it was a nervous sound. 'I think it's chilly enough in here as it is.'

'Do you want to sit?' I nodded towards the living room. 'New sofas and everything.'

'Thank you, yeah.' She reached forward to take her drink, and I waited until she'd walked towards the living room before I made to move there, too. 'I probably should have called first. But you probably wouldn't have answered.' She set her drink down on a coaster and sat tentatively on one end of the sofa. It occurred to me that she didn't know which side was mine anymore, which was my preferred seat. 'Are you going to tell me you would have done?' she asked when I took too long to find a response.

I shrugged. 'No.'

'At least you're honest.'

'I wouldn't have answered because I wouldn't have known what there was to say.' I took a seat in one of the armchairs, the greatest distance from her.

'Dotty, how I left . . .' She stopped and shook her head again, wearing that same look of confusion. 'I've done a lot of thinking, and how I left, it wasn't okay—'

'Caitlin, we really don't need to be the couple that does this,' I interrupted. I didn't want to stop her from speaking her truth, or whatever it was that she planned to do. But I wasn't in the market for an unnecessary conversation either. So, I sucked in a belly breath and, despite not exactly feeling it, I managed to drum up yet another bit of courage. 'I understand why you left.'

Her head jerked back in surprise. 'You do?'

I laughed. 'I mean, I told you to, didn't I?'

Caitlin laughed at that, too, and she seemed to relax. 'You seem to be doing well though, since . . . well, since everything?'

'New flat, *some* new clothes—'

'Probably not as many as Elouise would like for you,' she joked. There was an easy familiarity behind the comment. Of course, Elouise would have liked a whole wardrobe makeover for me. Of course, Caitlin knew me well enough to know that. 'New column, too?'

'Well, the same Dear Dotty in lots of ways.'

'And an entirely new one in others.'

My head shot up and I caught her smile. 'It's not a bad thing,' she added.

'No,' I answered, 'no, I suppose it isn't.'

'It's what I wanted for you, in lots of ways.'

I huffed a laugh. 'For me to change completely?'

'Goodness, Dotts, no,' she rushed out. 'Never completely. I just . . .'

'You just wanted me to care again.'

'Yes' — there was sadness around the fringes of her answer — 'yeah, I just wanted that.'

'Well . . .' I hesitated. 'I'm sorry I didn't give you that.'

Admittedly, if someone had asked me to imagine a sit-down conversation with Caitlin, there wasn't a single version in which *I* apologised. Or at the very least, not where I apologised first. But there it was, sitting on the coffee table between us, and it wasn't just lip service. I *was* sorry that I couldn't give her that, that I chose not to give her that. Caitlin had deserved more. It wasn't exactly my first time admitting it to myself, but it was my first time admitting it quite so easily. I'd found, recently, that there was a fine line between self-compassion and self-excusing. And this, this moment right here, I decided, marked out that line.

'I'm sorry that I let things slide how I did,' I continued. 'It wasn't my intention, but then, I don't know if anyone ever intends to do stuff like that.'

Caitlin inspected the words with a suspicious eye. 'I left.'

I lingered a second before answering. 'Yes, I . . . well, I'm not blind to that.'

'But *you're* apologising?'

I laughed. Her expression was so perplexed I couldn't help but find it amusing — find the whole situation amusing — that this person, this woman who had known me through so much, who had known me so well, now didn't know me at all.

'At least I can still surprise you.'

'Apparently so,' she answered with genuine warmth. 'And, for the record, I'm sorry as well. Not only for leaving how I did but for going about it with the whole' — she gestured with her free hand while the other still clutched the bag — 'letter and the sneakiness of it. For — *Christ* — even for starting to see Lili as soon as I did, that was, I don't know what that was, or what it is.'

'You met someone you want to buy Christmas decorations with' — I shrugged — 'that's allowed.'

Caitlin seemed to weigh up her answer with great care. 'Yeah,' was all she managed. And I decided to leave that dog sleeping where it was.

'I don't mean to rush this' — I glanced at my watch — 'but the girls are actually due here any minute, and while I commend your bravery in busting in on me unannounced—'

She let out a curt laugh as she stood from the sofa. 'You are absolutely right in thinking I don't want the same with them. I can't see them being quite so forgiving.'

I smiled. 'They're my friends. It's their job not to be.'

'Thanks for the water,' she said weakly as she moved towards the door, 'and for the time.' For a second we could no longer look each other in the eye. 'Dotty, are we . . .' she started the question staring into the hallway, but then turned quite deliberately to face me. 'Are we good?'

And to my surprise, I didn't even have to think about the answer. 'I think we are, yeah.'

I was already three glugs into my first gin when the girls arrived ten minutes later with enough food to feed an army.

Caitlin and I might have been good, but even bloody Superwoman needs a stiff drink after a shock.

CHAPTER THIRTY-SIX

I had spent months thinking that seeing Caitlin was nothing short of the worst thing in the world. After that first non-encounter, that had pushed me into leaving London altogether for a while, it worried me that another encounter, direct or indirect, might send me screaming to the Scottish Highlands to live out my days in solitude.

So after the unexpected visit, and the unwanted closure — a word that ordinarily made me recoil back into my own body — I kept waiting for the crash to come. I kept waiting for the unbearable burden of heartbreak to settle itself on me again, that would make words too difficult to write, food too difficult to chew, London too difficult a place to exist in, owing to the sheer proximity to Caitlin that the city afforded me.

So, imagine my surprise when, four days later, I was sitting in the window seat of my flat drinking tea like I always did, watching the city for another morning. I stayed tucked up beneath the warmth and comfort of a soft fleece blanket — I was still finding these stashed everywhere since Elouise had remade the place — and smiled to myself as Christmas lights came alive in café windows and people ordered their morning cinnamon-this and gingerbread-that to start their days. I even felt moved to switch on the lights of my own Christmas tree, although their magic was a little lost in the morning light. After a quiet hour of that I made toast, which wasn't too difficult to chew at all, and partway through eating that simple breakfast I went treading into my home office to tackle the Dear Dotty inbox that had gone unloved for two days owing to meetings with the marketing team, with Elza, and with the marketing team again.

Stepping up the column was amazing and all, but I was starting to worry that the column getting bigger and bolder in terms of publicity would eventually stop me from *actually being able to write the column*. It had been nothing short of absolute joy to sneak into my calendar the day before and block out *WRITING DAY* from nine until five — or, as long as things took me.

I was determined to work through every single letter, no matter how many rounds of toast it would mean eating.

I had answered six letters when I decided to upgrade my cup of tea to an entire pot. I updated my Instagram while the kettle boiled, then I made a pot of tea big enough to get me through to lunchtime. It felt quintessentially British to wander back into my office with an actual tray, laden with a teapot, milk jug, and mug, and featuring a muffin slathered in red and green icing that I'd nabbed from the office kitchen the day before. I hadn't quite upgraded to a cup and saucer yet, but I was sure that Mum would be elated when it inevitably happened. The teapot had been a present from her when Caitlin and I moved into the flat years ago, and I was sure that in that entire time, I'd used it maybe twice — both times when Mum had visited. I took a picture of my setup and sent it to her on WhatsApp, knowing it would take her at least two days to read, but it felt like an important moment of adulting to share all the same.

Even though I'd always told myself it was bad form to skim ahead through the inbox, specifically to seek out the juiciest subject lines, I couldn't resist a glance. I paused to pour out tea and I was midway to taking my first blissful sip when I spotted it — 'When she calls, do I answer?' — and I froze. My eyes shot across to the sender details and there was the validation I needed, enough to wind me into lowering my cup back down to my desk: Alia Kingsley.

Dear Dotty,

Life's a funny thing, isn't it? One minute you're minding your own business in a cooking class and the next minute you're giving your number to the woman you happened to be paired with to make seafood pasta. The thing is, she didn't call. And that's fine! I'm a grown-up and I wasn't exactly outlandish with my flirting — truth be told, she kind of made it hard to be. But then, after not calling, she pretty much sends up a blimp over the skies of London to tell me that she wanted to call. She even kept my number, so she said. She just still didn't know whether to use it. Now, I'm not normally one to be pushy with these things. But when a woman sends a blimp over London to say she wants to call you, it feels like a pretty big sign that she's looking for a nudge in a certain direction.

My worry, Dotty, is that if I nudge her, if I send up my own blimp to say, sure, I'll take the call, am I forcing her into it? Should she need a nudge? Maybe she just isn't ready to be dating, or in a place for it, and here I am cajoling her along. Argh, so many questions! But I suppose my own question, where I need a bit of advice, is if it takes her this long to call — assuming she does — should I answer? Would you?

Tell me your thoughts, Dotty, I wanna know 'em all.

With love and thanks,
Waiting On An Answer xxx

I read the letter four times, and then I threw back my lukewarm tea like I was taking a shot of something much stronger. I even glanced at the clock in the corner of my screen to see whether it was an appropriate time of day to actually take a shot but alas, the numbers were still on the wrong side of midday.

I ran my hands through my hair, poured another cup of tea, and then paced around my office while drinking it. Alia's letter hovered on the display of my screen, staring me down with every glance I braved towards it. I eventually caved and closed my browser window to see if it made it any easier to think.

'No, not a bit easier,' I answered aloud when my cup was empty again.

I went slinking off for a nervous wee and then, back in my office, I did the only sensible thing I could think of. I fumbled for my phone, thumbed through my contacts and hit dial.

'Can you talk?'

'Is it good news or bad?' Marissa answered. I heard her shifting around her office and imagined her shooing someone out, closing the door behind them. 'I've got a meeting in fifteen minutes.'

'Alia wrote back to me.'

'Who's Alia?'

I huffed down the line. Elouise would have remembered this sort of life detail. But then, Elouise couldn't be trusted for a sensible answer . . .

'Oh, wait! The cookery class woman? The woman on your fridge?'

'Yes, Marissa, the woman on my fridge.'

'Wait, she what?'

'You only have fifteen minutes, I need for you to follow this story faster!' My voice was filled with panic but I tried to steady it long enough to repeat, 'She wrote back to me.' I took a deliberate pause between each word. 'I just found the letter in my inbox from . . .' It occurred to me that I hadn't even thought to check when the letter had arrived — I'd been so blindsided by the mere arrival of it at all. 'Three days, it's been three days that I've been keeping her waiting for.'

'What did she even say?'

'She's asking for my advice on whether I'd answer if I called me after over a month.'

There was a long pause. 'I'm not sure that makes sense.'

'She wants to know whether to answer, if I call.'

'Good grief, it's like dating-ception.' Marissa sounded genuinely confused by the whole thing. There came a rustling from the background and then Marissa covered the speaker and said, 'This is an important call, can it wait?' A short pause before, 'Okay, thanks. I'll see you in the meeting.' She uncovered the phone and asked, 'So are you going to call her?'

'I don't know,' I whined, 'that's why I called you.'

I could practically hear Marissa thinking down the phoneline. 'How have you felt since you saw Caitlin?'

'What?'

'Just answer. How have you felt since you saw her?'

It was the second time in the space of a morning that I'd been blindsided. This wasn't exactly the approach I'd been expecting Marissa to take. I'd obviously told the girls about Caitlin's unannounced visit, and I'd also told them that I was fine with the whole thing. But now that I was backed into a corner of *really* thinking about it, I realised fine might have been an understatement. If anything, since seeing Caitlin I think that I'd been feeling—

'Lighter. I feel lighter since I saw her.'

'Then I think you should call this woman.'

I dropped slowly into my desk chair and pushed out a breath. 'Make your case.'

'Dotts, this might hurt a bit' — *Oh good* — 'but you checked out of yours and Caitlin's relationship a while before she left. I know the break-up came as a blow, naturally, because you were comfortable and you'd convinced yourself that comfortable was fine. But, for *months* now you've been going out of your way to bit by bit make yourself more uncomfortable with things in your life and if anything you seem, well, *more* comfortable. You seem more . . . Dotty. I think, if you're in the market for taking chances, which seems to have worked out for you just fine so far, then you should call the woman, go for a proper date drink, and hope for the best.'

I nodded along with Marissa's points, paying little attention to the sting of what she'd said about Caitlin — not least because I was slowly coming to terms with the reality that yes, I'd definitely been more checked out than I'd realised. But it had still been a blow and a heartbreak and a big thing to recover from. *Had I recovered from it*, I wondered, *or was I still in recovery?*

'Marissa, what if something goes wrong?'

'During *one* drink?'

'What if it's more than a drink?'

'What if it isn't?'

'It's like arguing with a six-year-old.'

'Dotty, please, you'd *know* if we were arguing about this. But there's nothing to argue about. You're going to call the woman, ask her for a drink, kiss her under some mistletoe and if nothing else you'll have had a nice holiday romance.'

'I'm not on holiday,' I answered flatly.

'My God, a *seasonal* romance then.'

I glanced around to my laptop and clicked open the letter again.

'All I'm saying,' Marissa started again, 'is if this woman is willing to give you a chance, a very public chance, might I add, to go for a drink with her, after *all this time* of waiting for you to call, I think, just maybe, it might be worth taking a chance on her.'

When I didn't answer she added, 'Consider it as taking a chance on yourself, too.'

I huffed a laugh. 'You ever think about switching careers?'

Marissa howled a curt laugh in answer. 'I'm far too close-minded to give people advice.'

'Well, you've done just fine this morning.'

'Just, think about what I've said, would you?'

I skimmed the letter from top to toe again. 'I will, I promise.'

'I love you, Dotts. Call me later.'

I promised Marissa I'd call, and then I spent another ten minutes staring at Alia's letter on my laptop screen. I grumbled and groaned and made some other nondescript noises before deciding that what I really needed was something else to drink. I couldn't stand the thought of any more tea — I didn't want something that would soothe me — so I took myself back to the kitchen with a quiet lie that I'd work out what to do after a tall glass of orange juice. Because that would help everything.

Aside from the fact that the orange juice was kept in the fridge. And the fridge was where Alia's number lived.

Dear Dotty,

    I've been doing some thinking about my break-up. Having seen my ex-partner recently, properly, for the first time since things ended, I've come to realise where some of the hurt really came from in the split. It wasn't just being left — although don't get me wrong, that leaves a sting for anyone. It was also losing the comfort of the life I had, which might be a big and bad thing to admit, but I'm saying it anyway. I was comfortable with my quiet London home and my quiet relationship that I'd settled into over the space of years. I didn't want the disquiet of navigating more nights out again to meet more people in the hope that someone might just like me. I was happy knowing someone liked me enough. But liking someone enough isn't always enough on its own. I can see that now. Sometimes you need fireworks, or at the very least sparklers. You need something that you're terrified to hold, or look at directly, because it's so blindingly brilliant that you don't know how you came to have it in your life to begin with. And NO, I'm not saying that's how every relationship needs to be — but I do think it's how every relationship should be at some point, whether that's the beginning, middle, or even the end. (No pressure, right?)

    Recently, a woman gave me her number for the first time since the break-up, and I didn't call. Then, I very publicly announced this fact through my column, as a big white flag that read: I wanted to call you, even though I didn't actually manage to do it. And she replied. She asked whether I'd answer, if I were in her shoes. The answer to that is that I really don't know, not least because that's not my thing to give advice on — not in this situation. But as to whether I will call, well, why didn't I to start with? Was I not ready then? Does that imply that I'm ready now? Gosh, does anyone ever know for certain if they're ready when one relationship ends, and you're thrown into the muddy terrain of another potentially beginning? Or am I simply asking too many questions

again, Dotty? I can't help but wonder how many hours of
my life have been spent asking questions that I can only get
the answers to by acting, not asking. And so here I am, a
woman who has spent the best part of a year making herself
uncomfortable — with introspection, wild water swimming,
and that one yoga class I managed — asking whether or not
feeling, living, being scared, might be better than asking all
these questions after all.

What do you think, Dotty?

With love, and a constant need for answers,
Dotty xxx

CHAPTER THIRTY-SEVEN

While standing bundled outside the Natural History Museum's ice rink, I was beginning to regret my offer of 'Lady's choice' when Alia had asked what I felt like doing for a first date. It was an awkward question to ask anyone, honestly, because who is *ever* ready to answer it? The prospect of offering her a simple drink felt utterly boring — especially after keeping her waiting on a phone call, and especially after she was kind enough to answer. Though she'd clearly been expecting a telemarketer from the tone she answered the call with. Still, when I'd handed the decision-making over to her, the last thing that crossed my mind was — I pushed out a shivery sigh — *ice-skating*. She'd suggested something festive, and I'd mumbled in agreement, mostly through nerves at what 'something festive' might mean. Then she'd suggested meeting at the ice rink, and I made the same noise again.

Now, here I was, wearing four layers and earmuffs on a first date.

I took another shaky glance at my watch and noticed that Alia was officially five minutes late. Naturally, I assumed she wasn't coming. *It's payback*, I thought. It's payback for me making her wait so long, so the advice columnist can write in her silly column about how she overshot things entirely and blew things with the first woman in over ten years to show a flicker of interest and—

Oh God, is that her?

I did a meerkat stretch upwards to peer over the huddle of teenagers that were shuffling about in front of me, and soon felt a rush — albeit a cold rush — of absolute relief. Needless to say, I hadn't exactly been calm about the prospect of a first date. Never mind a first date with someone who I perceived to be *entirely* out of my league. So it had been easy for the panic to spiral — not just today, but in the days prior to this, too. I'd lost count of the amount of worried phone calls the girls had had to field from me. I was fairly certain they'd even started answering in a rota system. But now, in place of a week's worth of panic, there came a rush of something more . . . *well, something!*

I waved to grab her attention and flashed my widest smile. Alia was wearing skintight jeans that were tucked into fur-trimmed boots, a jacket that I wagered was probably covering the same number of layers as me, and a beanie hat with a fur bobble on top that matched her footwear. Her hair was in loose curls that spiralled down from beneath the beanie and made her look the tiniest bit like the princess cartoons that so many of us had grown up with. She was, in short, quite gorgeous. And I was fast starting to regret the messy bun that I'd opted for, with only loose spirals hanging down around my face in what I hoped would look accidental and effortless — even though it had taken me nearly half an hour to get them right. The bun had seemed like a safe bet, though. Mum had always made me tie my hair up for sport, and ice-skating *was*, after all, a sport and—

Dotty, you are ridiculous.

I half-waved as she came a little closer, and when she smiled back it warmed me through.

'You look gorgeous,' she said by way of greeting, and I felt my knees buckle.

'That's the best hello I've had all week.' I hoped the reply sounded smooth. But when Alia leaned forward to kiss my cheek with a level of familiarity that I hadn't been at all braced for, I wagered that any smoothness I might have managed had now given way to the hot blush clawing up my cheeks. *Maybe she'll think it's the cold*, I consoled myself. I still tried to burrow my face a little further into my scarf as she pulled away.

'So, you finally decided to call, huh?' she said playfully. 'All that flirting I did over gin didn't give you the push you needed to begin with?'

Aha! So it was flirting!

'I'm just glad you decided to answer.'

She shrugged. 'Like I'd pass up a real date with *the* Dear Dotty. Just, ah, do me a favour?'

'Mm?' I murmured, my stomach tight at what might come.

'Don't write about the date?'

My face dropped.

Alia laughed and reached forward to squeeze my arm. 'I love that you write, and I think the column was perhaps . . . the *sweetest* way of apologising for not calling. But, I don't know, I'd just like it if some things weren't written about.'

Of course, it had crossed my mind that Alia might utterly hate the idea of me writing about her in the column. But I'd managed to knock the thought away, convincing myself that it was just another worry, just another over-feeling, of which there had been so many lately. I suffered the tiniest pang of guilt, then, that I'd brandished our meeting for all to read. Even though it had been done with the best of intentions.

'I can literally see you panicking,' she joked, 'but please don't? It was adorable. I'd just like to be able to sweep you off your feet without your readership knowing.'

'Sweep me off my feet, huh? Is that why you suggested ice-skating?'

She laughed again — a bubbly brilliant sound. 'I thought you said you'd been before?'

'I didn't say I was *good* when I came before,' I answered. 'Come on, you're going to have to do a lot of heavy lifting on this date.'

'Oh good' — she looped her arm through mine — 'that's exactly what I was hoping for . . .'

* * *

Despite the fact that I spent the majority of the ice-skating flat on my backside, there was an easiness to the whole date that I couldn't remember feeling before.

From the minute we set blades to ice, everything felt . . . natural. Admittedly, that might have been something to do with the physical barriers between us being instantly broken when I stepped from the side of the rink onto the ice and felt my feet whip out from under me, only to be saved by Alia's quick reflexes. From then on there was a lot of hand-holding and a lot of pulling. To my shame there actually *had* been a lot of lifting, too. But by the time our session was drawing to a close, Alia was cheering me on as she backwards skated in front of me, keeping her eyes on mine as I moved solo along the ice. Bambi-like in a way that she seemed to find endearing — *thank goodness* — I managed to move unaided back to the side of the rink without falling over once for a whole five minutes of our time there.

I tugged my feet from the skates, feeling child-like wonder at what we'd just done, and I couldn't decide whether it was the thrill of Alia, the experience of skating, the rush of cold to my burning cheeks, or a heady combination of all the above. But whatever the feeling was, I was desperate to bottle it. And, emboldened by that, I was even brave enough to ask—

'Do you want to grab a drink, before we call it a night?'

'A drink?' She looked up at me from lacing her boots. 'I'm starving after that!'

'Why don't we hit up a market, then? See if we can grab a cinnamon-dusted pretzel the size of our heads?'

Alia gave me a narrow-eyed look and a smirk as she stood level with me. 'I knew there was a reason I answered your call . . .'

Unlike my last first date — which had been approximately one hundred years ago, with Caitlin, when dinner counted as a share bucket of popcorn between us as we distractedly watched something at the cinema — the food on this date became an uninhibited experience. We both ordered warm cinnamon pretzels from the first Christmas market stall that we came to, and we ate them huddled to the side of the crowd, smiling at the sugar coating caught at our lips.

'How do you feel about eggnog?' Alia asked.

Eggnog sounded like the finest suggestion in the world to me in that moment. She and I held hands through the market under the pretence of not wanting to lose each other in the sea of bodies, but our hands stayed pressed tight together even as we huddled in the queue. We chatted effortlessly as we browsed the stalls and sipped our drinks, and I felt a swell of good feeling when Alia steered me to one side so she could buy a handful of Christmas decorations for her grandmother.

'She goes crazy for Christmas decorations,' she explained as she wedged her sparkly purchases into her bag. 'Now, next question, how do you feel about garlic bread?'

I narrowed my eyes. 'Is this a trick question?'

'A very important question is what it is.' She felt for my hand as we elbowed back into the crowd. And I found that I started to weigh the implications of her asking about something as potent as garlic bread on a first date. I mean, I *loved* garlic bread, obviously. But was it first date food? Was something *that* smelly really wise on a first date?

'You seem to be thinking very hard about your answer here,' she said when a few more seconds had passed.

'I'm weighing it up. If I say I love it, and you hate it, I could blow the whole evening.' I cast a sideways glance and caught Alia smiling.

'What if I say I love it, but I can't eat it alone because I don't want to be the only one smelling of garlic when I lean in to kiss you later?'

My face cracked open with a wide smile. I blushed and laughed and felt a rush of teenage feelings. Then I took Alia

to get warm garlic bread topped with melted cheese and car-
amelised onions. There was a thin string of mozzarella still
stuck to her bottom lip when I walked her back to the Tube
station — and it tasted fantastic.

CHAPTER THIRTY-EIGHT

The following morning I woke blissfully late, stretched out, and marvelled at the winter sunshine that was sneaking in through curtains I'd only managed to half-close the night before. After saying goodnight to Alia, I'd wandered home with the swagger of a woman on her third glass of wine.

We'd swapped messages to let the other know we were home safe — *Thanks for a lovely evening xxx* — and we'd established we would most definitely be doing it again. Alia had sent a message flooded with heart-eyed emojis by way of reviewing the garlic bread — *And the kiss wasn't bad either* ☺ *xxx* — and I'd decided that I would suggest Italian for our second date, somewhere with lashings of garlic on the menu. And the sleep that had come after that flurry of messages had been quiet and restorative.

Now, I skipped my morning scroll through social media, threw myself from bed with a groan befitting of someone ten years older than me — the bruises from skating were starting to form — and went straight to the kitchen to boil the kettle. I would have tea and sit in my window and bask in the quiet, I decided, and then—

Buzz. Buzz. Buzz.

The intercom to my building sounded. I was still sporting brushed cotton pyjamas with a polka-dot pattern of the Grinch's face. I had no make-up on, and my hair was still tied up in last night's messy bun — sort of. It had the added mess of a night's sleep. I glanced at my living room clock on the way to the door — heinously early for visitors, never mind unannounced ones — and clicked to waken the speaker.

'Hello?'

'Don't you *hello* me, missus, let me up,' Elouise's voice answered.

'Ah, okay, is everything—'

She must have snatched at the door in the same second that I'd unlocked it, because I heard the entry noise before I'd even finished the question. I left my front door on the latch and went back to the kitchen to add another person's worth of water to the kettle.

I heard Elouise stumble in seconds later, slamming the door behind her; then she appeared in the doorway clutching an armful of magazines. There was a moment of fast thinking when I tried to run through the modelling jobs she'd done recently. Had something gone to print this weekend? Had she decided she really did hate her natural hair colour and she wanted to be brunette again? I'd missed something, forgotten something, but Elouise wasn't filling in the blanks. She just stood there, three, maybe four magazines pressed to her torso like flimsy armour, with an eyebrow raised and her mouth bunched into a smirk that at least looked friendly and light, even if it didn't quite match her behaviour.

'Morning, El,' I tried. And that triggered something.

'Don't you *morning* me,' she parroted her earlier remark. 'Tell me all about last night.'

I huffed out a hearty breath that I didn't know I'd been holding, and a laugh followed it. 'That's it, that's all this is about? Good grief' — I turned to grab mugs from the cupboard — 'you're enough to give a woman a heart attack. I thought something was wrong.'

'Oh, there's nothing wrong. Only having to read about my *best friend's* first date with a woman from a cheap Sunday magazine.' There came a slap of something from behind me. When I turned, I realised it had been the magazines landing hard on the surface of my breakfast bar.

A mug slipped from my hand as the first headline leapt up and slapped me around the face: DEAR DOTTY'S BACK ON THE MARKET. The crash of porcelain was unforgivingly loud, and I flinched, as much at the headline as the noise, and for a second Elouise and I just stood there, neither of us saying a word.

'Babe, come on now, there's no need to go breaking things over it.' Elouise, perhaps sensing my shock, dismay, and utter raging embarrassment, leapt into action. 'Don't move an inch,' she said, staring at my bare feet now, 'and we'll get this cleaned up.' She trod around me to fetch my dustpan and brush from under the sink, and then set about collecting the shards of the mug. 'Okay, I think that's everything. Are you okay?'

It was a crap Sunday magazine — the sort that made Elza roll her eyes and shudder. But I was still news, and somehow, they'd even got a bloody picture of me and Alia to accompany their little story! Panic flooded through me then as I flashed back to the one thing Alia had asked of me: don't write about the date. And then the panic was swiftly replaced by a swell of sickly ill-feeling. *Don't write about the date*, she'd said, and here we were, newsworthy in our garlic bread bubble of first date-dom. *She'll never want to see me again* . . .

I managed to shake my head, and Elouise took that as an answer to her question. She guided me towards the breakfast bar, pulled out a stool, and gestured for me to sit. Then I listened as she took over the job of making tea.

'Tots and Marissa are coming over too.' I managed a nod. 'They stopped to get us breakfast.'

The slight mention of food made my stomach audibly churn. Elouise came around to the other side of the breakfast bar to take her own seat, and I felt her studying me while I was staring at the headline. I moved a shaky hand forward to reveal the magazine underneath — another Sunday weekly, thirty pages of poor writing that was hastily produced. But I saw my face again, albeit this time only in the side column of the page Elouise had folded the magazine open to: DEAR DOTTY'S DATING ANTICS: IS THIS THE GIRL FROM DOTTY'S OWN 'HAVE I LEFT IT TOO LATE' LETTER? I gulped, and Elouise set her hand on top of mine.

'That garlic bread looks amazing by the way,' she said. Even though I knew the comment was meant to be light-hearted, all I could manage in response was a painful groan. I snatched my hand away, rested both palms on my forehead, and let out another nondescript noise. 'I genuinely thought you'd already know about this, babe.'

'No,' I mumbled from behind my hands, 'I'd no idea. I— They— Why would someone *print* this? Why on earth would people even care?'

Elouise eased a hand away from my face. 'Dotts, you're kind of a big deal. Have you *seen* your Instagram followers these days?'

The truth was I tried not to look. It was easier to think of posting my emotional innards in the Dear Dotty feature every week if I remained ignorant of the sheer number of readers that might be out there paying attention now. But this, this was something much bigger than Instagram — and it would be much harder to ignore.

'There's nothing wrong with being a big deal, you know?' Elouise added.

'I'm not!' It wasn't a shout, but I felt my voice rise in my throat. 'I'm not a big deal, I'm just Dotty, I'm just some ten-a-penny columnist, I'm— Is that a third magazine under there?' I cut myself off, realising there was more to come. I reached out for it before Elouise had answered, and relief rushed out of me when I saw that she hadn't marked a page open in this one.

'You're in the gossip section on page thirteen.'

'I'm going to be sick.'

The front doorbell sounded.

'That'll be the girls with breakfast.'

I managed another groan.

'Imagine my dismay' — Tots burst into the room seconds later — 'at finding out my best friend had been papped and I hadn't even got first refusal on the pictures.' She threw her arms around my slumped form, still leaning over the breakfast bar. 'How you doing, lovely?' She kissed the top of my head. 'I'm guessing you've got some feelings about the magazine scoop.'

'Who even gives a toss about me dating someone?'

'Well, apparently lots of people,' Elouise answered.

'I'm not sure that's helpful,' Marissa said as she trailed in behind her.

I struggled upright, leaning on my forearms still, and pushed the magazines away from me. Marissa was brandishing two brown bags that were grease stained, and the smell was glorious. I'd swung around from being repulsed by food to wanting to comfort eat my body weight. She caught me eyeing her goods, too, and gestured with the bag.

'Breakfast?'

'What did you bring?'

'Avocado and cream cheese on a poppy seed bagel.'

I wrinkled my nose. 'That sounds far too healthy.'

'It should, because it's mine.' Elouise snatched the small bag that Marissa had just ferreted free. 'I'm on a cleanse.'

'When aren't you?' Tots snapped back.

'The rest of us have got fried egg and bacon on white bread.' Marissa set the bag down on the counter next to me. 'Will that ease your ills?'

'I could kiss you.'

'Ooooh,' Tots started, 'better not tell your new girlfriend that.' She tickled me with a childish glee that made me want to eat her breakfast sandwich out of spite. But that bitterness was soon undercut by the second wave of a much bigger, more terrifying thought.

'Oh. God.'

'What?' Elouise looked up from sniffing her breakfast.

'I have to call Alia.'

'You only went on a date last night.' Tots was somewhere behind me then, pulling small plates from a cupboard. 'Isn't it a bit soon to call her? Isn't there a three-day rule or something?'

I turned and slapped her arm with the back of my hand. 'Not about a date, Tots, about the bloody magazines. She specifically asked me not to write about our date, that's *all* she asked, that *one* thing.'

'Well' — Tots shrugged, a small plate in either hand — 'you didn't.'

'I think you're missing the point, Tots.' Marissa tried to mediate. She tucked an arm around my shoulders and gave me a squeeze that was uncharacteristically soft. 'Maybe you should try giving her a call while we plate up breakfast? Does that sound okay?'

'You're my favourite, did I ever tell you that?'

'Hey,' Elouise spoke around a bite of bagel, 'what did I do?'

I left the girls to find plates, ketchup, and brown sauce — which Tots definitely wouldn't find an ounce of in the entire kitchen, because I was of the (correct) view that it was disgusting. Still, I reasoned that telling her 'There might be some in the fridge' would keep her busy for long enough to call Alia and gauge her reaction, which I could only hope to heavens wouldn't be as torrential as mine.

I went back into the bedroom to grab my phone and decided to call from there to avoid the gaggle of noise erupting from the kitchen. It took three greedy and deep belly breaths for me to find the courage to hit call. She answered after the third ring, and by habit, I hit the button for the speakerphone.

'I wondered when I'd hear from you.'

I left a pause in case there was more to her welcome. When it became clear that there wasn't I shyly asked, 'On a scale of one to ten, how embarrassed are you?'

'Embarrassed? Not at all.'

'You've . . . You mean you aren't . . . Have you—'

Alia's bubbly laugh travelled through the speaker, and it was an instant balm.

'I've seen the magazines, yes. Well, not yes, actually, I've seen *pictures* of the magazines because my friend texted them to me this morning. But I'm not embarrassed, Dotty. Why would I be?'

'Ah . . .' I lingered. 'Because apparently our first date is newsworthy?'

'It's hardly *The Times*. It's just a few Sunday freebies. How many people even read them?'

Lots, actually. But I wasn't going to admit that aloud.

'But you asked me not to write about the date, Alia, you said—'

'I said please don't write about it, I remember' — that same laugh, already familiar and comforting somehow, broke through her sentence — 'but *you* haven't written about it. Some other . . . well, journalist seems a stretch, but some schmuck has. I'm assuming you didn't tip them off that you were going to be eating garlic bread at a Christmas market with me?'

'Christ, no, of course I—'

'I was joking.'

'Oh.'

'Dotty, look, I asked you not to and you didn't. Don't worry, okay?' She waited for me to murmur in agreement before she carried on. 'Now, I'm totally free today and it looks blisteringly cold outside. Why don't I meet you for a winter-time walk later?'

'I . . . Yes, that would be great. Lovely, in fact. It would be lovely.'

'Okay,' — I could hear her smile as she spoke — 'go and take some deep breaths. Have tea, herbal, if you have any, and I'll text you later on. We'll plan something.'

'Thanks, Alia, you're being . . . Just, thank you.'

'Oh, and Dotty, *now* you can write about the date.'

I stalled. False starts stuttered out of me, once, twice, three times before I managed, 'I'm not sure I understand.'

'They want to know whether I'm the girl from the letters, right?' Again, I could hear her smiling, though it sounded broader now. I imagined a full grin, even. 'Wouldn't it be fun if you told them? I'm imagining something like, *How soon do you call a girl after your first date?* She broke into a laugh. 'Though I guess in your case it's the next day.'

I matched her giggle and felt an instant ease of tension in my shoulders. 'I mean, I've only called you under *very* special circumstances.'

'Eh, they don't have to know that.'

I huffed, smiled, and stalled again. 'You're kind of amazing, you know that?'

'I've been told. Anyway, I'll text you later. Cool?'

'Cool. Thank you, Alia, again, and . . . thank you.'

When we ended the call I dropped my phone behind me onto the bed and then collapsed on it myself, arms outspread and a smile to match.

'I know that was a private conversation' — I lifted my head and caught sight of Tots standing in the doorway to my bedroom, clutching her breakfast sandwich with a great drip of ketchup that was threatening to blob onto the plate beneath — 'but I like her.'

'Me too' — Marissa appeared from behind Tots — 'and Elouise does, but she wants you to think she wasn't listening.'

'I wasn't listening!' El shouted. 'But I do like her!' she added.

Tots winked at me and gestured with her sandwich. 'You're out of brown sauce.'

Dear Dotty,

It's a tale as old as time. A woman gives you her phone number. You don't call, even though you want to. Then, you write a letter, in your own advice column, about wanting to call the woman. You are asking her, on a very public platform, if she'll answer your call after so long. She replies. Then you call and, wait, no— None of this is a tale as old as time! I did the brave thing, Dotty, I called the woman and I went on the date and I bruised parts of my body that I didn't even know had soft tissue during a very embarrassing but adorable encounter at an ice rink. And I ate garlic bread. Really good garlic bread, incidentally, with cheese and— I'm getting sidetracked.

Now the date is done, I suppose I'm writing to you to ask, what happens next? I'd like another date, and I think she would as well. But when do I call, Dotty? A day, three days? Are these archaic rules even still in place, or have we all reached a point, now, where 'playing it cool' isn't actually the cool thing to do anymore? The truth is, I'm a bit out of my depth in dating. It feels like learning the rules all over again, but in the time I've been sidelined — or rather, in the time I was in a relationship — the rules changed and now, when do I call? When do I text? Should I suggest the second date, or should she? Am I too old to even be worrying about this, when really I should just come out and say hey, I like you, and I'd like to eat more garlic bread with you when you're available for it?

Dotty, is playing it cool just a waste of perfectly good time?

Write back when you can, Dotty, and I'll try not to do anything stupid in the meantime . . .

With love and thanks, always.
Dotty xxx

CHAPTER THIRTY-NINE

While Instagram was my preferred social media platform for sharing my life with the world, there was one thing I'd never been able to wrap my editing skills around: reels. So I called in the experts! Elouise and Tots helped me to structure a video that featured one magazine article appearing after the other. We slammed them down onto my kitchen counter, leaving *just* enough time for the catchy headlines before ending with a quizzical and confused shrug from me.

'How do you think it looks?' I asked Marissa, who had respectfully excused herself from this bonding activity owing to 'not having a clue how the social media thing works'. Her own Instagram was square after square of home-cooked meals; aesthetically pleasing and good for the likes, but she was purely in it to show off her cooking skills rather than to gain followers.

She watched the reel quietly, three times. 'I think you're asking for trouble.'

'Oh, come on!' Tots chimed in from the kitchen, where she was brewing tea for us all — apart from Elouise, who declined in favour of water with a slice of cucumber. 'It's *her* social media, and didn't Elza *ask* for more content? This is less stylised, it's fun, it's—'

'Eye-catching.' Elouise beamed.

Marissa raised her eyebrow at me. 'Do you want to be eye-catching?'

My thumb lingered over the post button. 'I think I do, actually.'

'Well, there's your answer.'

'Just press post so we can start the film,' Elouise said as she snuggled into the sofa space next to me. She draped a soft touch blanket over the both of us and rested her head on my shoulder. 'It's just an Instagram post. How much trouble can you *really* get in for an Instagram post, Dots?'

Well, isn't that just the question . . .

'It's also an unofficial Dear Dotty letter,' Marissa added, as though the video were the only offending article in this discussion. But the video was captioned — and the caption most definitely wasn't Elza approved.

'I'm going to sit on it, I think,' I answered as I back-clicked out, saving the post to drafts instead. 'Let's throw the film on, and I'll see how I feel after.'

Tots handed me a mug of steaming tea. 'Chicken.' She winked.

'Yes,' I said, proudly, 'yes, I am a total chicken. Now put *The Holiday* on and get cosy. We'll make final decisions on the matter after two hours of Cameron Diaz and another three cups of tea.'

'Sure' — Tots landed in an armchair and pulled her legs up beneath her — 'because Cameron Diaz will help you think straight.'

* * *

London was alive with Christmas! And suddenly, I didn't mind one bit. The whole city had been made fresh with fairy lights, outlandish hanging decorations, and carols on every corner. I wandered into one of the many coffee shops down the road from my office, bouncing on the balls of my feet to Wham!'s 'Last Christmas', while the jolly server prepared my cinnamon and apple tea, and I wished her a very merry Christmas when she handed me back my thermos.

'Aw, thanks! Merry Christmas to you, too,' she answered with a tired smile that made me wonder how many times a day she had to say that.

Even though I'd left the song behind I found that I hummed it all the way to the office block. I took my Christmas spirit into the elevator, up to our floor, and I liberally sprinkled it over everyone in the office — an obnoxious serving of joy with my good mornings. But the office was another space that had been made fresh with Christmas: there was a tree in the far corner, bunting over every desk, and a smattering of Christmas cards propped up here and there from those conscientious enough to send them, rather than the 'Happy holidays!' emails that the lazy amongst us had opted to send instead. It was impossible to occupy this space and *not* feel some Christmas spirit in your veins.

But Elza was making a good effort at it.

'When did you last check your phone?' she called out before her office door had even managed to close behind me.

I didn't have an answer for her. My phone had been on airplane mode since the night before. And with good reason . . .

'Elza, remember what we said about taking a measured approach to this.' My head snapped around to where the extra voice had come from; tucked into the corner in a visitor's armchair, next to a squat Christmas tree that someone had deposited on Elza's coffee table.

'Morning, Dotty. You look pleased with yourself.' Candice smirked and sipped her drink.

The truth was, I *was* pleased with myself. But that didn't seem like The Mood I should have brought into this meeting with me. I tried to level my cheer into something that Elza might find less offensive before I spoke.

'Morning, Candice. This is a surprise.'

'I didn't want to miss all of the excitement.'

Elza huffed. 'Excitement is one word for it.'

She dropped her iPhone onto the desk with a heavy thud. Although I couldn't see the offending post, I knew it was there, hidden in the dim light of Elza's screen, goading her reaction.

'The publicity team are throwing their toys *right* out of the pram,' Elza announced. She ran a hand through her hair, then collected her own drink from the desk. 'Go on' — she nodded to where Candice sat — 'make yourself comfortable and start explaining.'

I had an abrupt flashback to the time when I'd been caught stealing from the tuck shop at school. It was trivial stuff: a Mars bar here, a Snickers there. I hadn't been the only one doing it, but I was definitely the only one who'd been caught red-handed by Mrs. Mullins, who stood with folded arms and a disapproving expression as she watched me duck back under the stable door that barred the tuck shop from public entry (if only the monitors ever thought to lock it). I'd been marched to the headmaster where I had to explain — well, that there *was* no explanation. It was wrong, and I was sorry. And to make up for it, I was more than willing to tot up the amount of chocolate bars I'd chewed my way through that term and pay back the appropriate amount of pocket money for it — which is about the time I also realised that I ate far too many Snickers.

But this was different. There was no crime! There was only a social media post. And, the last time I checked — in the first two days after posting — there were over forty thousand views, too.

I stared down at my drink; there was a small wisp of heat escaping through the hole at the top. 'Elza, I think what might have happened—'

'Dotty, you've gone viral!' she announced, and I winced — not at the announcement itself, only at the pitch of her voice. 'Why didn't you speak to us about this first?'

From the corner of my eye I saw Candice stifle a laugh. 'Which is a good thing, incidentally, Dotty. Going viral, that is.' I looked up at her then, my ally. I wondered whether

Candice was my ticket out of this mess. 'Elza's issue isn't with the post; I think it's important we establish that.'

'No, my issue is . . .' Elza started but then fizzled out. 'My issue is that you didn't *talk* to the publicity team about this.'

'Because it's *my* social media feed,' I protested, though I tried hard to keep my voice level. 'Elza, they took pictures of us; they made my first date into a headline. Why shouldn't I jump on the bandwagon of making a thing out of that? And besides' — I found the more I spoke, the easier my protest came — 'it's a *good* thing that Dear Dotty gets more media attention. Think of the book!'

'Exactly,' Candice chimed in. 'Elza, think of the *website hits.*'

Then and only then did Elza stop pacing. She sank into one of the free chairs and looked out of her office window — an office window that I only noticed then, was sprinkled with spray snow. 'Now tell me when you last checked your phone.'

I cleared my throat. 'It's been . . . a few hours.'

'It's been shared over twenty thousand times.'

'Right. And . . .' I hesitated over this next part, 'and does that count as viral?'

'Yes,' she answered flatly.

'Dotty, for the record' — Candice inched forward in her seat to speak to me — 'I think it was genius.'

I beamed. 'Genius?'

'Genius,' Elza answered, though it sounded like she begrudged saying it. 'Is she the girl from the letters?'

A laugh hiccupped out of me. 'Do you think I have some sort of harem?'

'Is it a holiday romance?' Elza asked, and the question stumped me. I sat with it for what felt like an especially lengthy time.

'I hope not,' I admitted. 'I like her, Elza. If I didn't like her, I don't think I would have posted the letter. It was meant to be . . . playful, and retaliatory, and, yes, it was meant to jump on the bandwagon of attention. And it worked, might I add.'

'You're putting your dating life on display for the public, Dotty,' she answered. 'Are you comfortable with that?'

I shrugged. Although it crossed my mind, then, that in amongst the publicity storm that I'd created for her, Elza's reaction might also be coming from a place of — dare I say it — care, concern even. 'It was already on display — along with everything else I've shared this year. A magazine literally printed a picture of our faces chowing down on garlic bread in the middle of a Christmas market.'

'It's an adorable picture, by the way,' Candice said. 'We might even make space for it in the book.'

'Let's not get carried away,' Elza cautioned her. Her demeanour seemed to soften, then, and I wondered whether Candice and I were beginning to wear her down — or at least, round off the sharp edges. 'I just want you to know that this has implications. You're going to need to talk to the publicity team, too, because if I fence one more email from them' — she held her hands up in defeat — 'frankly, I think I'll resort to taking holiday just so I can avoid them.'

'Wow' — I smiled across at her — 'things must be bad.'

Elza narrowed her eyes at me. 'You're too clever for your own good, Dotty. Did anyone ever tell you that?'

'Yes, actually,' I answered. And if I sounded smug, it's because I was — a little.

'Now the fireworks are out of the way, why don't we all tuck into these *delicious* gingerbread men that Sophie brought in earlier, and Dotty, you can tell us all about the mystery girl?' Candice nudged the plate of biscuits towards me. 'Doesn't that sound like a fine idea?'

Elza was the first to snatch a gingerbread man from the pile. She started with the head, which didn't surprise me at all.

'Well, to start with, the letter was *sort of* her idea . . .'

Elza rolled her eyes, but I could see the rise of a smile, too. 'That's just what we need; someone who's going to encourage you.'

'Quite frankly, Elza' — Candice snapped a leg free from her gingerbread biscuit and dunked it into her tea — 'I think that's *exactly* what our Dotty needs.'

CHAPTER FORTY

In a strange turn of events, two out of the three cottages that had been booked for the Women's Institute Christmas Vacation had flooded — thanks to a series of unexpected downpours and some ill-placed sandbags. That's how, two weeks later, my mother came to be pulling up outside of my flat in one of London's finest black cabs with a sack of presents that rivalled even Santa's.

I'd wanted to meet her from the train station — it was no secret that Mum hated everything about London, nothing more so than the travel — but I was up to my eyes in turkey . . . innards. I waved through the living room window when I saw her arrive, my hands still sheathed with my finest Marigolds, before stripping free of the gloves and rushing down to greet her. I launched myself from the bottom step of my building and threw my arms around Mum with childish glee, knocking a bag of presents out of her hand in the process.

I hurried to collect the bag. 'Oh, I'm so sorry. Was there anything breakable inside?'

'What does it matter?' Mum answered. 'For a greeting as lovely as that one.'

'I'm just so glad you're here, Mum.' I wrestled another two bags from her and headed for the open door of my building. 'The flat looks like a small grenade has gone off but you'll be impressed to know that the vegetables and pudding are prepped, and I've just finished doing some disgusting things to a turkey.'

Mum shrieked with laughter. 'I really can't believe you're doing everything yourself, love.'

I spoke over my shoulder as we climbed the stairs. 'The girls offered. They said they didn't mind helping. But, I don't know, something about this year makes it feel right to be doing it myself.' I kicked open the door to the flat, my hands still laden with bags. 'And I'd like to be able to treat you all to a nice Christmas dinner. Tots's Mum and Dad are having Christmas away, pointedly without the rest of the family. Marissa can't stand her own parents, still. And El, well, Elouise's family are still a bit frosty with her, since that lingerie campaign last year. So, a nice quiet Christmas dinner is deserved by all.' I deposited the presents on the sofa with a soft thud. 'Of course, it may not actually *be* a nice Christmas dinner, but at least I'll have tried.'

Mum leaned across to give my arm a squeeze. 'You can only ever try your best.'

'Now, tea?'

'Oh, I'm gasping.' Mum slipped her coat free and hung it on the stand in the hallway. 'And while you're making tea, you can tell me all about your new girlfriend.' She bunched her shoulders and smirked when she saw my expression. 'There's only so much I can learn about in the local magazines, you know . . .'

Alia and I had been on another three dates in the space of two weeks, and we'd fallen into a rhythm of speaking every day, too. Not *all* day, every day, but a 'good morning' text here and a 'how's your day been?' there. After the hiccup of the first date, we'd both become weirdly accustomed to the idea that someone, somewhere, might take a picture of us and send it to a magazine, or at the very least, post it on Instagram — usually tagging my Dear Dotty account, too. But given that Alia was perhaps the coolest woman on the face of the earth, she had made a running joke out of the whole thing.

On our second date — Italian, my choice, with boatloads of garlic bread — she had twirled carbonara around her fork with the ease of someone who knows their way around pasta, and said the only real impact the attention had had was making her think that bit more carefully about her outfit: 'If I'm going to get snapped, I need to look sharp.' She'd winked and tucked a forkful of pasta into her mouth, and I'd inelegantly necked the rest of my spritzer to give myself something to do. Otherwise, I might have just sat there, mouth agog in admiration.

She was out of the city for a few days to spend Christmas with her grandmother. And I was glad to be able to tell Mum that, because I just knew that otherwise—

'I was just going to say, you should have invited her.'

I laughed as I handed her a mug of tea. 'Too soon, Mum, too soon.'

* * *

On Christmas morning Mum and I curled up on the sofa in our pyjamas. Mum's, a plain but brilliant red with a crisp white trim. Mine, the same colour green as the Grinch's face with small Santa hats dotted all over them. We drank hot chocolate while we opened presents and listened to cheesy Christmas songs.

When the living room was covered in balls of wrapping paper — we'd been balling up and aiming for a rubbish bag in the corner, but it turned out neither of us was well-equipped for that game — Mum cosied up that bit closer to me and let out a hearty, soft sigh.

'I can't remember the last time I saw you like this, Dotts.'

Her head was on my shoulder, and I rested mine on top of hers. 'What do you mean?'

Mum took a long time to answer but eventually she decided on: 'Just . . . Dotty.'

It felt like a beautifully cinematic moment that I wanted to bottle. I imagined taking this exact scene and slipping it inside a snow globe — a shower of glitter tumbling over us whenever I shook up this memory.

Soon, though, the quiet bliss of the moment was disrupted by the beep-beep-beep of a car horn outside my apartment building. 'That'll be the rabble,' I announced.

Seconds later, Marissa, Elouise and Tots tumbled through my open front door brandishing bags and bottles. There was a flurry of excitement as they all found space around the living room to drop their belongings, creating small clusters of presents — arranged by recipient, to bring some order to the place, which was Marissa's trusty thinking — before hugs and kisses were thrown about like Christmas confetti.

'Mama Liz!' Elouise wrapped her arms around Mum. 'We're so glad you're here.'

'Oh, girls, you don't think I'm cramping your style?'

'Our style?' Tots threw open her trench coat with a dramatic flair to reveal Christmas pyjamas that were white all over with an obscenely large reindeer head in the centre of her chest. 'I think you're exactly on brand for what we're going for this Christmas, Lizzy.'

Mum shrieked with laughter as Marissa and Elouise made similar reveals.

'We decided that a Christmas day spent in pyjamas was exactly what we all needed.'

'We're not getting dressed?' Mum looked at me with mild horror. 'All day?'

'All day,' I answered. 'This is as smart as it gets. Hot chocolate?'

'Please!' the girls answered one by one. 'I've got some squirty cream in one of these bags somewhere,' Tots added, already ferreting through her belongings to find the tin.

'Oh, Tots, don't worry, I've got some open already,' I answered from the kitchen. As I filled a pan with milk I heard the rush of something being squirted in the living room. And

I looked up to find Tots, tin in hand, with Marissa kneeling in front of her with her mouth open.

'It's okay,' Tots explained, 'I found mine.'

I laughed on my way back in. 'You're animals, you pair. Mum, can you believe this?'

'Believe it?' Mum sat down on the sofa and tipped her head back. 'I think it's genius! Let's have a go.'

'If you make yourselves sick on whipped cream then I'll still expect you to eat dinner.'

Elouise crouched to take her turn. 'Please, there's like, nothing *in* whipped cream.'

'Do you need any help, Dotty?' Marissa asked, cream still clinging to the corners of her mouth.

'You can be on cup carrying duty. Mum, do you want another?'

Mum ummed and ahhed. 'Oh, go on, it is Christmas after all.'

Marissa and I trod back to the kitchen, and while I poured milk into mugs she tucked her arm around my waist and gave me a soft squeeze.

'You're not bad at this Christmas malarkey.'

'Eh,' I answered, 'maybe I've just realised Christmas isn't so bad after all.'

'You should be proud of yourself, Dotts.'

I huffed. 'For liking Christmas this year?'

'No, you daft idiot' — she squeezed me again — 'for this whole year.'

'Oh, babe, let's save introspection for New Year's Eve.'

Marissa let go of me and leaned against the kitchen work-top to get a view of my face as she spoke. 'I'm being serious, Dotty. If you think about the start of this year, if you think about *everything* that's happened this year . . .' she petered out, shook her head, and seemed to weigh carefully what came next. 'I just think you're pretty remarkable.'

I looked up at her and felt my eyes brim with tears. 'Marissa, that's . . .'

'Come *on*, you two!' Elouise interrupted. 'I've got you all really good presents and I want us to start opening them.'

'Can I get a splash of Bailey's in my hot chocolate?' Tots shouted. There came the rustle of bags and curse words muttered under Tots's breath before she announced, 'Aha! I knew I'd brought Bailey's, too.'

'You can add your own,' I answered. 'I'll leave enough room in the top of the mug.'

Marissa kissed my temple and took two mugs from me. 'Remarkable.'

I juggled the final three mugs and we distributed them accordingly: Marissa and I going for plain old hot chocolate, while Elouise and Tots sloshed booze into theirs. Mum took two sips from her drink to free up some space and then said, 'Oh, go on, it is Christmas after all,' when Tots reached out to her with the Baileys bottle.

'Right, Dotty, this is—'

'Els, before we do presents,' I cut across her, 'I just wanted to raise a little toast. I know I should probably save this for when the turkey is on the table, but I don't want to forget to say this, if that's okay?' I glanced around at their expectant faces. 'Girls, Mum, it's not exactly a secret that this year has been . . . transformative' — they mumbled their agreement — 'but everything I've done, everything I've tried to do, it's been held up by some pretty trusty scaffolding, and that's you four. One way or another, you've lifted me this year, and I can't . . .' I felt emotion catch in my throat and I blinked hard to try to focus myself. 'I can't thank you enough for being my scaffolding. I love you all, and I'm so glad we're spending Christmas together.'

There was a pin-drop quiet in the room then before Mum lifted her hot chocolate and said, 'To good scaffolding.'

'To good scaffolding,' the girls echoed.

Mum sipped her drink and slapped her lips. 'Oh, Tots, that's . . . that's bloody lovely.'

'Here.' Tots reached over with the bottle. 'Have some more.'

'You do realise,' Marissa said, 'that if you keep topping up the hot chocolate with Baileys, eventually it'll *just* be Baileys in your mugs?'

I giggled from behind my own drink and gave Mum a wink when she glanced my way. 'Oh, go on,' I said, 'it *is* Christmas after all . . .'

Dear Dotty,

Things are about to change. That's what I'd say, if I started this all over again. Things are about to change, and even though it mightn't feel like it, at all, things are about to change for the better. To your surprise, your heart isn't about to break clean in two, like you thought it might. Your world is about to spin off its axis, like you expected it to. Life will become a rollercoaster of feelings, like you've never known. And you will be fine. Let me lend advice to you now, Dotty, my love, because sometimes we need our inner voice to do the talking: You, will be fine.

Love and good things, always,
Dotty xxx

(P.S. When the book promotion happens, which you know it must, try to resist the urge to shrink. Fantastic things happen when we open our arms and take up space.)

271

CHAPTER FORTY-ONE

Eleven months later . . .

I set the loose pages down on the table next to me. Then I spread my arms as wide as I could comfortably reach and said, 'So here I am, taking up space.' It was a bold and theatrical gesture by my standards, but it paired well with the book extract. I truly thought the only way to survive this little shindig was to exude a confidence that I absolutely didn't feel — and the widespread arms somehow helped with that. 'I can't thank you all enough for turning up to celebrate *Dear Dotty*, or rather, the first wave of *Dear Dotty*. When Candice said she wanted to arrange a pre-order party, I actually laughed' — there came an echo of laughter from the room then, too — 'I laughed and said that I didn't think that was a thing. After that, I said, and I quote, "I'm not sure Dear Dotty deserves that".' I dropped my eyes to Candice who was brushing elbows with Elza at the front of the audience, and the pair of them swapped a knowing look. 'We were in a busy meeting at the time, surrounded by publicity wizards, and Candice gently took me to one side and' — laughter broke through my voice — 'and she told me I was being ridiculous.'

'Because you were, darling,' Candice shouted up from the audience bay.

'Ah, there'll be no heckling, thank you, at least not until the end.' I winked at her and she held her hands up in a defensive gesture. 'Candice told me I was being ridiculous, and I thought *she* was being ridiculous for saying that. But honestly, Candice, and Elza, too, Dear Dotty's guardian angels, I cannot thank you enough for all those occasions when you've told me I'm being ridiculous, or I'm getting what I deserve, or any number of other kind, supportive . . .' I laughed. 'Even sometimes quite brash things that you might have said to me, to get me here, and to get *Dear Dotty* here. It took a long time and a lot of hard listening, and I still don't feel convinced that I'm there, in terms of what *I* deserve. But I do know that the people who are writing in to Dear Dotty deserve this space that we're making for them. The letters from the vault deserve answers because *these* are the people, these are the qualities of *Dear Dotty* that keep the whole column afloat, and now, keep the whole book afloat, too. I realise I might have something to do with it' — there came another rumble of laughter from the audience — 'but I wanted to take this opportunity to thank each and every person who agreed to their letters appearing in the *Dear Dotty* book because their words, their time, their struggles, they are over and above anything I might write in a series of silly letters to myself.

'And I'm delighted to say they're all in the audience tonight, if we can have a round of applause for them, please?' There came a thunderous clapping from every corner in the room. While that rolled on, I took a tactical pause to sip water and scan the audience for my table. 'I won't embarrass my letter writers by calling them out one by one, but I will embarrass the loves of my life, in no particular order,' I made a point of adding this, because Elouise had already asked whose name I would say first. 'Tots, Elouise, and Marissa.' I raised my glass in their direction, and smiled as heads turned their way. 'Where on earth would I be without you? And of course, where on earth would I be without my gorgeous, glorious mum? You . . .'

The feeling caught in my throat again. I flashed back to last Christmas — to hot chocolate and Baileys, and to forgetting to turn the oven on (because there was *so much* Baileys). And I raised my glass.

'You four are my scaffolding.'

Mum stood bolt upright from their table, then, and holding her hands in my general direction she initiated another thunderous round of applause. She looked stunning in a black pantsuit that Elouise had helped her pick out during a shopping excursion only two weeks ago. Mum had paired it with a puckered red top beneath and layered gold necklaces that made her look every bit the style icon. And I was pleased to see, stylish in the seat next to her, Peter, the retired risk analyst. He looked just as sharp in a black suit and a crisp white shirt that he'd left open at the collar. Mum had sheepishly asked me two weeks ago whether it might be okay for him to come along tonight and I'd been secretly delighted. I hadn't looked him up on social media yet, but from everything Mum had told me, it looked as though Phil was turning out to be worth the twenty-year wait.

While Mum stood, still clapping like there was no tomorrow, the girls joined her. Tots, in her overpriced ripped jeans and crisp white shirt complete with a thin black tie; Marissa, in a deep green dress with a peplum skirt; and Elouise, who of course had come wearing a floor length red dress, looking every bit like she was ready to accept an award.

'We just want to make you proud, babe,' Tots had said only two hours ago when we were all clustered in my flat getting ready.

'You do, every day,' I'd answered, and I felt a swell of that now.

'And finally, before this speech turns into something befitting of an Oscar, I want to thank Alia.' I smiled as she stood from her post, next to Mum's seat, and jokingly bowed to the turned heads that surrounded her. And she was worthy of turning heads, too, in her white lace dress made up of a bodice and flowing skirt. She looked every bit the fairytale protagonist, and it suited her oh so well. I felt a wistful sigh escape me when I locked eyes with her. 'We didn't have the most conventional of beginnings' — I watched as her face broke into an embarrassed smile — 'given that I'm pretty sure most people can have a first date without someone taking photos of them. Unless that's a thing?' I shrugged to murmured amusement. 'But thank you, Alia, for every cooking class and every ice-skating experience, every wild water swim, and every piece of garlic bread. I have no idea who I am,' I admitted, though the unashamed honesty made my cheeks prick with heat, 'but I'm glad to be working it out with you.' I raised my glass again. 'Now, one final toast to *Dear Dotty* and I'll bid you farewell for the evening. Thank you so much, Candice, for arranging what is perhaps the most superb non-book launch I've ever been to. Enjoy yourselves, because Candice and her team worked very hard to make this happen. And make sure you sign the guestbook on your travels! I promise not to reprint anything you write in the *Dear Dotty* sequel.'

Then there came a deafening round of applause, the biggest of them all so far as I carefully trod my way to the edge of the stage. There was a young waiter in a sharp suit waiting with an outstretched hand to guide me down the steps, and my gratitude was immense. Elouise had me wearing heels that were so staggeringly high I thought they might induce a nosebleed before the evening was out — assuming I didn't slip them off under the table once I was back at my seat . . .

'Darling, you were bloody fantastic.' Candice rushed at me with a kiss on each cheek. 'You're very damp, though, Dotty, are you okay?'

I let out an awkward laugh. 'It's just nerves.' *Sweat. The biggest name in London publishing just kissed my sweat.* And I felt the colour of my cheeks deepen at the realisation. 'You're sure it was okay? I don't want to have let either of you down.'

'Kid' — Elza grabbed me by the balls of my shoulders — 'you couldn't if you tried.'

'There's a bottle of bubbly waiting on the table for you.' Candice winked. 'Grab a straw from the bar on your way past, you need to rehydrate.'

We shared more kisses on cheeks before promising to see each other again before the evening was out. There was such an absurd number of people crammed into the room that I wasn't sure whether we *would* see each other again, but it was a warming promise. On my way from the stage back to my table there were mini-applauses, bravos, and brief introductions, so much so that it may well have been another half an hour before I was back with the girls. But they'd patiently waited for me to open the bubbles that Candice had sent over.

'At long last' — Tots grabbed the neck of the bottle and yanked it free from its cooler — 'I'm parched.' She leaned back, aimed skywards, and popped the cork, beaming with pride as champagne started to overflow from the mouth of the bottle.

'Okay, well don't waste it,' Marissa said, scrambling for a glass to hold beneath the head.

Elouise tucked an arm around me. 'I can't believe you said me second.'

I laughed. 'Els, in *no* particular order . . .'

'Yeah, yeah. Champers?'

'Please!'

'Oh, my Dotty.' Mum threw her arms around me with such a force that she nearly knocked me clean off my stilts. She grabbed my upper arms to steady me. 'I'm so bloody proud of you, love. Just . . . would you just . . . I mean.' She gestured to the entire room. 'Just look at everything you've done! Everyone you've brought together.'

I smirked. 'I think the open bar is probably what brought people together, Mum.'

'Oh, shush now, Dotts, you can't push yourself down forever, love. Sometimes you just need to stand in the light.' She cupped my cheek with her warm palm and gave me such a loving look that I thought it might raise tears in my eyes. 'I do love you, Dotty.'

'Not as much as I love you.'

She narrowed her eyes. 'Let's not argue tonight.'

'Liz! Bubbly?' Tots pulled Mum's attention away.

'I thought I was going to be waiting for an audience with you all night.' Alia pulled me close to her and wrapped an arm around my waist. Her grip was strong, comforting. She leaned in to deliver a soft and singular kiss before moving away a fraction. 'Just the one,' she said with her forehead pressed against mine, 'you never know who might be taking photos.'

I rolled my eyes. 'In this room, I feel like *everyone* might be taking photos.'

'It was a great speech, Dotts' — she moved to kiss my forehead — 'I especially liked the named mentions. Nice touch.' Alia glanced behind her, as though to check no one else was within earshot. 'But, ah, you're allowed to call me your girlfriend, you know?'

My head jerked back. It might seem strange to some, but in the nearly twelve months that Alia and I had been dating, we'd only ever talked about this once. Six dates in — we were in a bread-making class and, spoiler alert, it turns out I cannot make bread from scratch — she'd told me how much she hated labels, how uncomfortable they made her, and how complacent she thought they often made other people. Since then, I hadn't even approached the subject. We were exclusive, I knew that much — we'd ironed that out ten dates in — but anything more than that had slipped through the cracks of date nights and sleepovers and weekends away.

'We never talked about you being my girlfriend,' I answered.

She smiled, tugged me closer, and turned to watch the girls filling our glasses — spilling offensive amounts of champagne across the table in the process. 'Maybe some things just happen, Dotty. Maybe some things don't actually need to be spoken about.'

'Maybe.' I leaned in to kiss her cheek. 'Maybe . . .'

THE END

ACKNOWLEDGEMENTS

The Break-up Before Christmas started out as a wild seedling of an idea that has grown into this book, and there are a few people deserving of thanks for that. My endless thanks to my agent, Andrew, for seeing something in those early emails that was worth carrying forwards into a fully-fledged story. Thanks to Jasmine, for also believing in this story, and for being so thoughtful with your edits; you helped me to bring *The Break-up Before Christmas* together in the final stages, and she is all the better for it. Thank you to the entire Choc Lit and Joffe team for their care and attention, too. It takes a village to raise a book, and I am endlessly thankful to the editors and publishers, both for this book and for my others, who have helped my stories to become real, breathing creations in the world. Finally, thank you to my beautiful big sister for listening to me talk about Christmas in the middle of a heatwave, as I carefully weaved seasonal cheer into the parts of this story where it was lacking, and thank you to my Max, for reading chapters and re-writes and snippets, and for offering me tea and Pringles as required.

THE CHOC LIT STORY

Established in 2009, Choc Lit is an independent, award-winning publisher dedicated to creating a delicious selection of quality women's fiction.

We have won 18 awards, including Publisher of the Year and the Romantic Novel of the Year, and have been shortlisted for countless others. In 2023, we were shortlisted for Publisher of the Year by the Romantic Novelists' Association.

All our novels are selected by genuine readers. We are proud to publish talented first-time authors, as well as established writers whose books we love introducing to a new generation of readers.

In 2023, we became a Joffe Books company. Best known for publishing a wide range of commercial fiction, Joffe Books has its roots in women's fiction. Today it is one of the largest independent publishers in the UK.

We love to hear from you, so please email us about absolutely anything bookish at choc-lit@joffebooks.com.

If you want to receive free books every Friday and hear about all our new releases, join our mailing list here: www.joffebooks.com/freebooks.

www.ingramcontent.com/pod-product-compliance
Lightning Source LLC
Chambersburg PA
CBHW011450170626
46816CB00009B/2605